A DEADLY GAME

When he spoke, Dagger's voice was low. "Paige, what, exactly, do you want me to do?"

"I want you to help us. I want you to prove my brother and the others were killed by agents of the United States government — murdered! And to help us bring those people to justice."

He stirred. "I don't know, Paige." Before she could protest, he said, "I think you and the others are marked. I think they would like to scare you all into silence. All of you. They've stolen your documents, now all they have to do is steal your confidence."

"And if they can't do that?"

The words from his mouth were spoken with a deadly tone. "Then they'll have to kill you all."

DAGGER

WILLIAM MASON

ZEBRA BOOKS
KENSINGTON PUBLISHING CORP.

ZEBRA BOOKS

are published by

Kensington Publishing Corp.
475 Park Avenue South
New York, N.Y. 10016

First printing: June, 1984

Printed in the United States of America

Earl of Sandwich: 'Pon my honor, Wilkes, I don't know whether you'll die on the gallows or of the pox.

Wilkes: That must depend, my Lord, upon whether I first embrace your Lordship's principles, or your Lordship's mistresses.

John Wilkes

PROLOGUE

February. Washington, D.C.

"I can't touch it," the assistant director of the CIA's European division said. He spoke from the deep shadows of the expensive hotel suite. "Again, gentlemen — no."

"I don't believe you are fully cognizant of the gravity of this, ah, particular situation," the second man in the semidarkened room said. "These people of whom we speak have information — indeed, the *proof,* we believe — to destroy us and the plans that have taken so many years to build to this point. Practically a point of no return. We don't know much about them, but we do know they have met and talked of naming names, dates, places, events. Senator Larkin and Representatives Cassard and Ballard are very upset at this news. As are several very important men and women of commerce and industry. All could be damaged, indeed, destroyed, if this surfaces. Needless to say, I don't have to mention the, ah, other matter."

"No," the Company man said, his tone adamant. "I am telling you both it is just too soon for Go. We can't get involved in this."

"Would you become involved if, ah, you personally might be exposed?" A third voice was added to the discussion. The voice spoke from behind swirls of fragrant pipe smoke. He smiled at the Company man. "Or someone very high in our, ah, other operation?"

The Company man sighed. Cursed under his breath. "Yes. Of course. Should that occur, our involvement would then have to be considered."

"Well, then." The voice seemed smug and supercilious behind the cloud of smoke, annoying the Company man. "Let me say those we seek to . . . silence, for want of a better word, have knowledge of the Jasmine Affair."

"That is impossible!" the Company man flatly rejected the claim.

"April the seventh, 1969. Baton Rouge. Tucker, Webb, Lester, Young."

"All right—perhaps. Yes, your facts are correct as far as they go. But I must remind you— both of you—those men are no longer with the Agency."

The pipe smoker laughed derisively, arrogantly. "But they were with your group during the time of the Jasmine Affair, were they not?"

The Company man nodded his head.

"They were the agents assigned—directly—to

carry out the plan?"

Again, the slight nod of the head.

"And they, shall we say, got a bit out of control, did they not?"

"They were young agents at the time. We prefer to say they were a bit overzealous in the performance of their duties. But they were reprimanded for their overenthusiastic indiscretions."

The pipe smoker laughed, laughed so heartily he almost choked on his smoke. "Reprimanded, sir? Indiscretions? Really! What you mean is they were slapped on the wrists for the deaths of five people. And they were acting on their own, outside the Agency."

"It produced the desired results, though, am I correct in saying that?"

"For a time, Fritzler," the pipe smoker said. "Only for a time. But now, two brothers, a sister and two children of those people killed that evening are preparing—have almost concluded—a report of what happened in sixty-nine. And, sir," he said, punctuating his words with stabbing motions, using the stem of his pipe, "they might be able to prove a great deal of what they have prepared."

Fritzler's eyes grew cloudy. He pursed his lips in thought. "How . . . much can they prove?"

"According to our sources—our reports—more than enough to cause trouble. Make big waves when we need the seas calm. Enough, perhaps, to take the dossier to an investigative reporter—and one has been suggested to them from the Times-Picayune/States-Item out of New Orleans—and let the reporter carry the ball from that point. I would not like that to happen."

"Burn the reporter," Fritzler suggested.

"Don't be an idiot!"

Fritzler ran his fingers along the carefully pressed seam of his trousers. Again, he sighed. "I don't have to remind you gentlemen the Agency has taken a battering over the past decade. We have had to—out of sheer desperation—become quite respectable. At least in certain areas. One of the reasons we all . . . slid away—" his eyes touched both men—"is the fact the liberals in America cannot seem to get it through their thick skulls one must fight fire with fire. Gentlemen, the Jasmine Affair occurred years ago. There is not one agent left in our employ who had anything to do with that . . . unfortunate event."

The second voice in the room came to life, contempt heavy in his tone. "Mr. Fritzler, don't insult us and don't bullshit us! You are not dealing with idiots. One section of the Agency was directly responsible for what happened in Louisiana that night. And you, Mr. Fritzler, gave the green light for that operation."

"With your knowledge and duplicity," both men were reminded.

The second man waved that off with a curt slash of one hand. "And for you to now tell us that Tucker, Webb, Lester and Young are no longer employed by the Agency is a lie I find personally insulting!"

"General . . ."

"Shut up. I served my country well for thirty years. I am very comfortable in my retirement and my position as advisor to the president. Our plans are coming along well—very well. It goes down in April. It must go down in April. And I don't need to remind you how deeply you are personally involved. I—we—don't want any boat-rocking. I do not savor the feeling of finding myself in the spotlight, attempting to explain away my involvement with a quartet of fools who killed five civilians—you bastard!"

"Now, you see here," Fritzler said, rising from his chair. "You can't talk to me—"

"Shut your mouth!" General Mitchell snapped. "Shut up, sit down and listen to me. Here is where we stand: Mr. and Mrs. Tom Shaffler, Mr. and Mrs. Alex Burrell, and Alice Volker were killed April seventh, 1969, in Baton Rouge, Louisiana, under an assignment code-named the Jasmine Affair. Shaffler had two younger brothers, Mike and Jimmy. Burrell had a sister, Paige. Alice Volker lost her husband in Vietnam—a war hero, you fool—they had two children, Ralph and Kit. Those five people have spent the last year compiling a dossier on the Jasmine operation. They worked with a New Orleans private detective named Rossieau."

Fritzler stirred in his chair. "I know all that," he said peevishly. "The P.I. is dead."

"Yes," the pipe smoker said. "We had him killed. He was getting too close."

Fritzler allowed himself a tight smile. "I thought as much when I heard it. It had all the markings of a touch. A young, very healthy man in his late thirties drops dead on a Baton Rouge street. A doctor just *happens* to be near; a doctor who just *happened* to be involved with the Phoenix Project in 'Nam. Heart attack, the doctor proclaims, after working on the man for a few moments. End of case." Fritzler again touched the seam of his trousers. "All bullshit, of course."

General Mitchell said, "We know that Rossieau had a few contacts, enough to allow him digging room. He found more contacts, then dug more deeply. He had to be stopped. We didn't want to burn him, but we felt we had no choice. Now the dossier is almost complete. We've brought the project to a standstill, but for how long? So you, Mr. Fritzler, had best stop vacillating and get cracking from your end."

The pipe smoker said, "Young, Lester, Webb and Tucker are still in the Company's employ. If we —" he indicated the general — "can dig that up with little effort, so can a lot of other people."

The assistant DCI nodded his head, reluctantly capitulating. "If the Shafflers, Volkers, and the Burrell woman die, the dossier recovered . . . that still leaves loose ends flapping about."

"Yes," Mitchell said. "Quite a few of them. All depends on how many agents used."

Fritzler met his eyes. "And?"

General Mitchell shrugged.

"You're talking about many deaths, General."

General Mitchell smiled. *"I'm* not talking about any *deaths,* Fritzler. That's your department. I just want this put in a box, wrapped up and tied neatly. Then we can shelve it, forget it, proceed with our more pressing plans."

"Damn!" Fritzler said. "Always something."

The pipe smoker puffed and said, "A name keeps cropping up. A name the survivors — according to our intelligence — will, in all probability, contact for help. Dagger. S.B. Dagger."

Fritzler's head jerked up, eyes alive and shining. His expression was that of a man just goosed with an electric cattle prod. "Dagger! I don't believe it. Dagger stopped any type of mercenary work about four years ago. Quit it cold. He will occasionally work as a bounty hunter, but the case must be something that appeals to him. He will go after a child molester, a pervert, something of that nature. His sister, much younger than Dagger, was raped and sodomized and murdered when she was quite young. That's the reason for Dagger's choosiness. It's said when he caught up with the three men who . . . did those disgusting things to his sister, it took the men several days to die. Horribly. Too . . . repulsive to even discuss. Dagger was quite inventive with the men, so I'm told." Fritzler shuddered at the recall. "The initials are just that. S.B. Stand for nothing. Some people say S.B. stands for son of a bitch; I don't doubt it a bit. He lives in the hills of Missouri. Gardens for a hobby—raises flowers, of all things. We watched him quite closely for a year after he retired from the field."

"For some reason," Mitchell said, "we can't get anything on him, other than the standard BS, that is. How does he live?"

"Draws the standard bucks from the government to keep his mouth shut. He's also a Medal of Honor winner. When his parents were killed in an auto crash, he was left quite a sum of money. He invested it wisely. He is very comfortable in his retirement."

"Age?"

"Forty, forty-one."

"Dangerous?" the pipe smoker asked.

Fritzler laughed. "Every intelligence agency from ours to the KGB ranked Dagger as the most dangerous man in the world when he was active. When he was just a little boy, he found some books on the art of Ninja. It fascinated him; he was a natural for it. He was a killer before he was fourteen." Fritzler took in the startled looks of the men. "True. Killed a grown man in Springfield. Man tried to take Dagger's movie money. Dagger left him in a gutter with two broken arms and a broken neck. When he was fifteen, his football coach cursed him for some play that was not performed to the coach's satisfaction. Dagger, in the words of the principal, 'beat the shit out of the coach, the assistant coach and some bystander who was there watching the practice.'

"He was expelled from high school. Parents sent him to a military school in Tennessee. Or Virginia. Dagger graduated top of his class. Continued to perfect his martial arts skills. Went directly into the army. NCO school. Infantryman, paratrooper, Ranger, Green Beret—every survival school known to exist. Only God knows how many men he killed in Southeast Asia. He won every medal America had to offer and every medal the Vietnamese government had to offer.

"Dagger left the American army and joined the French foreign legion after telling a group of reporters if he had his way, he'd line every goddamned one of them up against a wall and shoot them. Dagger does not like the press, to put it mildly. He doesn't much care for liberals. Again, putting it mildly. Nor does he care for judges or attorneys. I don't know that Dagger likes anyone. He seldom talks to anyone—that we are aware of. He's a loner."

"You certainly make him out to be one bad customer," Mitchell said.

Fritzler nodded. "S.B. Dagger is the toughest, meanest, nastiest son of a bitch on the face of the earth."

1

"If you'll hold still," Dagger said to the squirming little puppy, "I'll get this thorn out of your paw and you can be on your way."

Dagger petted the puppy, calming it, talking gently to it. The little cocker spaniel finally relaxed and looked up at Dagger with liquid, trusting eyes. Dagger pulled the thorn from its paw and released it. The puppy licked Dagger's hand, licked the small wound on its paw, then ran barking and playing down the road.

Dagger smiled and watched the puppy race toward home, more than a mile away, down a seldom-used gravel road. There was little chance of the dog being hit by a speeding car. No one raced vehicles up and down this road. No one. Not since Dagger jerked two hulking teen-agers out of a jacked-up-in-the-rear hot rod and used his wide leather belt on their respective butts. Dagger opined the young men—ages seventeen and eighteen—could probably heat their own bath water for a week just by sitting in it.

Their parents were outraged at this overt act of brutality directed toward their little darlings. They went to the sheriff of the county. The sheriff told them the only way he would attempt to arrest S.B. Dagger was if he had the entire Eighty-second Airborne backing him up. And then he'd have reservations.

"Besides," he told the parents, "your kids have been needing a good ass-busting for several years."

The parents said they would go see this barbarian themselves.

The sheriff asked them their next of kin.

The parents left Dagger's property walking very stiffly and sweating a lot. Dagger had greeted them politely, listened for a moment, then motioned the parents out to his back yard. There, he smashed a concrete block with his bare hands. Broke several bricks. Bent a horseshoe. Put soda pop bottle caps between his outstretched fingers, brought his fingers together and bent the caps. Dagger then picked up a large anvil and, standing there, with no apparent effort, asked the man and woman if there was anything else on their minds.

They thought not.

Goodbye.

Dagger watched the puppy race away, barking. He smiled, but the humor did not reach his eyes. His eyes were blue. But they appeared to hold no warmth. They looked cold and savage. The eyes of a viking. Dagger was not a huge, towering, overpowering man in appearance. He was six feet, one inch tall. But his weight was very deceptive. People usually guessed him thirty pounds lighter than he really was. His wrists were huge and his musculature heavy. He was barrel-chested, lean-waisted. His hands were big and calloused. He was deeply tanned. Dark brown hair with just a touch of gray.

He had never married. His sex life was adequate by arrangement with several local women who preferred being well-loved to being well-gossiped.

He seldom went anywhere off his one hundred acres of wooded land. He was, as some residents of the county maintained, self-contained.

Dagger would bother no one who did not first bother him.

He was left alone.

But he had his memories.

He tried not to think of most of them.

Especially of that one woman. But she still popped up in his mind occasionally. And his dreams.

From long habit, Dagger, on this day, carefully prowled the acreage immediately surrounding his home. He looked for anything out of the ordinary: a bit of broken wood, a bent twig or flower, a disturbed bird or a suddenly alert squirrel.

Nothing.

But Dagger had a feeling deep in his guts that something was wrong. He couldn't pin it down. But it would come to him. In one way or another, it always did.

He looked up into the leaden sky, filled with rainclouds. The sky appeared cold, like Dagger's eyes.

And lonely.

"Don't count Dagger out," General Mitchell said. "Men like that seldom stay retired."

"Kill him," the pipe smoker said.

"No!" Fritzler said, his tone leaving no room for argument. "That would open up a brand new can of worms. Believe me. Dagger is not without friends. Lethal friends. Some of them would come snooping. He may be a hero from an unpopular war, but he is still a national hero. That would raise too many questions, for Dagger is not that easily killed."

"I agree," Mitchell said, "but he needs to be placed under some kind of surveillance."

"He'd pick up on it immediately," Fritzler said.

"That's probably true," Mitchell agreed. "All right. Judging from Dagger's past actions, it's doubtful he would take the job even if offered. We'll put people on the survivors. You know the agents to get, Fritzler."

"Lester and his old group?"

"Yes."

"I was afraid you'd say that." Fritzler sighed audibly.

"We're going to need them," the pipe smoker said.

Fritzler shook his head.

"And we will live to regret not burning Dagger," the pipe smoker maintained.

"I don't see it that way," Fritzler held on.

"Fritzler, we did learn that Pig Lester hates Dagger," spoken through clouds of smoke. "Dagger whipped him badly in a fight, years ago. Put Pig in the hospital for several weeks. Think about it. This could be the way to get rid of both of them. If it comes to it, let Pig kill Dagger. Then Pig could have an accident."

Fritzler liked that. "You have a point."

Mitchell said, "The DCI should have had Pig iced years ago. After that rape incident."

"The DCI didn't know anything about that," Fritzler told both men. "Besides, it was all smoothed over. The girl's parents were compensated; the girl was given the very best of medical and psychological care. She has, according to the last word I received, only a fuzzy, hazy recollection of what . . . occurred that night."

"Had," the pipe smoker said.

Fritzler looked at him. "What do you mean 'had'?"

"The woman is dead. Killed herself months ago. Something triggered a remembrance-response in her mind. She wrote a long letter to a friend, telling all. Then she blew her brains out with a shotgun. Obviously you have not kept the file open or you would know of that."

"Well," Fritzler said, "that is unfortunate. But why keep a file open? How does her death concern us? Dagger has no knowledge of that. He was in Vietnam."

"Dagger doesn't have any knowledge of it — yet. But Lester bragged about it to a buddy. They were drinking, in a bar in Baton Rouge. The buddy told a buddy, and so on down the line. You know how your Agency's grapevine works: quietly, but you still have one. The P.I., Rossieau, got word of it, tracked down the dead woman's letter, made a copy, really started snooping. Looking under rocks, so to speak. Then he made a copy of the copy and gave it to the Shaffler brothers."

Fritzler shook his head. He looked perplexed. "This is getting complicated. Too many people involved. I don't like it . How in the hell did Rossieau get wind of an incident that occurred more than a decade ago? There was no newsprint or electronic coverage of the rape."

"You can't break wind in Cajun country without half the parish knowing of it," Mitchell said. "The P.I.'s grandmother lives — or lived — out in the swamps. She was somehow related to a friend of the raped woman. Rossieau heard his grandmother talking to one of her cronies — this was years ago—about a friend in New Orleans suddenly and mysteriously coming into a large amount of money, large to her. Rossieau was just back from Vietnam, working as a deputy in a South Louisiana parish. He tucked the information back in his head and thought no more of it until a few months ago. After he was contacted by Shaffler, Burrell and Volker, he began tying up loose ends, thought of the little bit of information and decided to check it out. It seemed to fit somehow. He snooped some more and came up with a bag full of damning suspicions—but no hard proof."

"You're sure Dagger has not been contacted?"

"You keep coming back to him, Fritzler. He's just a man. No. He has not been contacted. We are reasonably certain of that."

"If Operation Jasmine is uncovered," Fritzler mused, "then it's only a matter of time before more will be exposed to the light: ten killings in a matter of a few months, five of them for no apparent reason. Ten lives snuffed out with tacit government approval. There are a number of ramifications that must be considered in this . . . affair."

"Yes," Mitchell said with a smile. "As I mentioned, a few heads of government that are still in office. Especially those who turned their heads while Section Five was being formed. Perhaps, Fritzler, you should consider re-forming that section. How many agents of Five are still around?"

Fritzler looked glum for a moment. He had worked long and hard to get to his present position within the Agency, and he knew only too well it could all crumble and fall around him, taking him with it, if the matter now before the three men was not handled with the utmost delicacy. Very quietly, and very efficiently. "There was strong opposition within the Company to that section being formed. Much relief when it was dissolved. Dagger worked for Five. But he was overseas personnel; clean stateside."

"That doesn't answer my question. How many agents still alive?"

"I'd have to run a records check. But I would say, oh, fifteen or eighteen still operational."

"And those people would have friends scattered about, men and women who at one time or another, and for one reason or another, worked for Section Five?"

"Certainly."

"Bringing the total to?"

"Twenty-five to thirty-five."

"And those people would not want their covers blown." It was not a question.

"That is correct."

"It's in your lap, Fritzler," the pipe smoker said.

The man from the CIA nodded curtly and rose from his chair. He looked at the men. "I'll get right on it." He stepped into the hall, quietly closing the door behind him. His footsteps were hushed and muted on the thick carpet of the expensive hotel.

The pipe smoker looked at General Mitchell. "Nothing must stand in the way of Eagle-Fall. Nothing."

"Yes, sir," the general said.

In the private living quarters of the president of the United States, President Menen was speaking with the head of the Secret Service, Lorne Holt.

"What have you discovered for a fact, Lorne?"

"No hard facts, sir. Just rumors. But they keep coming. The Agency's mole in Moscow says you are to be assassinated this spring."

"When this spring?"

"Around the last of April."

"That would coincide with the trip to Los Angeles, when I address the western governors."

"Yes, sir. I believe that is when the attempt will be made. Mr. President? It is very difficult for me to believe the Secret Service has been compromised. I just . . ." He shrugged his skepticism.

"Every law enforcement agency in the nation has been compromised to some degree, Lorne — over a period of years. And not just government. You have seen the proof that all the majors have been penetrated."

The Secret Service man nodded reluctantly.

"And my own staff, I believe," Menen said.

"Perhaps the inner circle, but I hate to even think of that. I don't know where to point the finger. Lorne, I think it's time we started firming up our long-range plans."

"With all due respect, sir. Right now, I'd rather talk about keeping you alive."

The president glanced at the man.

Lorne chuckled as he lit his pipe. "Doctor took me off cigarettes but let me keep my pipe. Hell, sir — what difference does it make? I'm dying and know it. But I want to prevent your death. Mine can't be prevented — yours can."

"The liberals can't understand there is no way to prevent a nut with a gun from shooting a public figure — or anyone else for that matter. And they can't seem to understand that gun control is not the answer. Not in America — we'd have a civil war attempting to enforce it. I don't have to convince you of that, Lorne."

"No, sir. I don't believe in gun control." He puffed clouds of scented smoke into the air. "We're still a couple of people short, sir."

"You told me you had someone in mind."

"Yes, sir. I think he's our man."

"All right, then, Lorne. Start the ball rolling and firm it up."

"You're that certain, sir?"

"I'm ninety percent sure, yes. But nothing will be put into effect — nothing physical and final — until that last ten percent is cleared up in my mind."

"How much money do we have banked?"

"Millions. All drawing top interest for years—adding more millions to the millions. There is no way it can be traced to any one group or individual."

"All right, sir. Now let's talk of keeping you alive and who we can trust while doing that."

"We've got several months to worry about that, Lorne. Whatever you come up with, we'll keep it between ourselves until the last possible moment."

"And when Harrison of the Agency or Powell of the Bureau get wind of it—and they will—what then?"

"We're surprised, Lorne—what else? We can't do a thing until we find out who we can trust in this matter. Doyle? It's unbelievable."

"He's clean, sir. We've checked him all the way back to practically the moment of conception."

The president looked relieved. "Are you sure, Lorne?"

"As sure as we can be, sir. Doyle is clean."

"Who else would stand to gain, Lorne?"

Lorne shrugged his shoulders. "I can't think of a single person here in the White House, sir. We've checked them all out—quietly—both before they came in here with your administration, and over the past few months, as well. It's . . . confusing, sir. It's the very first time in my memory I can recall where we have any proof at all—however slight—the Reds are really planning to hit a U.S. president."

But the president was not thinking about his planned assassination. It was as if his life—laid alongside the broader aspirations of his plan—was inconsequential. "The streets are jungles," Menen said, as much to himself as to Lorne. "Many of our elderly live in fear of their lives—when they aren't starving to death on the miserable pittance this government allows them. The goddamned doctors in this nation have become mercenaries; our courts are a disgrace; our schools are breeding grounds for graduated ignorance; coaches are being paid more than many teachers." He sighed in disgust. "The military has no morale or discipline to speak of; our morals are at an all-time low; criminals—with the help of so-called legal-rights groups—are crapping all over the rights of the law-abiding citizens and victims. The list is endless," he concluded, abhorrence in his voice. He rubbed his face; his eyes felt gritty and tired. "Ninety-five percent of my mind is now made up, Lorne."

"Is there any possibility of it getting out of hand, sir?"

"Yes," Menen admitted. "A slight one. But there is more risk walking the cities' streets. We have taken—this country, Lorne—a very slight turn back to the right; but not enough of a turn. These people, Lorne, these ten people we have chosen—are they the best we can find?"

"Yes, sir. Nine people, if we go with the man we

discussed earlier."

"Very well, nine is enough. I believe we can stop it at that number."

"Yes, sir." The agent smiled. "A pity I won't be around to see it. I would like to see the ACLU and some of those other moaners and bleeders pee on themselves and wallow in it. When they put it all together—and they will, to some degree. Along with a number of other people."

"But they will have no proof, Lorne. Not one modicum of proof. And they won't be able to *get any proof*. That's the beauty—or the deadliness—of it all. We are going to bury these nine so deeply, we are going to give them so much built-in protection—quiet protection—they won't be touched." He shook his head. "It isn't foolproof, Lorne. But it is time for it."

"I certainly agree with you on that. How long do you anticipate them lasting, sir?"

"Ten years, minimum. Twenty years, maximum. The first group. Whether there will be a second group . . . well, that all depends on an international assemblage that will meet in ten years. If the laws of this nation have been changed to protect the innocent and punish the guilty, the nine will be ended. If not . . ." He shrugged.

"Their monies, sir?"

"They will be paid through a very complicated system, Lorne. Complicated to anyone not familiar with it. Very simple to one versed in money matters on the international scene. Switzerland is beginning to open up some of their accounts. So the monies are being quietly transferred out, to a . . . let us say more closed-mouthed nation — and a very stable one. I have the feeling the group will be in operation long after my death."

"Speaking of that, sir."

"All right, Lorne. All right. Let's discuss keeping me alive against the unknown enemy. That's the only thing that's going to make you happy today. But one more item before that. What about this Dagger?"

Lorne sighed, dug in his briefcase, and handed the president a folder.

Menen laughed at the expression on his friend's face, then turned his attention to the subject matter. He read for a few moments then said, "God! This Dagger is a randy son of a bitch."

"Yes, sir." Lorne's reply was cutting in its dryness. "To say the least."

2

March. Baton Rouge, Louisiana.

"All right," Paige Burrell said. "We were all followed here this evening. It's been going on for ten days—that we know of. At least that long."

"It's got to have something to do with our attempting to reopen the killings of 1969," Kit Volker said. "I'm scared, Paige. Is our own government doing this to us?"

"Who else?" Paige said sarcastically.

"I say we get in touch with Senator Bodine," Kit's brother, Ralph, said. "Just lay it on the table and tell him what's been going on."

"No hard proof," Jimmy Shaffler said. "We don't know if it is any government agency. We don't know who it is."

"I read somewhere," Kit said, "about these new listening devices. They don't even have to bug your house anymore. They just point some kind of long, skinny microphone at the house, maybe from like a mile away, and then listen to everything that is said."

No one spoke for a moment. The they were all up on their feet, moving toward their jackets and sweaters, heading for the front door of Kit's apartment.

Paige stopped, whirling around, her face flushed with anger. "This is ridiculous!" she snapped the words from her mouth. "We're talking about our homes, our apartments. We're not criminals; we haven't broken any laws. Damn this! I've had enough."

Ralph walked across the room to the stereo, clicking it on, turning up the volume. His smile was rather sad and self-conscious. "Just in case," he said. "I've seen them do it in the movies."

All turned to look at Paige.

Her hair, now slightly mussed from her quick movements, was black as midnight. Her eyes were a deep blue. She was tall—five feet, eight inches—with a magnificent figure. Thirty years old, she owned a string of very profitable dress shops in the cities of Louisiana. She had never married, and had never really regretted it. She worked, not because she needed the money, but to have something to do. Her parents were rich— very rich—and Paige had come into her full inheritance when she was twenty-one. After taxes, she earned, from many sound investments, almost 150 thousand dollars a year—not counting the money from her dress shops. Shoppes, that is. At thirty, Paige was well-fixed monetarily.

Paige returned the stares from her friends.

The three men and two women were as different in personalities as in appearance.

Paige, strong-willed and stubborn, was sometimes impatient with those less intelligent than she. Which was about seventy-five percent of the population. She confided in no one, keeping her innermost feelings to herself.

Mike Shaffler, who had spent several days in the nation's capital in February, was a college jock-type who was not quite good enough for the NFL. He had tried the Canadian league, but since he really didn't have to work—didn't need the money—he couldn't make it up there either. But he could not forget the roar of the crowds.

Mike's brother, Jimmy: a totally different type of young man—almost the opposite of his brother. Jimmy had been a good athlete at LSU, a running back. But Jimmy, unlike his brother, had not kept in shape by pumping iron. He kept in good shape with swimming and tennis and handball, but had lost the look of a jock and no longer followed the sport with the crazed fanaticism of a religious zealot about to touch the nail-scarred hands of Jesus.

Ralph Volker had been tagged since grade school as a coward. That title was false and undeserved. A CPA, owner of his own firm, Ralph earned a good living. Behind his glass-encased eyes was a mind with the fantastic memory recall of almost ninety percent. And Ralph, though he

33

never spoke of it—even his friends did not know it—was skilled in savate and held a black belt in karate.

Kit Volker, a pretty woman, but without the head-turning beauty of Paige. A talented artist and, like her brother, extremely intelligent. Kit had a very active sex life. Very often. And very inventive.

Paige motioned for the stereo to be turned off and the five of them filed out of the apartment and onto the street. They did not speak until they were on the sidewalk.

Jimmy said, "I am still against using that Missouri man. There must be a better way."

"Rossieau told us he was the best in the world—if he would work for us," Ralph said. "Paige? I think we're in trouble. We need help."

Mike snorted his contempt and lit his pipe. "Big deal. Some goddamn mercenary, strutting around, flexing his muscles. I bet he's not much."

Ralph looked at him with ill-concealed dislike, knowing the feeling was mutual.

"I remember going to a lecture one night," Kit said. "It was something to do on a boring evening. Some Green Beret type was speaking. He said the most dangerous men in the world don't look it—usually."

"That is probably very true," Ralph said.

"What the hell would you know about it?" Mike asked him.

Ralph smiled at him. "Someday, Mike, I might

just decide to show you." He looked at Paige. "I think we should contact this Dagger person. Do you want me to go?"

"No," she replied. "I'll do it. I can best afford to leave town."

Mike stuck out his chin belligerently. "What the hell do you mean, Ralph: You might decide to show me? Show me what? How quick you are with a pencil?" He laughed.

Ralph ignored him. As he had done for years. "Dagger has an unlisted phone number, Paige. All Rossieau gave us was the general area where the man lives."

"I'll find him," Paige said.

"We lost her," the man said. "She picked up on us tailin' her and lost us. She knows this country down here — we don't."

"We're spread too thin," another man observed. "We've got to get more people in here to help us. Why are we waiting? Damn it all, let's take them out — now!"

The man who was once in charge of the Agency's clandestine and now-defunct Section Five laughed, an ugly overtone to his chuckling.

"Two cunts, a fairy and two ex-jocks, and ten trained agents can't handle them. God, you people are pathetic." Dan "Pig" Lester let his contemptuous gaze sweep the eight men and two women in the room, touching each person.

Pig continued. "You, J.B., you got a nice little sporting goods business down in Florida. Little live-in gal to keep you happy when you get a hard-on. You want all that destroyed?"

J.B shook his head.

"Bitsy? You make your living as a writer now. You want all that ruined with the knowledge made public you were a paid gun for the Company? Or that you like your sex so kinky even a porn movie looks tame when compared to you."

She shook her head, something close to fear in her eyes.

"Carl—you're all happy raisin' hogs in Illinois. All that could be wiped out in a matter of minutes. Same with you, Art, Peter, Les, Rich, Dean. You're all settled in, all—for the public's eyes—straight and legal and doing well. Just a little job for the Company every now and then to keep your hand in it and to pick up some extra pocket money. All of you had best think how much you have to lose if your covers are blown."

"I've just about reached the point where I don't care," Dean said. "Hell, Pig! The Vietnam thing is old news now. So what if we rousted some war protestors, leaned on a few professors, and violated some civil rights down the line? So what if just a little bit of our cover is lifted? Jesus, all that was *years* ago, back in the sixties. Who gives a damn now? And what the hell could anybody really prove?"

Pig smiled. Shook his head. "Boys and girls,

you all have short memories. Dean, I seem to re-call you enjoyed using a cattle prod on a couple of gals to get information on the whereabouts of that Jew activist. I seem to recall you enjoyed it so much you got a little carried away and stuck it up one of those young gals." Pig shrugged philo-sophically. " 'Course you had no way of knowing that little gal had heart trouble, now, did you?"

Dean lifted his shoulders in a so-what? ges-ture. "She's just another runaway of the peace and love generation, Pig. Her body will never be found. And after all these years, there is nothing left except some rotting bones."

Pig's smiled never left his face. "Maybe so, maybe not." He turned to another person. "Art? You're not forgetting that night in Virginia, are you?"

Art Tappen shuffled his feet nervously.

"You and that high-yellow nigger gal had quite a tussle, didn't you?"

"I get your meaning, Pig," Art said, keeping his eyes downcast.

"I don't think so. You thought she was just an-other cotton patch nigger from Mississippi, didn't you, Art?" Pig laughed. "Turned out her daddy was a doctor in New York City and worth quite a bit of change." He looked at each person in the room. "Everybody—all of you—had a taste of brown sugar that night." His eyes lin-gered on the two women. "One way or another. How many years did that high yellow spend in the loony bin, gang? Four? Five? I forget. Now we don't know if these people we're chasing have any information on that . . . but who wants to take a chance?"

The men and women looked at each other. Shook their heads.

"Mel?" Pig wouldn't let up. "You and that Jewboy had quite a time in St. Louis, didn't you? Tough little bastard, wasn't he? You didn't know he was ex-Marine Force Recon, did you? You think he'd recognize you if your ugly face hit the TV or the papers?"

"All right, Pig," Peter Cooper said. "No need to go into all these past details. If we weren't afraid of having our covers blown, we wouldn't be here, would we?"

"No, Pete—there is a lot more to it than that. It's time."

Every man and woman in the room stiffened. Each dreading that phrase they knew Pig was about to throw at them.

"Eagle-Fall," Pig said.

"But the Bear . . ." Lisa said.

"The Bear knows what to do. The word comes from the Bear. Now then," Pig went on. "I think you all need your memories refreshed. You've all become complacent, secure, and you all know better. Or should have. You, Pete, you've got quite a bit to lose if what you did ever hits the news. Lacing that bowl of booze with LSD wasn't very nice, was it? Still some folks playing out in never-never land from that night. And you've got bodies to your credit.

"Lisa? You like your lovers young and kinky still? I thought so. And like Pete, baby, you've got kills on your file.

"Les? Some John Doe warrants floating around, all they need is your name on them. Rape, breaking and entering, assault with a deadly weapon, blackmail, strong-arming. Can you afford to lose what it's taken you years to build? No? I thought not.

"Rich? I understand you're quite a respected businessman now; some folks even think you'd make a good mayor for that hick town in Washington. How long you think you'd last in that conservative community if they knew you were queer—had a black lover back in the sixties? You want to come out of the closet, Rich? No? Ah, well, I thought not."

Rich Bowman looked at the floor. He would meet no one's eyes. "I never thought I'd hear the words Eagle-Fall again," he said.

"You thought you were taking the man's money for free?" Pig asked. "Don't be stupid."

Art asked, "Pig, are there still records around on Section Five that would link us directly to the Agency?"

"I don't know," Pig admitted. "That section never officially existed. It would be difficult to prove. But that isn't the point now. Eagle-Fall is rolling, and we've got to keep it ticking. If it fails, it's prison for all of us—or worse. You all know that." A flash of irritation crossed his face.

Pig was aptly nicknamed. He looked like a hog. Dagger had once told him he was the ugliest bastard he'd ever seen outside of a freak house or a geek in a carnival.

That was just seconds before Dagger whipped Pig, putting him in the hospital.

Pig's head was shaved and bullet-shaped. His eyes were close-set and buggy. His nose was pug and his mouth a wide, cruel slit. Pig was just under five-ten, and carried 210 pounds. He bore a striking resemblance to a butcher's block.

A small notation on his Agency's eyes-only file stated quite simply that Daniel "Pig" Lester was thought to be insane.

But he had served his department well for more than twenty years. After graduating from a small college in Iowa, where he had played defensive right tackle, Pig was recruited by the Agency.

Pig was a master at, and enjoyed, torture. Stateside, he was responsible for at least five deaths from his sadistic enjoyment of torture. No one knew how many had died in Southeast Asia during his tenure there. Pig knew he was red-tabbed for assassination by a half dozen countries (including two groups and one Dog Team in the U.S.) but that knowledge did not seem to worry him. He knew as long as he did a good job for his chiefs at the Company, he was relatively safe. But he lived daily with the knowledge that some day, some place, he would have his ticket punched. It was the only way a man like Pig could go out.

Pig was a senior agent, always working clandestinely, and no man with Pig's years in the field is to be taken lightly: too much power and inner-office influence can be built up over those years.

"We have to play the game," Pig said. "The Bear gave those orders."

"You think Burrell was going to see Dagger, Pig?" Les asked.

Pig grinned. "I hope so. I hope she gets to him and hires him. Then I can kill him."

J.B. looked at Pig, amusement in his eyes. "Dagger is no sweetheart, Pig. He's got more snuffs than any of us—including you. Lots of people have tried to take Dagger. He buried them all."

Another agent in the room laughed and lit his pipe.

Pig flushed, the color rising to his face. "If I say I'm going to kill Dagger—I'll kill him."

Doug Farmer, analyst for Internal Affairs, spoke to the director of Central Intelligence. "Thought you might be interested in seeing this, sir." He placed a sheet of paper on the DCI's desk. "One of our operatives in New Orleans reports seeing a number of ex-agents and a few working agents gathering at a motel in Metairie. That's just outside the city."

The DCI glanced at the sheet of paper. "I was not aware our field agents had conventions."

"They don't," Doug spoke around the stem of his pipe. "At least not openly."

"Who are these people? These ex-agents?"

Doug hesitated a few heartbeats. He knew the ex-agents were ex in name only; they still worked for the Agency in some capacity. But if the DCI didn't know that . . .

Doug knew about Section Five. Knew a great deal about it. He also knew when to keep his mouth shut and when to open it.

So the DCI was being deliberately kept in the dark.

Interesting.

Doug had spent years within the confines of the Company's HQ. Knew about the sudden transfers of Young, Lester, Webb and Tucker back in late sixty-nine. And knew why. Knew about the new and highly covert missions of a number of other agents, too.

Doug knew a great deal he was not about to tell the DCI. For various reasons known only to a few.

He lit his pipe. "I don't know, sir. They've been out of the Agency for years, most of them."

"All the way out?"

Again, he lied. "Yes, sir. Full civilian status."

The DCI picked up the sheet of paper, started

to hand it back to Farmer, then hesitated. He was relatively new to the job, having been confirmed when the administration went in, eighteen months back. The new DCI had no knowledge of any special groups that once existed within the Company. But he knew it was odd that this many past and currently employed operatives should all get together. That was solidly against policy. He lifted his eyes.

"This is to remain between us, Doug. *Only* between us. Do you fully understand that?"

"Yes, sir."

"I will inform our man in New Orleans to keep us informed of any odd behavior these agents might exhibit. Understood?"

"Yes, sir."

"It's probably nothing. But let's be certain."

"Right, sir."

Doug left the room, leaving behind a trace of fragrant pipe smoke.

3

April. Missouri Ozarks.

Dagger was restless, pacing his spacious den. Restlessness was something alien to him, and he did not like the feeling. It interfered with his normal cool control.

And it usually meant something was about to pop in his life. Good or bad.

He heard a car come down the gravel road, go past his turnoff, then stop and back up. He opened a desk drawer and took out a .41 magnum, checking the cylinder to see if it was fully loaded. It was.

He heard his gate open and a car rattle over the cattle guard. A Cadillac El Dorado pulled into view, a woman got out. One hell of a woman. Dagger appraised her with an experienced eye. High fashion boots, jeans, and fashion denim shirt, which she filled out quite well. The gems on her fingers sparkled in the April sun, the colors jumping with pure brilliance, the gold gleaming

44

in the background.

He stepped out onto the porch of the native rock house, the .41 shoved behind his belt. He made no effort to hide the butt of the pistol.

"I don't like company, lady," he bluntly informed her.

"So I gather," she said, never slowing her stride toward the porch and man. "It took me three weeks just to find the area in which you live, another week to track you down."

"Yeah, I know."

That stopped her. "You *knew* I was searching for you?"

"Yeah."

"How?"

"Desk clerk up at The Lakes called me. Told me. I keep her on retainer, so to speak."

Her eyes drifted to the butt of the big pistol, back to his cold stare. Unblinking. She felt like she was looking directly into the eyes of a cobra. "It must be expensive keeping her on a retainer."

"No, I just screw her every now and then."

Deep color crept up the woman's face. Her eyes flashed a warning at him. He caught it, ignored it. "She must like crudeness, then," Paige said.

Dagger told her how the woman liked it — bluntly.

Paige looked at him for a moment, then a smile began playing around the corners of her mouth as she tuned into his game. "It won't work, Mr. Dagger."

"Just Dagger, lady. Drop the mister. What is it that won't work?"

"Your game. Your crudeness game. Care to try another tack?"

Smart lady, he thought. Dagger shrugged his pretended indifference. "How'd you get my name?"

"From a private investigator."

"Who?"

"Rossieau."

Dagger grunted. "What do you want, lady?"

"To speak with you."

Dagger looked at her for a long moment. Paige felt she was being undressed. She was. She felt like he was spiritually making love to her. He was. It was . . . disconcerting.

Dagger finally nodded his head. "Pull your Caddy around to the side of my house. Park it by my truck."

"Why?" she challenged the order. She had never liked to be ordered about.

"Because I told you to, that's why."

He watched her walk to her car. Sensational derrière. A lot of woman, he thought. More than most men could handle. Dagger did not doubt his ability to handle her in the least. He had yet to find the woman who could best him in bed. Or any other way, for that matter.

Just that green-eyed lady he had found and couldn't keep. And sex had had nothing to do with that.

He shook that thought from his head and pushed it back into a vault. Locked it. But she would be back. She always managed that.

Dagger motioned the woman into the house and she stood for a moment, amazed at the interior.

The home was lushly furnished, everything in excellent taste. A bit too modern for her tastes, but done very skillfully. The carpet was thick and expensive and muted. The furniture all leather. The lamps chrome and glass and gleaming. The paintings were tastefully hung, spaced so one did not take away from the other, and they were originals — known names. Music pushed softly from huge but not vulgar speakers. She would have expected some whiny hillbilly singer. What she was listening to was Rachmaninov's Piano Concerto number two.

She looked at Dagger. She could not read his eyes. She doubted anyone could. "I'm impressed," she told him.

He shattered that. "It was done by a queer and a dyke from Springfield. They bitched at each other all the time. Half the time I couldn't tell male from female." He pointed to a sofa. "Park it there."

Again, she got the strong impression he was saying those things just to get her reaction. His faint, mocking smile confirmed her suspicions.

"Why do you pretend to be something you are

not?" she asked.

"Do you want something to drink?" he side-stepped her question.

"No."

"Fine."

She sat down.

"So talk to me, lady."

"My name is Paige Burrell. I'm from Baton Rouge. That's in Louisiana."

"Yeah," he said dryly. "I know, lady. Means Red Stick."

"Have you ever heard my name before?"

"No."

"Would you tell me if you had?"

"Yes."

"Man of few words, aren't you?"

"Until I get to know you better. If I choose to get to know you better." His smile was sarcastic and sardonic.

It was infuriating to her.

Exactly what he wants, she reminded herself. "I don't think I like you very much, Mr. Dagger."

"I'll live with or without your approval, lady."

Her eyes again found the butt of the pistol. "Why are you armed, Mr. Dagger?"

"I might decide to shoot you and skin you and have you mounted. Nude."

"Your humor is grotesque."

"So I've been told. Along with other parts of me." He said it flatly.

She had already noticed he was amply endowed. Unless he had stuffed a banana down the front of his khakis. She doubted that. She fought her rising temper and bested it.

"I might like to employ you, Mr. Dagger."

"Dagger. Just Dagger. Drop the mister. I'm very expensive."

"I can afford it, Dagger."

"Probably. Employ me to do what? I'm retired."

"I doubt that last bit. But . . . well . . . I'm really not sure what I—we—want you to do, Mr., I mean Dagger."

Annoyance flashed across his features. "Lady, that is a very stupid reply."

"I want to tell you a story, Dagger. I must find someone to help me—us. My friends think you are the right person for the job. Most of them. None of us know where to turn, who to trust. Do you know that feeling?"

His short bark of humor—if that's what it was—told her he did know, very well.

"In the spring of 1969," Paige said, after expelling a deep sigh, during which Dagger noticed she had great-looking breasts, at least as far as he could see, "just outside of Baton Rouge proper, five people were killed in what the police called a gangland-style slaying. Among them was my brother, Alex Burrell, and his wife, Lydia."

Dagger sat down in a chair and leaned back, listening.

"I was at LSU at the time," she continued, her

voice throaty.

And I was taking R&R in Australia, Dagger thought, about to meet . . . her.

"Naturally, it was a great shock to all concerned," she said, her eyes misty in sudden remembrance.

"How were they killed?" Dagger asked.

"The car blew up. They had been to a concert, then stopped at a restaurant for something to eat. When they got in the car and started the engine, the car exploded. And I mean it really blew up. There . . . wasn't much left of any of them."

"What kind of car?"

"Cadillac. Four door. Blue. Why do you ask?"

"Go on." Dagger did not have any idea what this woman expected him to do—if anything— but he did not want her to leave. And he felt the surgings of buried fire building within him, just under the surface, smoking.

He also wondered what Paige would look like naked. Waiting, her dark hair fanned out over the whiteness of pillow.

"A few months later," she said, "another car blew up. Five more people were killed in the same manner."

"What kind of car?"

Her smile was grim and knowing. "You catch on very quickly, Dagger. A Cadillac. Blue. Four door."

"It happens. Mistaken identity. The last five to die, who were they?"

"Anti-war activists, from New Orleans and from back east. I don't remember all their names — I have that information in the car — but one of them was Karl Crowe."

Dagger finally smiled in a friendly manner. It changed his entire face, making him appear much younger, more human, much more appealing to Paige. "I'm familiar with the name Karl Crowe," he said dryly, obvious dislike in his tone.

"You're a fighting man, Dagger. Naturally you would not care for a pacifist."

Dagger laughed at her. "Hell, lady! Karl Crowe was no pacifist. He was a known Red agent. The FBI couldn't get enough proof together to deport him back to Russia, where he belonged."

"You're joking!" She almost came off the sofa. "But a lot of us at LSU attended his lectures and read his books."

Dagger looked at the woman for a moment, then solemnly scratched the side of his face with a finger, deep in thought for a moment. "The gullibility of the public," he said. "Crowe changed his name years ago, from Crovonovich, or something like that. He was directly responsible for the deaths of at least three CIA people: deep cover agents in Europe. That is fact, Ms. Burrell. One of those men was a very good friend of mine."

She touched him with her eyes. Almost a physical caress. "Live and learn, I suppose, Dagger.

College students are very susceptible, just the right age." She dismissed Karl Crowe with a wave of one jeweled hand. "Forget him. I came here to ask for your help."

"Fine. Just as long as we know where the other stands when it comes to defending men or women who are dedicated to bringing down this government. As bad as it is, it's still the best one on this planet."

Paige watched his face, his eyes. She decided this man could be—probably was—very dangerous. She wondered about his mental stability.

Dagger said, "Go on with your story. I gather the police never caught the men who killed your brother and the others?"

"Not just the police—the FBI as well."

A silent bell donged in Dagger's head. But he could not determine what triggered the bell. So the Bureau blew what appeared to be a simple case. Odd.

That bell donged once more.

"How long did the FBI work on it?"

"A long time."

"And?"

"The same agents interviewed us all, many times. Then . . . the case was just . . . I guess shelved is the right word. My parents put their grief behind them; I went back to school."

"Did you know the others killed with your brother?"

"Yes. Knew the children better. All went to the

same school, all went to LSU. Then, early last year, Ralph Volker, that's the brother of Kit, called me, said he wanted to reopen the case — the investigation. Said he felt there was a cover-up going on, right from the start."

She looked at the toe of one boot. "We all agreed with him — all but Jimmy. But we finally convinced him to go along with us."

"Jimmy who?"

"Jimmy Shaffler, brother of Mike."

"Did this Ralph tell you why he felt there had been a cover-up?"

"He said everything was too pat. Said when it happened, we were all too young to think about things like that, but over the years he'd been giving it a lot of think-time. And something just smelled bad — to use his words.

"None of us mean to imply the police were in any way involved. None of us believe that. They worked for months on it. So did the FBI. Nothing. The only thing we were told was the type explosives used."

"And that was?"

"Plastic. One detective called it C-4."

Dagger smiled.

Paige stiffened on the sofa. "I see nothing at all amusing about the deaths of five — no! ten — people. Why are you smiling?"

"It was probably an Agency hit, out of Section Five. That's Pig Lester's style. He likes to blow things up." Another man who liked to blow things up slipped into Dagger's mind — The Gunner — and he wondered why he would think of him at this time. The two had never gotten along. "And from sixty-seven through sixty-nine, Pig and his bunch were going full-tilt here in the States."

Her eyes widened. When she spoke her voice was filled with controlled rage and incredulity. "Are you telling me you *know* who killed my brother and all those other people?"

"Sure — probably. But you'll never be able to prove it. I was in 'Nam in sixty-nine, but the grapevine still worked, even over there. I heard a hit had been ordered on Crowe. Later still, I heard the hit had gone sour. Then Crowe was taken out and the entire unit — Section Five — disbanded." He was silently reflective for a moment. "Really, Paige, the section should have never been formed. Not here in the States. It wasn't necessary — then."

"You mean you believe it is now?"

"Yes," he said simply and quietly and surely. "It's a jungle out there." He waved to the outside. "People are afraid in their own homes, and that is a sad commentary on the justice system prevailing in America."

She stuck out her chin, eyes flashing at even just the thought of citizen action. "I don't agree with you."

"Of course not. I would imagine you're quite well off. Comfortably fixed. You can buy all the protection you need." He smiled that infuriatingly knowing smile once more. "Just like—in a sense—you are attempting to do now."

"You want to argue about that? Debate it?"

"Not me, lady. I was merely stating a fact."

The thought flitted through her mind that this man had probably killed many times. She wondered if he ever thought about the people he'd killed?

The answer would have surprised her.

"Did you—any of you—go to the police with your suspicions?" Dagger inquired.

"No. We hired a private detective—Rossieau—told him of our suspicions, and handed him a blank check, so to speak. I—all of us—are of some means.

"Rossieau wanted to quit several times; he just couldn't come up with anything. He said he felt he was taking our money without producing results. We begged him to continue. Then he remembered something he had overheard his grandmother saying, some years back. He wouldn't tell us what it was, at first. Said the two events were probably not related. As it turned out, they were. Very much so."

"Tell me."

"Between the time my brother was killed, and Crowe was killed—and his party—there was a rape just outside New Orleans. Actually, between Baton Rouge and New Orleans, just off Highway 61. Outside of a little Cajun bar is where it all began. The girl who was raped was a distant relative of Rossieau's grandmother, or a daughter of a friend of hers—something like that. Then, suddenly, the raped girl comes into a sum of money and certain police are asked to back off; maybe it wasn't rape after all—this is according to Rossieau. The girl was placed in a private psychiatric hospital and stayed there for a long time."

"How did your P.I. put the events together? Tie them all in?"

Paige shrugged, her breasts lifting with the movement. Dagger watched the lift and gentle fall with an appreciative eye. "He had what he called a cat man break into the hospital's records room and take pictures of the records of the girl and who was paying the bills and from where."

"And?"

"The money was coming from a bank in Central Virginia. After that, Rossieau said it was easy. I mean, armed with that knowledge, he said he just placed a few calls to friends—Rossieau had been in some kind of high-level military intelligence—and they firmed it up for him. The money came from an Agency slush fund, to use Rossieau's words." She stared hard at Dagger. "I assume he meant the CIA."

"Paige," Dagger said slowly, "you have to understand something: Ninety-nine percent of what the Company does is very necessary, the world being in the shape it's in, and I don't mean round. But every organization—if it's of any size, and the Agency is very large and complex — be it gov-ernment, military or civilian, will have its share of rogues. They just don't and can't have the wherewithal to weed those people out — not all of them. I know for a fact the DCI — "

"The what?"

"The director of Central Intelligence did not have any, repeat, did not have *any* knowledge of the existence of Section Five. Neither did State, the president, NSA, Joint Chiefs, NSC or a lot of other people in very high places. Section Five was the brain child of three men, only one of whom worked, works, for the Company."

"The Company being the CIA?"

"Right. And not only that, but all who did work for Section Five were not killers or rapists."

"And how would you know that?"

He met her slightly hostile stare. "Because I worked for Five for a year."

"Rossieau obviously did not uncover that odious fact," she said. She seemed to shrink away from him without actually moving from her spot on the sofa.

Dagger had to hide a smile at her revulsion. Goodness! I'm sitting in a room with a man who actually zapped people. Mr. Alda's boy would probably go into an absolute snit.

"Paige, I never raped anyone in my life. I have killed on orders, and will admit enjoying some of those kills to the point I knew I was ridding the world of filth."

She bit at the fullness of lower lip. "I see."

"I doubt it, lady—few civilians do. Go on with your story."

"There isn't that much more to tell." Her body English told Dagger he was forgiven for his past work. "Rossieau put what he had together: not many facts but quite a lot of damning hypothesis, and gave us each a copy."

"Where are the copies?"

"All but one was stolen over the past two months. The original copy is in a safe-deposit box in Baton Rouge." She stopped to stare at his knowing smile. "What is so funny, Dagger?"

"I'll bet you it isn't in that box."

She sat up straight on the sofa. "Dagger, there is no way anyone could get into that box without my permission."

"If it got to the box at all. Which is doubtful. Paige, you just don't realize the power of the Agency. Few people do—outsiders. It can't be proven—of course—but they touch every department of government. The computer room of the Agency—and that is only one of many—is the most awesome thing you or anyone could ever witness. Every friendly government around the world has tie-ins with Langley—and many of them don't even know they are being monitored, their computer codes broken. The Agency has—and there again, it can't be proven—stringers all over the nation and the world. Which is how, I'm certain, that original copy got switched, right in front of your eyes."

"I don't believe it!"

"You put the copy in the box personally?"

"Well, ah, actually I gave it to my banker."

"Uh-huh."

She slumped back on the sofa. "Stringers, Dagger?"

"Informants, if you will, although it goes much deeper than that. No, it isn't Orwell's *1984* or Big Brother."

She was surprised he even knew of Orwell.

"It's just the way the world is, that's all. If Sam Funk, who is president of the First National Bank of Podunk, has an affair with his secretary, well, that information might be useful some day. If the owner/editor of a newspaper has a drinking problem, or a gambling problem, that will be useful information. So on down the line.

"Now, before you get all worked up, full of indignation—righteous or otherwise—about people in government snooping on you . . . don't. Unless you have reason to come to the Agency's attention, or the attention of a dozen other agencies and groups, they don't even know you're alive. But—" he held up a warning finger—"cross them, and you could find yourself in serious trouble.

"IRS says their files are confidential—maybe they even believe it—but don't you believe it. There is no doubt in my mind that the Company has computer tie-ins with the IRS computers.

And they can punch up your records any damn time they please. And so can other groups in government.

"The Company's been a good boy—so to speak—for some years now. The quote/unquote bad asses purged. Don't you believe it." His smile was suddenly very unpleasant. "All that means is they've been transferred to a civilian-appearing job market: They run a grocery store in Queens; a sporting goods operation in Moline; a shoe store in Seattle. Whatever. And most of the time, the businesses are self-supporting, make a profit."

There was humor in his face as he waited for her inevitable question and response.

"And the money is deposited into an Agency bank?" she asked, interest on her face.

"You're learning," Dagger said, thinking: very quick, lady. "Or, as in most cases, the bank president is on a Company hook, or he's really a working agent. The same can be said of all government operations."

"The government has something on these people and they are forced to go along?"

"That's it, lady."

"The way you say it, Dagger, it sounds as though you approve of this type of . . . deception—skullduggery."

"I'm not opposed to it."

"But that's unconstitutional!" she yelled.

His laugh was deep and genuine, a bark of

humor from a man who had lived, worked and fought in countries where people could not even pronounce constitutional rights, in any language, much less tell you what it meant. In Vietnam, most of the people in the country wanted no more than an acre of land on which to plant their rice to feed their families. Most of them wouldn't have given a damn if Kermit the Frog ran the country, just as long as they were left alone.

"Sure it is," he said. "But the Bill of Rights also guarantees an American citizen the right to be safe and secure in their homes and papers and effects. And if you believe that bullshit just shoot someone who is attempting to steal your lawn mower or your car and see how fast you come to trial and how fast you end up in prison. The constitution, Paige, is so contradictory as to be practically unworkable. It's as bad as the Bible: open to hundreds of opinions and interpretations."

She studied him silently, thinking: This man is no fool. As a matter of fact, he's damned intelligent.

She stood up. "Let me get some papers from the car." She was very conscious of his eyes on her body as she walked out the door.

Back in the house, seated on the sofa, she opened her brief case and removed a folder. She met his gaze. "I still maintain it is unconstitutional."

His steady gaze, so cold she could practically

see the fiords in his eyes, bore into her dark eyes. "What would you have to fear if you have nothing to hide?"

She was silent for a moment. Mercenary or not, she thought, the man is quick. "The constitution also guarantees a person the right to a trial, Dagger."

"Like I said, it's contradictory."

She shook her head and laughed. "All right, Dagger. All right. We'll argue this later."

She wrapped up her story: Rossieau's death; the very convenient doctor, that she and her friends had been constantly watched and followed for several weeks.

He sat quietly, listening. He wondered if the woman was afraid of him. Most people were. And Dagger could never really understand that. Not the source of the fear. He had concluded long ago that most people must have a great deal of deep-rooted fear within them. Either that or they lacked confidence. Or both.

Paige was not afraid.

When he spoke, Dagger's voice was low. "Paige, what, exactly, do you want me to do?"

"I want you to help us. I want you to prove my brother and the others were killed by agents of the United States government—murdered! And to help us bring those people to justice."

He stirred. "I don't know, Paige." Before she could protest, he said, "Let me finish. After all this is over, I may—repeat: may—be able to help you prove who killed your family and friends. But I am not a detective. I think we should do first things first."

"What do you mean?"

"There were never more than fifteen to eighteen agents assigned to any one section of Five. So I think the section who hit your brother and friends have gathered in Baton Rouge to finish what they started, years ago. They have to, to protect themselves."

"I don't . . . I'm not sure what you mean."

His eyes held no warmth as he said, "I think you and the others are marked. I think they would like to scare you all into silence. All of you. They've stolen your documents, now all they have to do is steal your confidence."

"And if they can't do that?"

The words from his mouth were spoken with a deadly tone. "Then they'll have to kill you all."

4

Her face drained of color at his words, words that shocked her. "I . . . felt it might come to that," she said haltingly. "But . . . I kept telling myself: This is America, this can't happen here. Well, I guess it is happening. And you say Big Brother doesn't exist, Dagger? You're wrong."

She rose from the couch to stand in front of the barren fireplace. After looking into the empty fireplace for a few seconds, she turned and began pacing the room. Dagger watched her, taking in her grace and beauty.

She whirled around, fire in her eyes. "Well!" She spat out the word. "I suppose we now do what we should have done in the first place."

"And that is?" Dagger knew but wanted to hear it from her. He needed a good laugh.

"Ralph wants to go to the police."

Dagger laughed at her.

High color rose to darken her face, the color accentuating the fiery blue of her eyes. "Well . . .

we can't go any higher than the FBI. How about them?"

It had been a long time—too long, really—since Dagger had had a good laugh. He would rather not have had it at this woman's expense, but he couldn't help it. He howled until tears misted his vision, while Paige stood a few yards in front of him, her face dark with anger, hands on her hips.

"Paige," he said, wiping his eyes with the back of his hand, "I needed that. I just can't believe the average public mentality. It's a constant source of amusement to me."

Then she let him have it. Both barrels, as is said. Her father's people were Old English, but her mother's people were Acadian French—Cajun—and her French inheritance boiled to its explosive surface.

Dagger sat with a smile on his lips as she cursed him, unaware—or just not caring—as she slipped from French to English and back again, as she worked off her mad at his expense, just as he had given way to laughter at her expense.

She slowly wound down. Normal color returned to her cheeks and her breathing evened. Dagger sat quietly in his chair.

"That's quite a present you just handed me, Paige. I don't believe I've ever had my ancestry traced from the present back to the trees, and beyond, quite so eloquently."

She glared at him. *"You* speak French?"

"I speak several languages, Paige."

She stared at him. Shook her head in disbelief. "You are a man of many surprises, Dagger. Will you help us?"

"Maybe." But he knew he was going to help. The case, he felt, was much bigger than any of the five civilians realized. And he wanted to get next to this woman. "What's it worth to you?"

"We paid the private investigator two hundred and fifty dollars a day — plus expenses."

Dagger shook his head. "Not enough. This one is going to involve killing." He watched her for some kind of reaction.

Her face paled slightly and her eyes widened. "You said that with no more emotion than asking someone to pass the salt."

Dagger lifted his shoulders in indifference.

"You can't know for certain," she said. "The killing, I mean."

"Yes, I can, Paige. I know Pig and his bunch. And I know Section Five."

"Five hundred dollars a day, plus all your expenses," she offered. "Plus a . . . five thousand dollar bonus at the conclusion."

He rose from his chair and walked the short distance between them, putting his big hands on her waist. She turned, putting her back to him. He moved his hands upward, cupping her breasts, at the same time pushing his groin against her buttocks.

She offered no resistance.

She felt the bulk of him against her.

He slipped his hand downward, to stroke her denim-clad belly. But as he slid his hand further downward to cup the mound of her, she slipped away. Out of his grasp, she turned to face him.

"I'm not a honky-tonk girl, Dagger. Such as the kind you're accustomed to, I'm sure. I make the decision as to where and when I play. And with whom."

"Si fait." He smiled at her. "Just clearing the air, baby."

"I'm not your baby. Don't call me that."

"OK, baby."

He was playing again. Paige wondered how many personalities the man could bring to the surface, and if he knew when he shifted from one to the other?

"The bonus comes up front, Paige."

Her smile was victorious, her eyes shining. "I anticipated that. I had a cashier's check made out before I left Baton Rouge." She walked to her purse and dug at the contents, handing the check to Dagger.

Their fingers touched. His fingers, hard, blunt-ended and calloused. Her fingers, soft to the touch, carefully manicured.

He tucked the check away in his pocket. "I'll button up the house after I get my gear together." He looked hard at her, his mind working swiftly. He knew Pig and his boys could have silenced this bunch of amateurs with no more effort than swatting a fly. So something bigger was at stake, something Paige and her friends either didn't know about, or thought they didn't. He made a mental list of the gear they might need.

"Be sure, Paige — about this thing. Pig — if he is involved — plays rough. Get ready to spend some money, and I'm talking ten or fifteen thousand more dollars. At the low end. If Pig and his boys and girls are after you people, we'll probably have to run for it as soon as he discovers I'm in the game. And running gets expensive. You sure?"

"Yes," she said quietly.

"All right. From here, we go to Georgia."

"Why Georgia?"

" 'Cause that's where the man is. Don't interrupt. I'm going to need some expensive gear. And there ain't no charge accounts with this man."

She stared at him, not having the foggiest idea what he was talking about.

"I won't kid you, Paige: If Pig is in on this, it's going to get rough. If he gets his hands on you, he'll torture and rape you before he kills you — and I am not joking. Pig doesn't have both oars in the water."

"Nice company you used to keep, Dagger."

"I despise the bastard."

"That makes me feel a little better."

When Dagger decided to move, Paige noticed, he did not waste time — or any motion. He packed swiftly, locked up his house (it was then she noticed how much the home resembled a fort, with small windows and steel-reinforced doors), and they were moving within the hour.

Dagger told her they would drive straight through to Atlanta. As they drove, she told him how she had taken evasive action leaving Baton Rouge, finally losing her followers.

"Smart on your part," he complimented her. And she got the impression that compliments from Dagger's lips were rare. "Shows you have a survival instinct built-in. Tell me about your friends."

"Well . . . Mike Shaffler appears to be the toughest and strongest of the men—but I don't really know. I don't believe any of them have ever been in any real crisis situation."

"Any of the men ever pulled any military time?"

"No."

"Wonderful," Dagger said sarcastically.

She ignored that. Then she decided to defend her friends. "But Mike was a star football player at LSU, and so was his brother."

"I'm so impressed," Dagger said.

Paige looked at her arm to see if any tiny flecks of ice from his tone lingered on her blouse.

"Tell me about Mike. What does he do?"

"Nothing," she said bluntly and honestly. "He doesn't have to work, so he doesn't. He's been married twice, divorced twice."

"Playboy."

"Well, yes. But you must understand that all of us are of some means and social importance."

That got her a dirty look.

She kept her eyes on the road. "Mike and his brother, Jimmy, came into quite an inheritance. Mike chose to become a gentleman farmer, rancher, and . . . playboy. He owns quite a large sugar plantation in south Louisiana and a very large farm in north Louisiana. A big cattle ranch somewhere. But I don't believe he's done a day's work in ten years."

"Sounds like a real winner," Dagger muttered.

Paige smiled, only a faint curving along her lips. She did not tell Dagger her own opinion of Mike was even lower than his. For a variety of reasons.

She said, "Mike's brother, Jimmy, is another story. Just the opposite of Mike. Jimmy works and works hard. Owns several farms and businesses, stays on top of them. Isn't afraid to get his hands dirty. I think Jimmy would probably stand up to any bad situation.

"Kit Volker is a playgirl. Nothing more than that. Divorced. Marriage didn't last long. Pouty. Spoiled. Has to have her way or she is hard to handle. She has quite a lot of money and is a talented artist, but she won't work at it. She could be quite a well-known and respected artist, I believe. She just doesn't have the drive or discipline to achieve it. She has experimented with almost every kind of dope known to exist, and her morals are, shall we say, rather loose."

"Screws a lot," Dagger said.

"Crude, but correct." Paige glanced at the man. That damnable smile was playing on his lips.

"Go on."

"At first glance you won't — at least I don't think you will — believe it. But Kit's brother, Ralph, is the strongest of the five — myself included. He looks rather frail. But he isn't. I get the impression he is quite capable of taking care of himself — if he's pushed to it. Rumor has it he is black belt in karate, although he never speaks of it. He is a CPA, owns his own firm. Does quite well. That's a thumbnail sketch of us."

"All but you," he corrected.

"What do you want to know, and why?"

"I want to know everything. Why? Because I'm a curious sort. Something you say could well save your lives, give me an angle on which way to go. And you haven't painted a very admirable picture of the people you've hired me to help. Half of them don't sound as though they're worth keeping alive."

She glanced at him, something odd shining in her eyes. "You're not God. That isn't for you to judge."

"I've judged a hell of a lot more people on a hell of a lot less information, lady. And left them to rot on the ground."

"You've killed many times?" A look of horror

and revulsion on her face. Same look of people walking through a snake house at the zoo.

Look, look, mommy! Ohhh!

A dime's worth of orgasm.

"Yes," Dagger said.

"Does it ever bother you? I mean, like dreams or nightmares?"

Or daymares, Dagger thought. "No, almost never. And then not for very long."

She thought about that reply for a few silent miles. "Dagger? Why did you laugh at me back at the house. I think I know why, but I want to hear it from you."

"Because you people are in a box, and you can't, or won't, recognize it as such. You are, I would imagine, all of you, law-abiding people, trusting in the law to help you out of any mess. But the law won't be able to do a thing with this one. You have no proof. A good investigative reporter—and it hurts my mouth to say it—with time and money and a big daily or network behind him, might, *might* be able to prove something on Section Five. Obviously, that's the way the agents from that old section see it. But rather than letting you go and taking whatever lumps might come their way because of past actions—if any—they're taking the easy way out. If they can't frighten you into silence, then they'll just have to kill you. All of you."

She shivered beside him. Dagger imagined she felt chill bumps crawl over her flesh like maggots working on the cold flesh of the dead.

Dagger said, "Other than the few names I've mentioned, none of you has any proof to take to the police or the Bureau. You can't prove anyone has been following you. You can't prove anyone is trying to harm you. No proof that anyone broke into your homes or apartments and stole anything. You don't have anything solid. Civilian police sure as hell never heard of Section Five. I doubt very seriously the FBI ever heard of it. And if they did, they sure as hell won't admit it. To do so this late in the game would destroy their credibility. And they can't afford that.

"If Pig Lester is involved in this—and I strongly suspect he is, probably in charge of it— all he has to do is lay low for a time and he'll get you all.

"The Company, Paige, *has* to take care of its own. They have absolutely no choice in the matter. Calmer, cooler heads might not want to, but they will have no choice, not in the final breakdown. Five more deaths, as compared to the shattering of morale, more disgrace on the nation, the interruption of vital information flowing from all countries . . ." He let his silence tell the rest of it. But he was thinking: It's got to be something bigger. Nothing else adds up.

He was to find it was bigger than anything he could have possibly imagined.

"Are you playing devil's advocate, Dagger? Which side are you on?"

"You hired me, Paige. I'm on your side. I can't be bought off. Believe it or not, that is the unwritten code a merc must abide by."

"Are all mercenaries this honest?"

"Most of the ones I know, yes."

"Interesting," she muttered. "What do you intend doing about these . . . animals stalking us?"

He thought for a few seconds. "First of all, I intend trying to convince all of you to drop your pursuit. Let the dead lie. If I can do that, then I'll try to set up a meet with Pig, ask him to ease off and back off. You people will forget it if he'll do the same. Go on back to your jobs and everything will hopefully be copacetic."

"Be what?"

"OK."

She chewed at her lower lip. "But you don't think this . . . Pig will agree to that?"

"That's right."

"Then?"

"I take them out while protecting you people. That's the only other way I can see — at this time."

"Kill them?"

"That is correct."

She looked at him strangely and was silent.

Dagger's mind was racing out front, mentally determining what equipment he would need. He knew the odds of Pig backing off were astronomically high against. Whatever it was, it was big, too big to plan on making any deals.

Dagger had his .41 mag, but in some instances

that would prove too big and make too much noise. He would have to get a Colt Woodsman, maybe a couple of them, barrels machined for a silencer. He would need a small, easy-to-handle machine gun. An M-10, 9mm, would be the best for this job, he believed. Thirty-two-round clip. He'd get two of them if he could, putting one back for a spare. There would perhaps be occasion for some long-range shooting, so he opted for a model 70 Winchester, .338 magnum.

And there was other equipment he'd pick up when he met the man in Georgia.

If the man would meet with him. For if this was a government-backed job against Paige and her friends, the word would have gone out: no cooperation.

He would cross that bridge if he came to it.

Dagger noticed the small plastic strip in the window of the Cadillac. "This a rent car?"

"Yes. I thought I told you. Why, what difference does that make?"

"Time," Dagger said shortly. And he knew from the slightly knotted-up feeling in his guts this job was something very big. Dagger had learned a long time back to trust his hunches. "We could have been to St. Louis by now. We'll head for Memphis. Pig will guess you came, or are coming, to see me. And he'll put it together. They don't dare put a bug or a tail on me; I'd pick it up as soon as they did. Pig will probably have Springfield and St. Louis staked out. He won't figure on Memphis. I hope. We'll turn the car in and book passage to Atlanta under false names. Use cash. You have bank cards?"

"Of course." She glanced at him. "Doesn't everybody?"

"No. That's just another way for people to keep track of a person. Can you get cash with them?"

"Certainly." There was a fair amount of indignation in her tone.

"Get the limit on each card."

"But I have several thousand dollars in traveler's checks."

Dagger looked at her and concealed a rueful smile. He didn't want to unduly alarm the woman, but he knew if the Agency—any part of the Agency—was behind any of this, they had the power within the IRS to freeze bank accounts under any number of false charges. He didn't feel it the time to explain to her that Big Brother has a person by the balls anytime Big Brother wants to apply the pressure.

Or in Paige's case—by another part of her superb anatomy.

"I want us to have at least five thousand in cash," Dagger told her. "Ten thousand if you can swing it. Some of Pig's people may be hungry enough to be bought off. Are you scared enough yet to spread your legs for a guarantee of safety?"

The look she gave him was not at all friendly.

"Who has hold of my ankles?"

"Pig or one of his men."

"No way, Dagger!"

"Just asking. When we get to Atlanta, we'll pick up another rental car for the run to Baton Rouge."

"Why not fly?"

"Can't risk it with all the equipment we'll be carrying. If we're caught, the police would put both of us under the jail."

"Sounds like you plan on starting a minor war."

"Just a little brush fire," he told her. "Paige?"

"Yes?"

"From this moment on, I'm the boss. Don't question what we'll be doing or why. When I tell you to do something, do it."

That defiant jutting out of the jaw. Her eyes darkened. "That sounds like an order."

"It is, Paige. If you want to stay alive."

She forced a grin. "Yes, sir."

But Dagger did not return the grin. He had suddenly untied the knots in his guts and put a piece of the puzzle together. And he did not like the picture the puzzle might present. He knew, only too well, the awesome power of a government agency — any government, any agency — gone haywire. Knew it could get bloody. He had been there before.

And it looked like he was returning for a replay.

Full dark when their flight touched down on the tarmac of the Atlanta Airport. The night was cool and cloudless. Renting a car, Dagger drove west for a time, then turned straight north for a few miles. Just outside of a small town, they checked into a motel, paying cash for the rooms, signing false names. Paige suspected he would try to register them as man and wife. When he did not, signing her as his sister, she did not know if she was angry or disappointed.

Or both.

They had stopped at a number of banks along the way and in Memphis, Paige using her bank cards for cash advances. She had given the money to Dagger.

He said, "Stay put. Don't answer the door for anyone except me. Chain the door and stay in."

He was gone into the night.

At a service station, he placed his call.

"Haven't heard much about you for a few years, Dagger," the man said.

"I've been out of the business—so to speak."

"So I heard. You back in?"

"For a time."

"Don't con me, Dagger. And even more important, don't con yourself. Nobody comes back in for a one-shot."

"Could be you're right."

"What'd you need, Dagger?"

Dagger told him.

"No sweat. If you've got the cash."

"I've got it."

"Dagger, I owe you a favor or two—maybe three, so I'll deliver the goods this time. But I know what you're up to; the word is out on you. Came down hard, if you know what I mean." He paused. "Aw, piss on this. Hell with it! Come on out to the old house. We got to chew and spit some."

Dagger wondered if the old merc was setting him up for a touch. He felt the butt of his .41 mag. "OK. Is the old way still the best way?"

The voice chuckled. "You haven't forgotten a thing, have you? Yeah. I'll meet you by the ruins. Give me ninety to get the gear together."

Dagger traveled the old back country roads, taking his time, feeling his way, the headlights like twin eyes in the darkness. He was alert for any tails. None. He pulled onto a dirt road and drove up to the fire-gutted ruins of a once-magnificent ante-bellum home, the columns standing like tall black sentries in the night. A man limped out to meet him. They shook hands.

"Long time, Dagger."

"Seventy-seven. When we went into the Comoran Islands."

"And how is Le Colonel—Le Affreux?"

"Haven't seen him since. That was one of my last ops. If Bob has any sense, he's peddling cars in France."

"Do any of us have any sense, Dagger?"

"Good point. We are, old friend, what we make of ourselves."

"Age brings out the philosopher in us all, eh, Dagger? And now you're back in business."

"I got restless."

"This time, *mercenaire,*" the older man said, "you might well get dead."

"A chance we all take, Dog." Dagger used the man's cover name, hung on him when he was a very young mercenary in Southeast Asia in the early fifties, fighting for the white planters against the communists from the north.

All that changed at Dien Bien Phu.

"You're lookin' good, Dagger. Still keepin' in shape, I see."

Dagger nodded. "I try. How's the cancer, Dog?"

"Still with me, but I'm fighting it. It'll get me one of these days, though. All right, old son—I brought you a couple boxes of .41 mag ammo, figured you still carried that goddamn hand cannon. Got you two M-10s—9mm—five hundred rounds of ammo. Four clips per weapon. Got your Colt Woodsman, two of them, tapped for silencer, and a good silencer. Ammo for the Colts. Tossed in a good .22 mag derringer—hideout gun just for luck, and you're going to need all the *bonne chance* you can get on this caper, son. Told you a lie about the .338—thought I had one. Didn't. Had to run in a sub. Been a lot of calls for long rifles lately. So I brought you a—" he grinned—"Weatherby, .460 mag."

"Jesus Christ!" Dagger said. "What do you think I'm hunting, Cape Buffalo?"

The old Dog laughed. "No, just a big, bad Pig, that's all—and believe me, old son, that's enough."

"He's a big, lard-assed loony, Dog."

Dog shook his head, his white hair picking up shards of moonlight. "He's still tough and mean, Dagger. Don't sell Pig too short—and he hates you." He was silent for a few seconds. "Dagger, reassure an old man that you're not taking on the Company single-handedly. The word is out on you, Dagger. You're not supposed to get any co-operation from old friends. You know the drill, boy: too many markers out on too many of us, and they're being picked up faster than bald on a buzzard. The big hand coming from D.C."

"Not the whole Company, Dog. Just an old section that's been reactivated—very quietly, and, I'm sure, without the knowledge of the DCI. And I don't know what it's all about—not really. Not yet. But I think it's bigger than people realize."

"Section Five?"

"Yeah."

The Dog swore softly in the night, his voice and his words tainting the softness of early spring in Georgia. He put a hand on Dagger's shoulder. "Son, back off from this one. It's too big. Too many folks in high-up places involved, and they're not going to let you smear their names all over the TV."

"The folks I'm working for are clean, Dog. They're being chased and hounded because they uncovered a cesspool. And I believe in what they're doing. I took their money; I gave my word."

"Give them back their money, Dagger! Tell them to stuff it. Listen to me on this one, boy. There's something big in the wind. I don't know what, or I'd tell you and to hell with the word. But be careful, Dagger. Be very careful who you trust in this caper; all may not be what it seems."

"What's it all about, Dog?"

"I don't know, boy." The older man shrugged. Sighed in the night. "I've done all I know how to do, Dagger. I tried." He looked hard at Dagger. "You're stubborn, boy. Just like a damn Missouri mule. All right. I brought you a box full of assorted goodies: some C-4 and timers, other explosives, other stuff. I think you'll need them all in this suicide mission."

"You really believe it's that big and that bad, Dog?"

"Goddamn it, boy, you know it is—you've been in the game too long not to be able to sense it in your guts. So stop playing dumbass with an old man. What are you trying to do: Come back in a flash and go out in a blaze of glory?"

"Aren't you planning the same thing when

what's eating on you starts taking too big of a bite, Dog?"

That stopped the old mercenary. Then he smiled. "You never were one to play patty-cake, were you, boy? Yeah, OK — you're right. Let's get this gear transferred. After this, Dagger, don't count on old friends — you'd be putting them in a hard bind and maybe signing their death warrants. But there is one they either can't or won't touch — and he's down south. You know who I'm talking about."

Dagger nodded.

"I've loaded you up the best I could, Dagger. All I can say is watch your back."

"How much do I owe you, Dog?"

The old merc, beat-up and scarred from more battles than he could even remember, looked at Dagger for a very long moment. He knew; he would do the same thing were he standing in Dagger's shoes. He finally smiled: the smile of warriors that only warriors understand, men who have stood and laughed at death and loved life and tasted the sweet and sour of it all. He knew.

"Nothing, boy," Dog said. "This one is on the house."

"You know," Dagger said, allowing himself a tight smile, "I kinda figured it would be."

"Arschloch!" the Dog cursed him in jest.

Dagger switched languages. *"Bordel de merde!"*

"Now that we have that out of our systems," the Dog said. "Let's get to work."

The men worked for a few moments in silence, transferring the lethal cargo from one car to the other. Then the cancer-stricken older merc and the young merc stood for a time, sharing silent memories of battles past and friends long dead and rotting in faraway graves, remembered only by fellow warriors, almost never held in any special reverence by those civilians they fought and bled and sweated and died for. And the two men shared silently the unfairness of it all. Without words.

They looked at each other. Then, as if on cue, they shook hands and turned away, walking back to their cars, without ever acknowledging they had ever spoken or met, ever fought together, ever known the horror or the high of combat.

And then the Georgia night was silent as death.

Only the dead but still moving memories remained by the ruins for a time, the ghosts of warriors past, and then they, too, were gone.

And the night was silent.

5

He tapped lightly on Paige's door. "Dagger," he softly called. Chain noises on wood and metal and the door opened. "Get your gear together, we're pulling out — now."

"What?"

"There you go again, questioning orders."

"Sorry, sahib," she muttered. "I'll be ready in a few minutes."

"Please take your time," Dagger said with a smile. She wore no bra under her thin shirt and Dagger took in the nipples pushing against the fabric.

"Getting your eyes full?" she asked him.

"Yes. And my hands are so jealous."

She grimaced and shut the door in his face.

Dagger laughed at the closed door.

They headed southwest on Interstate 85. They got sandwiches to go at a truck stop and then continued rolling through the night.

"Why are we doing this?" Paige asked. "I was

looking forward to a night's sleep."

"Sleep forever when you're dead," was Dagger's response. "Pig may have had the Dog staked out, so we put distance between us and them and get to your friends as quickly as possible. The Dog told me the word's gone out — come down — that K Teams are looking for me."

"Dog! God, what disgusting names you people give each other. What in the world is a K Team?"

"Kill Team." The faint odor of nervous sweat clung to him, not unpleasantly so.

A reminder to her of the strain he must be silently enduring.

Despite herself, and the knowledge that he was the type of man she didn't particularly care for, she felt an attraction — of sorts — toward him.

"I napped while you were gone," she told him. "Why don't you rest and let me drive."

Dagger gave her the wheel and told her to wake him in two hours.

Two and a half hours later, on the outskirts of Montgomery, she woke him. She was startled at his sudden alertness, for she had not touched him, merely extended her hand toward him before his eyes popped open, pale and expressionless, staring at her.

"You sometimes frighten me," she told him.

His reply was a grunt.

They picked up Interstate 65 and headed for Mobile.

Too keyed up to sleep, she asked, "Dagger, despite all you think is going to happen, you like this, don't you? The excitement, I mean?"

"Yes, I suppose that's true."

"Then why did you retire?"

He slowly expelled a breath. "I . . . got tired of the blood and the sweat and the . . . I just got disgusted with it all. War is a futile gesture. The strong hammering the weak into submission. But out of the weak, there are always men and women of strength, and they form guerrilla bands—it never stops. Soon it will be occurring in this country. Bet on it. But . . . I thought I could put it all behind me. I was wrong, I suppose."

She stirred on the seat beside him. "You really believe there will be war in this country?"

"It's inevitable. We came very close to economic collapse last year. And in a nation that is filled with petty, greedy, grasping, spoiled and pampered people, that would have spawned riots and anarchy. We are rapidly approaching a turn-row: two or three liberal, Democratic presidents in a row, with liberal houses to back them, and this nation will be a socialistic form of government. That has been foreseen and forewarned by men and women much more knowledgeable than this soldier. Should that occur, some of those in the opposite camp will turn to guns to settle it. We have too many people in this nation who not only want but advocate a free ride—and there is no such thing.

"We have too many haves and too many have-nots. This nation simply cannot provide the jobs for its citizens. It's physically impossible with the world market the way it is. In three to five years, the communist guerrillas now in Central America will sweep through Mexico and be camped on our southwestern borders. By then it will be too late to stop the guerrillas, for the malcontents in this nation—and there are many—will be only too willing to join the guerrillas, and in a nation the size of America, a full-scale guerrilla operation will be impossible to stop."

"Where do you keep your crystal ball, Dagger?"

"I have eyes, ears and a brain, Paige. If people will use those attributes to their maximum, that's all it takes."

"Then . . . you're back in your . . . business to stay?"

"If I—we—live through what's ahead of us, yes."

"I see."

"I really doubt it, Paige."

"I know you are a decorated war hero," she said.

"There is no other type of hero, Paige. Regardless of what some writers claim. The difference is, most of us don't take the title too seriously, even though we genuinely earned it."

She thought about that for a mile or two.

When she brought her thoughts back to the

present, Dagger was saying, "Decorated for doing exactly what hundreds of other guys did. Only difference being I was seen doing it and they weren't."

"I think you're being overly modest. I know you won the Congressional Medal of Honor."

"For whatever it's worth. One guy who won it, so I heard, is washing dishes in a cafe in Peoria, Illinois. Only job he could find. Americans really think a lot of their genuine heroes."

He looked at her in the dim light from the dashboard. "How did you know about the congressional?"

"I know a great deal about you. A friend of yours who was with the Cuban resistance movement told Rossieau about you."

The man down south the Dog spoke of. "Ah, yes. Has to be Hank."

"Yes, that was the name. You were a paratrooper, a Ranger, a Green Beret, a member of the French foreign legion and a mercenary. You have a peculiar moral streak in you. You're a loner, never married. You were—or are—considered to be a very dangerous man. You can kill without remorse."

"Interesting," Dagger said.

"That I would know so much about you?"

"Yes. Why?"

"I'm a curious sort," she fed his words back to him.

He smiled.

"Why did you never marry?"

Green eyes came to him in a rushing flood of emotions. Memories so real they seemed to be alive. The scent of her, softness of her hair, the touch of her, the—

He rudely pushed her away.

"You'd better get some sleep," Dagger said gruffly. "I'll wake you if I get tired."

Hours later, when he shook her awake, they were approaching New Orleans. He had driven through Mobile while she slept.

She rubbed her eyes and looked at him. "Why didn't you wake me, Dagger? I could have spelled you at the wheel."

"You were sleeping so soundly I didn't want to disturb you. It's been years since I was in New Orleans. How do we get to the airport?"

"Pull over. I'll drive."

"Is that an order?" he said, smiling.

"Yes." She laughed and, oddly enough, felt closer to him.

Opposites attract, she thought. But in this case, is it worth the risk? We are so different, from such alien worlds.

She looked at his profile, and the woman in her softened.

EAGLE-FALL + 14

At Dagger's instructions, they rented another car at the airport, a full-sized Chevy, and drove across the Pontchartrain. He found a small motel and they checked in: two adjoining rooms. They checked in under assumed names, paying cash in advance. Paige stayed in the car.

"Some motels, the larger ones," Dagger said, "have begun asking for IDs at check-in. Stay with the smaller units, they're safer if you're trying to hide."

"I'm picking up all sorts of useful tidbits from you," she replied, rather a jaundiced look in her eyes.

Dagger ignored the dryness. "I'm going to get some sleep. Stay close and out of sight. Tonight, I start hunting them."

She noticed he was smiling as he said that, and there was a grim look of satisfaction in his cold eyes.

She said nothing.

* * *

She had drifted off to sleep in her room, fully clothed, on the top spread. Then she was vaguely aware of a shower running in Dagger's room. When the shower stopped, she again dozed. The scent of after-shave assailed her head. She opened her eyes. Dagger was standing over her.

She rolled over on her back, fully aware of his eyes on her body. They traveled from ankles to eyes.

"Get up, Paige. We've been spotted and staked out."

Absolutely no romance in the man's soul whatsoever, she thought, swinging her feet to the carpet and running her fingers through her thick hair.

"How did they find us?"

"Leg work," he said simply. "They knew you rented the original car. After that, it was simple: They just staked out the airports in Baton Rouge and New Orleans. Well, I wanted them to know I was in this game, but it means more trouble a little quicker than I thought."

She began brushing her hair. "What do you mean?"

"Someone within the Agency is working with them. It doesn't come as any surprise to me. Either there, or in some intelligence group, at least. Pig has been in the business for a long time, and he's done a lot of favors for a lot of people, intentionally doing them, building up brownie points just in case something like this ever happened. Or else he . . ." Dagger trailed off, lapsing into silence.

"Or else what?" Paige prompted.

"Nothing." Dagger shook his head. "Thinking out loud, that's all. Well," he said with a sigh, "it's happened, and it complicates matters."

"How? I don't understand."

"It means I can't go in shooting at anything that moves. Even if they are on his side. Some of the men and women he may have pulled in from the outside will have no knowledge of what you and your friends are really attempting to do. Pig will have convinced them you're all traitors of some sort, that you're attempting to destroy our intelligence networks for the Reds, or flooding the country with funny money made in Russia. There is no telling what kind of crap he may have fed them, backed up with very convincing proof — even without any proof, Pig can be very convincing and humble when it serves his purpose. I've got to get to a safe phone and call in to a friend of mine with Army intelligence. Maybe he'll help me, maybe not."

She watched him slip into and then lace up his low-quarters. "Most men wear loafers," she said absently.

"Ever try to run quickly, for distance, in slip-ons?" he countered.

He thinks of all possibilities, Paige thought.

I'll remember that.

"Paige? Have you told your parents about this — anything about it?"

She shook her head. "No. I haven't seen them in weeks, and I didn't see the point of worrying them about any of this — until we had any proof. Besides, they're in England for the summer, then Europe. They'll be gone for several months. Father has extensive business holdings over on the continent."

How sophisticated and urbane, Dagger thought. On the continent. "Any of the others told their friends or relatives?"

"I'm . . . I'm sure they haven't. We agreed not to. Besides, the Shaffler parents are dead. Ralph and Kit have relatives in Dallas, but they are not close. No, no one knows."

Dagger was thoughtful for a moment. "Your parents live where?"

"They have a home here in New Orleans. But they have just purchased and renovated a huge, old mansion just south of St. Francisville."

"Servants?"

"Not yet."

"Utilities on?"

"Yes. Certainly." She caught his drift. "Yes, it would be perfect. It's really quite isolated, a lovely, old ante-bellum home. And it was bought under a corporate name, not under our name." She smiled. "Yes, let's go there. It's quite romantic."

Dagger ignored the last bit. "Maybe. You say it's secluded?"

"Very. Sits in the middle of . . . oh, I don't know how many acres."

She went into the bathroom to freshen up and put on makeup. When she returned, Dagger was screwing something onto the barrel of a pistol.

"What's that thing?" she asked.

"Silencer."

She watched him check the clip. "It's getting down to the wire, isn't it, Dagger?"

"Pretty close. Look out the window, tell me if you recognize the man in the blue Buick parked next to the alley opening."

She peeped out through the drapes. "He's the man who has been following me from the outset. He's grinned at me several times, a nasty grin. I don't like him at all."

"That's good."

"Why do you say that?"

His pale eyes touched her blue ones. "Because I'm about to kill him, probably."

A vein began throbbing at her temples.

"His name is Les Kates. He's got more John Doe arrest warrants floating around for him than John Dillinger ever had: rape, assault, strong-arm tactics, torture, civil rights violations — you name it, he's done it. He will not be missed."

"You're assuming a lot, aren't you? They haven't tried to harm us in any way. At least, not yet."

Dagger's smile was wan. "Getting cold feet, Paige?"

She glared at him.

"I listened to the news while you slept. Call your friend, Miss Volker. Ask her what happened to her early this morning."

She paled slightly, put her hand on the phone, then withdrew it. "This phone might not be safe."

"You're learning."

"What happened to her?" There was almost a little-girl quality to her voice. A very scared little girl.

"Someone tried to kidnap her. She started screaming bloody murder and they had to abort the mission. Kit wriggled away." He looked out at the afternoon sunlight. He looked at Paige. "Still think I'm opening this dance, honey?"

Paige sat on the edge of the bed and fought back a watery flood of emotions. Through a silvery mist, she heard Dagger say, "You sit there and blubber for a while, Paige. I'll go earn my money."

"Son of a bitch!" she cursed him.

He laughed at her. "S.B. That's me."

The door opened and closed. Paige sat on the side of the bed. She wiped her eyes. She did not want to peek through the drapes and witness a cold-blooded murder. At least that's what she tried to tell herself it would be. Somehow the silent words fell flat in her mind.

Kates watched Dagger walk slowly to the car

parked by the alley. No one else could be seen. There had never been any love between the two men, and Kates felt the old hate well up strong within him. It was jealous hate, but Kates would never admit that.

"Hello, son of a bitch," Kates said, his words laced with venom.

Dagger said nothing. His Woodsman was tucked between the waistband of his trousers and his skin, over his rear pocket. Tucked loosely, so the silencer would not catch on the cloth of his trousers when he jerked it out. Dagger noticed a .38 snub-nose on the seat beside Kates. But Dagger knew Kates well, knew that the obvious .38 was a decoy. Kates was an admirer of Mike Hammer and carried a .45 auto in a speed rig under his left armpit. The weapon would be on half-cock. Not the smartest or safest way to carry a big automatic.

But as someone had once observed: It sure made Mickey a lot of money.

"You bought yourself a mess of grief this time, Dagger baby. You should have stayed retired and away from the big boys."

"I want a sit-down with Pig, Kates. Try to work something out."

Kates's laugh was the nasty kind. Dagger noticed his breath was strong enough to stop a fly in midflight. "Too late, Dagger."

"What do you mean?"

"SOS, S.O.B."

Dagger nodded. "OK. But don't try to tell me the Company is all the way in on this. The DCI would have no part of something like this."

"I think two full sections will be enough, Dagger."

Twenty-four agents, minimum, Dagger mentally tallied up the score. More with maverick agents from other departments and those who were sucked innocently into the operation. Make it an even forty.

Dagger had been told he was SOS. Now he had to make certain. "Five or six more bodies, Kates? When does it all end?"

"When you're all dead, Dagger. That word comes from the assistant DCI and Mitchell." He laughed, once more offending the air. And Dagger. "Funny thing is, Dagger, you can't prove a thing. Fritzler is covered head-deep to the good — clean. And nobody can tie General Mitchell in on any of this."

"Only one man," Dagger stabbed in the dark, searching.

Kates shook his head. "You've been out of it too long, Dagger, my boy. No one knows the third man."

So the mysterious third man was still operating. Rumors of him were kicking around when Dagger was operative. Some said he worked out of California; others said he was full-time District of Columbia. Some said his base of operations was Wall Street. Others said he didn't exist.

"You're sure you want this, Kates?"

Kates grinned. Dagger noticed his teeth needed cleaning. "I pick up a few coins for this touch, Dagger."

Using his left hand, partly hidden from view by the door, Kates unbuttoned his jacket.

"You're just as big a fool as you always were, Kates."

"Goodbye, Dagger."

Dagger slipped the Colt from his waistband and shot Kates in the temple, almost at point-blank range—just as the agent reached for his .45. The small slug jerked Kates to the right, stretching him out in the front seat, his head resting on the right-side armrest.

Kates would no longer offend people with his stinking breath.

Dagger took the .38 and the .45, rolled up all the windows and locked the doors of the car after removing the keys from the ignition. He walked back to the rooms.

He told Paige, "Get a towel and wipe off everything you might have touched. We've got to travel. The word is out on me, and on you and your friends as well—SOS."

She had changed clothes, dried her eyes, and regained composure. "SOS?"

"Shoot on sight."

Dagger drove aimlessly, to see if they were being followed. No tail that he could spot.

Paige asked, "That man you just . . . killed—" she seemed to gulp the word—"did he have a family?"

"I don't believe so. He was married once for a short time. Divorced years ago."

"Any children?"

"No. That I can tell you for sure. Put those thoughts out of your mind, Paige. You can't think about that, can't dwell on it. These people have been sent here to kill you and your friends— and me. Kates confirmed that. And it's even bigger than I first thought. You first thought. One of the top men in the Agency is involved and he's part of the big picture, I'm sure." Or the bigger picture, Dagger kept that to himself. "But a man once considered for a post in the National Security Agency is ramrodding this operation. And the third man. The mystery man. But he doesn't bother me as much as the general. He'll have friends in the active military that owe him."

"One great, big fraternity," Paige summed it up accurately.

Dagger abruptly pulled off the road and into a service station, parking by the phone. Paige watched him exchange green for coins, feed the machine and talk for a long time, twice going back for more change. She heard the conversation change from harsh profanity to a more buddy-buddy type of chatting of old times and distant places.

Driving away, pulling out onto the highway, she asked, "Well?"

"The army's out of it. At least for now, that is. I laid it on the line to my buddy—he's a colonel. A captain when I knew him well in 'Nam."

"Was the army . . . in on it?"

"Yes. A certain branch of it."

"What branch?"

"You would never have heard of it, Paige. Not very many people have. Be glad you never came in contact with this branch. Just be glad they are not in on the hunt." Dagger was silent for a moment, lost in remembrance, thinking of a good friend of years past. Terry Kovak. One of the original Dog Team members. He sighed. Long dead. "They were approached by Pig to join the hunt. He fed them a line of bull about how I'd turned traitor. That was the wrong tack to take and Pig should have known better—shows he's slipping. The Reds approached me years ago, offering me a lot of money to change sides, work both sides of the street as a double agent. I went straight to my section leader and, under his orders, took the job, eventually breaking up a spy ring. The Reds have me red-tabbed in their files."

"What's that mean?"

"Kill me if they can."

"Wonderful," she said dryly. "Now I see why you are so cautious."

"Anyway, my buddy is contacting his counterparts in other branches, telling them, asking them, if they're approached, to hold off."

"Will they?"

"My friend thinks so."

She was silent as Dagger's mind worked over-time. He was doubtful he would be able to make another kill as easily as he had hit Kates. From this point on, Pig and his people would be very careful in dealing with Dagger.

Dagger wondered if Kates had been able to re-port in while he was watching the motel. There had been no handie-talkie in the car, and no CB. Dagger reviewed the kill scene, the car. It had been a rented car. But he didn't know if Kates had left the car to call in. He thought not. Kates would not have risked letting his prey slip away.

"What are you thinking, Dagger?"

"We've got to get word to your friends to leave the city. To meet us. Got to buy a little time."

"The phones are bugged? In their apartments, I mean?"

"I'm sure of it. And I can't risk leaving you alone while I go in after them. Not until I'm a little more certain of their moves."

She gave him a curious gaze. "Am I more im-portant than the others?"

He was silent for a mile, the hum of the tires and the rush of air the only proof she was not by herself. "Yes," he finally spoke.

That confused her already-troubled emotions. "Why, Dagger?"

"Maybe it's because you hold the money," he

said with a smile.

"I gave it all to you, remember? But thanks anyway," she said dryly.

He had an idea. "Do any of your friends speak French?"

"Yes. Ralph Volker. I see what you're getting at. But what if the person listening in speaks French?"

"Chance we have to take. Speak very fast when you talk to him. And speak Cajun; use as many colloquialisms as possible."

She touched his arm and was amazed at the hardness under her finger tips. Not just firm—hard. "Ralph goes to a private health club every day after work. Surely they wouldn't have those phones bugged."

"Probably not. I doubt they have the personnel to do that. As much as they'd like to." He signaled for a turn and pulled into a service station by a motel. "Call your friend," he said, glancing at his watch. "It's past five; he should be working out now. Tell him, in French, to get his sister and both of them pack some clothes and get as much cash as they can. Be at his apartment at ten o'clock tonight. Tell them to be ready to move quickly."

"How will you get them out?"

"I don't know," he admitted.

6

It was raining hard, and that suited Dagger just fine. The heavy downpour would be a blessing, covering any noise he might make in the alley leading to Ralph's apartment. Dagger had spotted one person he believed might be one of Pig's men. He felt sure there would be another. But where was he?

"All right, Paige, here it is: If anyone tries to snatch you, blow the horn, turn on the lights and scream like a banshee, understand?"

Her eyes were wide and she looked a bit shaky. She nodded her head. "I'll lock all the doors and hunker down in the seat. You won't be gone long?"

"Only as long as it takes."

He handed her the second Colt Woodsman and showed her the safety. "If all else fails, Paige, push this, point the muzzle toward your assailant, pull the trigger and keep pulling it. You might not hit anyone, but you'll sure scare the piss out of them. Just try not to zap some citizen, huh?"

She looked perturbed, brows knitted. "And just how do I determine that, General?"

"I was a sergeant, Paige—not an officer. If the person's got a gun or a knife or a club in his hand, trying to jerk open the door of this car or smash out the window, I believe you can be reasonably certain said person is not trying to sell you Girl Scout cookies."

"But suppose it's just a drunk trying to break in, looking for a place to spend the night, to get in out of the rain?"

Dagger looked at her. "Then he won't have to worry about a hangover in the morning, will he?"

He slipped out of the car and was gone into the black, silver-spotted night.

She lost sight of him in two heartbeats.

She was alone, listening to the heavy rain hammer on the roof of the car.

She hoped nothing went wrong.

Dagger had no choice but to go in the front door. The back door of the apartment complex, according to Paige, was locked and barred at nine o'clock. Could be opened only from the inside, easily, in case of fire. Dagger thought he'd buy a little insurance. He moved silently through the rain to the car parked across the street. A car, Paige said, she'd seen following her several times. Slipping up the sidewalk behind the car, on the passenger side, Dagger smiled when he saw the rear door unlocked. He jerked the door open, sat down in the back seat and pointed the Colt at the man's head.

"Give me straight answers and you'll live," Dagger told him. "If you're ready to die, just get cute one time."

"I hear you. You kill Kates this afternoon?"

"You got that right, ace. Put your hands on the steering wheel and do it slowly. Herky-jerky gets you a bullet in the head."

The man did as ordered—slowly. "I don't want to die, Dagger."

"Then you give me straight answers. How'd you know my name?"

"Man! The word came down you were back in the game. Had to be you."

Dagger didn't believe him. He let that slide for the moment. "Where is the second man?"

"In the alley behind the apartment. Please take your finger off the trigger, Dagger."

"Just answer my questions."

"Ask them!"

"How much money is on my head?"

"A bundle."

"Start the car and drive around to your buddy—do it."

"Anything you say, Dagger. I got a wife and kids, man."

"You're breaking my heart. Drive."

The man slowly pulled into the street, driving with both hands on the wheel, at ten and two. As he drove, Dagger frisked him, the Woodsman pressing into the man's neck. Removing the pistol from leather, Dagger shoved the .357 behind his belt.

Turning into the alley, Dagger asked, "What's the recognition signal you're coming up?"

"Dim, bright, dim. Then he touches his brakes once."

"Do it, and it better be right."

"Jesus, Dagger, it's right!"

The man flashed his lights and the driver of the parked car touched his brakes, the red lights jumping out of the rainy night.

"You got a signal for one or the other to get out?"

"No," the man said. Sweat beaded his forehead and ran down his face. Dagger was retired, his file clearly stated that — but it also stated that Dagger was a very dangerous man, and had many, many kills to his credit. Snuffs, as many call them. "I'm senior, so he'll probably get out and walk back to me."

"If you're lying, you're dying. Surely you realize that."

"God is my witness, Dagger. I'm not lying. I don't want to die."

The back alley agent opened the door to his car, walked back to the rear car, passenger side. The rain obscured his vision. He did not see Dagger until it was too late. He had the door open, his hands occupied. He grunted his surprise but made no hasty moves. He had been well-trained.

"Open your raincoat," Dagger told him. "Let me see your pistol."

He opened his coat.

"All right," Dagger said. "Button your jacket and your raincoat — all the way up, both of them. Then get in the car and put both hands on the dashboard. Do it slowly."

The agent did as ordered. Unless he had a hide-out gun in the pocket of his raincoat, his weapon was effectively sealed beneath suitcoat and rain-coat.

"You couldn't be part of Pig's bunch," Dagger said. "You're both acting far too intelligently. Who are you?"

The men glanced at each other. The senior agent said, "Navy intelligence."

Dagger's astonishment came through as he blurted, "You've got to be kidding! I just spoke with O'Brian in army MI this afternoon. He said he was calling his counterparts in the other branches, asking them to back away from this one. I can't believe your boss didn't buy his story."

Again, that look passed between them. Dagger picked up on it. "All right, boys. Something smells here. Let me have it."

"O'Brian's dead, Dagger. Killed late this after-noon. It looked like a heart attack; but some-body pumped him full of a stimulant that brought on the attack. The word's come down you're working on the Red side of the street; they got to you. These people you're trying to protect are not only tied in with the Reds, but have organized-crime connections. It's so big, the Justice Department called us in on it."

"O'Brian dead," Dagger spoke from the shadows of the back seat. "Well . . . his phone would be tapped. I didn't call on any scrambler line; hell, I don't know any of those codes anymore."

"It won't wash, Dagger," the second agent said. "My boss was reluctant to believe it, but the evidence against you is overwhelming. And from the way she looks, the Burrell woman probably has some fine sleeve. You wouldn't be the first man to let pussy override common sense. Give it up, man."

The word "sleeve" pegged him. Dagger was certain the men were navy intelligence and not part of Pig's bunch. "Oh, come on, boys!" Dagger said, anger in his voice. "You guys and your boss have been had. You came into this too fast. You should have checked me out. You'd have found I'm very comfortable. My bank records are open for inspection. If I turned down a quarter of a million dollars back when I was drawing a sergeant's pay, I goddamn sure would do it now. As far as pussy, boys, I get all I can handle whenever I need it. You could have checked that out as well. And you should have checked out the fact that I've been out of the game for almost five years."

"You say, Dagger."

"That's right — I say." The rain and wind picked up, slamming against the car. "Look, boys — I don't want to kill any innocent. Let me prove to you both that you've been had."

"You've got the gun, Dagger."

"Back this thing up and drive into the parking lot of the complex. Pull alongside a dark blue Chevy. I've got to convince you both you're mistaken in this."

The senior agent looked at his partner. "It won't hurt to listen."

"Hell," his partner replied, both hands on the dashboard, disgust evident in his words. "Do we have a choice?"

Pulling up alongside Paige, Dagger rolled down the window. "Go get Ralph and Kit. Check in at that motel where I made the second call. The one by the service station. Do you remember it?"

She spoke through the pouring rain, her eyes taking in the two men in the front seat, sitting tensely, their hands not moving. "Yes."

"Register us as Mr. and Mrs. Curt Jackson, Ralph and Kit as Mr. and Mrs. Morton. Adjoining rooms. Pay cash. We'll be right behind you."

The men from navy intelligence — if they were and if they were on the level as to their innocence in this operation — listened intently as Paige and Kit and Ralph told their stories. They left nothing out.

Dagger knew then, with a sinking feeling, the men were working with Pig. They did not record any of the story or make any notes.

After several seconds of silence, the men shook their heads, the senior agent saying, "I believe you. It's just too weird not to be true."

"I'm gonna buy it," his partner agreed quickly. Too quickly.

Dagger sat quietly, letting the two agents — both of them not yet out of their twenties — talk among themselves.

"It won't take long to check out Dagger's story."

"Something else, too. If Pig's people have penetrated navy intelligence — and you can bet they have — we're running the risk of going out like O'Brian."

"Yeah, I thought of that, too."

"You guys have names?" Dagger asked.

"I'm Crowson," the senior agent said, "This is Knight."

Sure, Dagger thought, and I'm Burt Reynolds. He could have blown that up in their faces by asking for ID. But he wanted them talking. He nodded his head at each man, accepting what he would bet were false names.

"Ladies and Mr. Volker," Crowson said, smiling at Paige and Kit. "We'd like to speak to Mr. Dagger alone. With Dagger's permission, of course."

Dagger nodded.

Kit held a copy of the evening paper in her

hands, folding to the crossword puzzle. "Does anybody have a pen. I like to work the crossword."

Knight handed her a silver-colored pen.

Paige looked at Dagger. He jerked his head toward the adjoining room. The trio marched out, Paige leading the way.

"OK, Dagger," Crowson said. "We'll buy your story. And what those three in there said as well. So we'll lay it out for you — on the level. We'll compare notes."

Dagger put the Woodsman on the bed and smiled. He did not mention the .22 mag derringer tucked behind his belt buckle.

Knight sighed audibly. "I cannot tell you how much that relieves me, Dagger. Your file states you are not known for a gentle trigger finger."

Mistake number two, Dagger thought. You've been stalking me for a time. No way for you boys to get the word of O'Brian's death, read my file, and get down here from D.C. all in a few hours, in time to stake out anyone's apartment. Keep talking, boys.

Dagger sat on the side of the bed, the fingers of his right hand hooked behind his belt buckle, touching the small butt of the derringer. He watched as Crowson began pacing the motel-room carpet, pausing on each return in front of the bureau where Paige had left her jacket.

"The way it is," Knight said, looking at Dagger with that intense stare of a man about to tell a lie, "We had to have a fall guy."

Dagger watched out of the corner of his eye as Crowson slipped something into the pocket of Paige's jacket.

Neat, Dagger thought. Clumsy, but neat.

"And you're it," Knight said with a grin. "Sorry, Dagger, but we had to play along with Pig in order to gain his confidence. It wasn't our idea or decision." He kicked responsibility up to the top. "It came from our boss."

"Give us time to work on this," Crowson said. "And we'll clear your name. Just keep Miss Burrell and her buddies out of sight for a week or so. That's all we ask."

"Two weeks tops," Knight said.

His partner blistered him with a look.

So it's two weeks to something, Dagger thought. He kept his face impassive. But what is going down in two weeks?

Crowson's face was red from anger at his partner's slip.

God, you boys are amateurs. "What happens then?" Dagger asked.

Crowson relaxed visibly. "It's over. Miss Burrell and her friends get justice on the guys who did the number on their relatives, and you can go on back to merc work."

But I never told you I was going back to mercing, Dagger thought. He reviewed it in his mind: Pig would know if I came back in; if I once got another taste of it, I would be back to stay. Pig and a lot of people in and around Swampy Bottom,

D.C. So Pig—and his boss or bosses—are tied in with all the intelligence agencies. It's big.

"How much money is on my head and who put it there?" Dagger asked.

"Twenty-five thousand," Crowson replied. "And going up. I don't know who hung it on you. So you can see how it would behoove you to stay low and out of sight."

I can guess who hung it on me. Dagger's expression did not change. Pig. Fritzler. Mitchell. The pipe smoker. "Why? What do I know that is worth twenty-five big ones?"

"We told you, Dagger: It's that made-up Red connection," Knight spoke.

Sure it is. "How about the Shaffler boys?"

"Air force intelligence is loosely tailing them, in addition to Pig's bunch. They know what we know—which isn't much."

Dagger maintained his passive expression. So all agencies of military intelligence have been penetrated. Dandy. How big is this thing and what the hell is it? And where do I fit in this puzzle? Mitchell was air force head of intelligence at one time. So he would have friends there, left over from before he unofficially headed up Section Five along with Fritzler and the pipe smoker.

Dagger looked at the navy men. They're setting me up, he mused. But why? And it's big—real big—and it goes down in two weeks. But what is this line of BS about me and these civilians being Red agents? Am I carrying something around in my head that is so important I must be killed to shut me up? And how does — or did — Karl Crowe really figure in all this? And those five dead civilians and these five relatives of theirs?

It's all flapping around in the wind — too many loose ends that need securing.

"All right," Dagger said, playing the game. "I want the Shaffler boys free and clear."

"Good," Crowson beamed the word. He was certain he had Dagger, hooked and kicking. "I'll call air force and tell them you're on the way for the boys. Get them, and get out of sight for a couple of weeks."

Crowson dialed a number and spoke softly for a few seconds. He hung up and turned around. "Everything is all set for you, Dagger." He scribbled a number on a slip of paper. "That's the number you are to call to tell us of your whereabouts, and after that, to give us any information you think we might need." He held out a hand. "Good luck."

Dagger shook the hand, thinking: You're a lying son of a bitch. You'll never get any call from me. You're setting me up sure as hell. Getting me out — or trying to get me out — of circulation for a couple of weeks.

But damned if I can figure out why.

7

Walking with Paige and her friends out to the rental car, Dagger cautioned, "Don't say anything about our destination when we get in the car. Keep the talk light. I'll explain later."

In the car, Paige and the others noticed Dagger's set jaw and cold eyes. They spoke nothing of substance and kept the talk airy.

Dagger drove to the apartment of Jimmy Shaffler, where Mike was also staying. Both of them waiting for Paige.

"Go in and get them," he told Ralph. "Tell them to follow us in their car."

The CPA opened his mouth to protest.

"Do it!" Dagger said.

Dagger checked the area, quickly spotting the men supposedly from air force intelligence. They were parked in front of the apartment building, a very loose surveillance.

Ralph was back in ten minutes. He got into the back of the Chevy with his sister. "I told them to follow us. They'll be in a Trans-Am."

Dagger pulled away from the curb when the Trans-Am grumbled up behind him.

Checking the rear-view, he noticed he was not being followed — except for the Trans-Am.

At least, he thought, not closely.

He smiled knowingly.

Dagger stopped once to buy flashlights and a dozen batteries. He volunteered no information and his passengers asked for none. He constantly checked his rear-view for a tail.

None.

He pulled into a truck stop outside Baton Rouge on I-10, and tucked the rented car in between two rumbling eighteen-wheelers in the parking lot. He motioned for his passengers to get out.

Standing on the blacktop of the lot, Paige finally asked, "Dagger, what is going on?"

"I noticed Crowson standing very close to your jacket several times," Dagger said. "Then he put something in your side pocket." He looked at Kit. "Just before you went into the adjoining room with Paige and your brother, Knight gave you a pen to work the crossword puzzle. Let me see it."

Mike and Jimmy Shaffler stood close by, looking on, saying nothing.

Dagger hefted the pen and said, "Too heavy." He unscrewed the cap. Using his flashlight, he looked into the top of the pen. Metal gleamed back at him. "It's a tracking device, a transmitter," he said with a smile. "A beeper or toner, if you will. I felt they were setting us up."

Dagger looked at the faces around him. Kit seemed awed by it all. Ralph and Jimmy looked puzzled. Mike lit his pipe and looked amused as he puffed fragrant smoke into the misty air, cool now, after the hard downpour. Paige just looked scared.

"Let me see your jacket," Dagger said.

He fanned the coat, finding a quarter in the side pocket. He compared it with a quarter from his own pocket. The quarter from her jacket shone too brightly and was just a bit heavier than his own.

Dagger took the quarter and the pen and placed one in the cab of an eighteen-wheeler and the other in the cab of a bob truck, tucking them under the driver's seat.

"That ought to keep them busy for a day or so," he said, as much to himself as to the others.

Dagger carefully inspected both cars. After twenty minutes of crawling in, under and around the cars, getting filthy, Dagger found what he was seeking: two magnetic-backed discs, hidden under the bumpers of the cars.

"Mr. Dagger," Jimmy said, stepping forward, holding out his hand. "I don't believe we've been properly introduced. I'm Jimmy Shaffler, and this is my brother, Mike."

The men shook hands. Jimmy asked, "What

were those things you removed from the cars?"

"More tracking devices. This way, Pig and his people don't have to keep us under visual surveillance. But they'll still know exactly where we are at all times." This was the one among the five who did not want to hire Dagger. Dagger studied the man; he seemed likable enough. But Dagger knew that accounted for nothing.

"Why would they want to do that?" Mike asked, impatience in his tone. The tone of a man used to getting his own way. "Those men from the air force said they were on our side — just like the guys from the navy. I believe them."

Dagger ignored him. He had taken one look at Mike and pegged him as a spoiled playboy. Dagger instantly disliked the man. Dagger viewed men who must constantly keep in style with the ever-changing fads in clothing and hair style with suspicion — and amusement.

Dagger glanced at Paige. "I can't be sure I found all the tracking devices, but we can't stay here any longer. I need a quiet place to think. We'll head for your parents' plantation home. You know the way, you drive."

"Now see here," Mike protested. "I —"

"Shut up," Dagger said quietly. "If you want to live, do as you're told. You people hired me, so follow orders and knock off the mouth."

Mike flushed, the anger creeping up his neck and face. He balled his big fists. Dagger, at least ten years older than Mike, stood calmly, loosely, his expression not changing.

Mike did not realize he was staring into the face of much hurt, broken bones, bruises and possibly death.

Jimmy picked up on the hostility between the two men. He didn't need that—not at this juncture. But he understood it very well. His brother had proven himself very good at one thing: he excelled at irritating the hell out of people.

"Get in the car, Mike," he told his brother. "For once, do as you're told without making a federal case of it."

"No pun intended?" Dagger said with a smile.

Ralph laughed.

The younger brother and Ralph got a hot look, but Mike turned and walked around the Trans-Am, getting in without comment.

"He's been under a lot of strain," Jimmy said, feeling obligated to defend his kin.

"From what?" Dagger asked innocently. "I wasn't aware your brother ever did anything." He motioned his passengers back into the Chevy and pulled away from the grumbling lines of eighteen-wheelers.

Back on the highway, with the taillights of the Chevy in view, Jimmy said, "Don't crowd this one, Mike. Mr. Dagger will have you for an hors d'oeuvre and then look around for the main course."

"He's an old dude," Mike retorted. "I could take him with one hand."

Sure you could, Jimmy thought. "We've got too much riding on this, Mike. Far too much. Keep that in mind at all times. We don't need any of your macho bullshit screwing things up."

Mike said nothing.

"Why was O'Brian murdered?" DCI Harrison asked Dave Church, a friend and veteran field agent for the CIA.

It was raining in Langley, Virginia, the rain spotting the window behind the DCI's desk. The reports of O'Brian's death — the news of his being murdered would not now, or ever, be released to the press, only that he had a heart attack and died — had disturbed Harrison. And who, or what, he had been asking himself, is S.B. Dagger?

"We don't know, sir," Church replied. And he didn't know.

The assistant DCI, Fritzler, didn't like or trust Church. Church, like so many top people in the Agency, was of the Ivy League — one of the gang.

Fritzler had graduated from a small teachers' college in Illinois.

"Was he involved in something we need to know about?" Harrison asked. "Anything we need to stay on top of?"

"Sir, before I respond to that, may I say something?"

"Of course, you may, Dave."

"Sir—I've been with the Agency twenty-four years. I got this feeling—this feeling I am now experiencing—just before the Bay of Pigs went down and sour. I got it during the big flap in Munich some years ago. And I've had it several times since, when things were about to pop. But never this strong and with such a feeling of—" he sighed heavily—"impending disaster. Something, Mr. Harrison, is very wrong around here."

The DCI leaned back in his leather chair. "The sun's over the yardarm, Dave." Harrison had been in the navy. "Let's fix us a drink and talk about this . . . emotion of yours."

Drinks fixed, the men returned to their chairs, informally denoting positions of authority in the pecking order of the Company.

Senior agent Dave Church looked at the DCI and said, "I don't know who to trust, sir."

Harrison looked at the rain-spotted window, swung his chair back. Looked at Church. "You are certain this is not an over reaction, Dave?"

"Positive, sir."

"You know Doug Farmer well, Dave?"

"Yes, sir. Well enough to trust him. We have . . . well, walked around this topic a couple of times the last few days."

"I see." Harrison sipped his Crown Royal on the rocks. "Go on, Dave. We'll return to Doug in a moment."

"O'Brian got a call from just outside New Orleans a few hours before the hit was made on him. From S.B. Dagger. I'll tell you about Dagger, sir. First this: Our Como Sat fed the call to us. Sir, had I not been in that particular section of the computer room at the right moment, I would never have learned of that call. The woman working it is a close friend of my wife; they play bridge together. She told me she was ordered to put a hold on that info and to not include it in her daily report. Don't even tell her section chief. She said that order came from you."

Tension headache number twenty-eight came on Harrison with a vengeance. He rubbed his aching temples with his fingertips. "That's a damned lie, Dave. I gave no such order. You're going too fast. What about our Como Sat?"

"Using our communications satellite, sir, we can monitor any call coming into any intelligence agency of this government anytime we wish to do so. You know that, sir."

"I also know we can listen in on anyone's private conversations—if we choose to do so, correct?"

"Yes, sir. Of course, the intelligence agencies' calls are usually scrambled—this one wasn't."

"And private citizens' calls are almost never scrambled, are they, Dave?"

"No, sir."

"And we do listen in occasionally, do we not?"

"Yes, sir."

"You are aware that is a slight violation of the Privacy Act." Not a question.

"Yes, sir."

"I believe it was Henry Stimson who disbanded the State Department's Black Chamber of code experts just after World War I, was it not?"

"Yes, sir."

"I believe Mr. Stimson said, 'Gentlemen don't read other people's mail,' did he not?"

"Yes, sir."

"As long as we understand each other, Dave. Go on."

Church could not hide his chuckle. He also saw the corners of the DCI's mouth lift in humor. Very little changes from DCI to DCI: Do it if you have to, just as long as I don't know about it.

"The man who told her the orders came from you, sir, was Bennie Warwick."

"I see," Harrison said. He watched as Church lit his pipe. Good tobacco the man used. Very pleasant scent. He absently traced the thin moustache above his upper lip. He smoothed the already impeccably groomed hairline. "First Doug comes in here with information about a number of ex-agents gathering outside of New Orleans . . ."

Church sat upright in his chair. He almost spilled his drink. "What agents, sir?"

"Well . . ." Harrison shuffled papers in a desk drawer. "Their names were not at all familiar to me." He located the folder and handed it to Dave.

Church quickly scanned the list and slumped

back in his chair. "Damn!" he exclaimed in a huff of explosive profanity. "Pig Lester and his bunch of Section Five personnel. I wonder what possessed Doug not to tell me about this?"

Harrison could but stare at him. Finally, he said, "Dave, what, or who, is a Section Five?"

"I . . . really don't think you want to know, sir. Believe me."

"But I do want to know, Dave." The DCI's gaze was unwavering.

Dave nodded, took a deep breath, then crisply and concisely told the DCI all he knew — which was considerable — about Section Five's work, for as long as it had lasted. He left nothing out.

Sherman Harrison, lawyer, past college president, and all-around good guy, looked at the senior agent in absolute astonishment. He used to love to read spy novels. He didn't do that anymore. Not since taking this job. He was finding out what he had always assumed was fiction was, indeed, fact.

"Good lord!" he finally blurted. "I can't believe any of our past presidents would actually condone such a group."

"None of them did," Dave said.

"But, well, this section was disbanded in . . . when was it disbanded? God, don't tell me we still have it operational?"

"No, sir. It was disbanded in late sixty-nine or early seventy. It was, as you can well imagine, very covert."

"Yes. No doubt. Who set it up?"

"General Mitchell — when he was still active in the military; Fritzler . . . yes, sir, our Fritzler; and one other party that has remained unknown. I'm reasonably certain more were involved, but it was the brainchild of those three people."

"And it was set up to combat . . . what? Communist agents here in the country? What?"

"No, sir. Pig and his bunch were head-knockers. Dagger's group in 'Nam did the commie-hunting. Out in the field. I think it was in 'Nam — I may be wrong — when Dagger whipped Pig's ass. Dagger doesn't like Pig, didn't like Section Five's operation in this country."

Harrison realized that Dave had just spoken a lot of words and really hadn't told him a hill of beans about the original question. But he was used to that. Some agents employed by the Company would make a priest committed to a vow of silence appear talkative.

"Did Nixon learn of it and bring it to a halt?"

"Somebody did, sir."

"Dave — speak English to me. Stop waltzing around and give me straight and direct answers to my questions."

"Yes, sir. He did."

"Nixon?"

"To the best of my knowledge, sir. I was not privy to Oval Office meetings."

Dave's way of saying: Don't put too much pressure on me. Sir.

126

"Thank you, Dave. I realize and can appreciate your loyalty to past presidents. Tell me more about this S.B. Dagger. Does the man have a first name?"

"No, sir. Just S.B. Although some people do maintain the initials stand for son of a bitch."

The DCI allowed himself a tight smile. "Literally, Dave?"

"No, sir. Dagger is just such a mean bastard, that's all."

"All right, Dave. Now tell me everything you know about Dagger. You think this man had anything to do with O'Brian's death?"

"No, sir. I don't." Again, crisply and succinctly, Dave Church gave the DCI what he knew, and again, it was plenty, about S.B. Dagger.

"So," Harrison summed it up, "Dagger has killed, but he is not, per se, a killer for hire."

"That . . . is one way of summing it up, sir."

"But he is a dangerous man?"

"Extremely so. A modern-day ninja."

Harrison sighed. "Dave, I don't care what you are currently working on—drop it. I want you—personally—to find out what is going on. Bypass our people in New Orleans for the time being. I don't care where you have to go to get it done, but find out and report to me on a daily basis. Use my private line. For the time being, Dave, this is between us."

"Yes, sir."

EAGLE-FALL + 13

All through the early morning hours, the two-car caravan snaked a winding route to St. Francisville. Dawn was breaking when they pulled into the old plantation home. A magnificent, two-story structure — a monument to the glory days of the Old South.

Paige handed Dagger the keys and he unlocked the iron gates leading to the curving, tree- and shrub-lined drive. They drove up to the home.

It was impressive, even to Dagger, who was difficult to impress.

The home was built along almost the same lines as Bon Sejour, the house of good sojourn, located in St. James Parish.

"Beautiful," Dagger said.

Twenty-eight modified Doric columns surrounded the classic facade of the Burrell home, each column helping support the second-story gallery, rising to a moderate cornice.

At first Dagger thought the balustrades on the

upper gallery were wrought ironwork. A closer look revealed they were not, but a stacked-grain design.

Matching balusters on the belvedere connected the tall chimneys, blending into a sense of harmony.

The grounds were filled with live oaks, flowering shrubs and a running hedge.

"The jasmine won't bloom for about another month," Paige told him. "It's even more beautiful when they are in bloom."

"And fragrant, I should imagine," Dagger said.

"Quite."

"Get them in the house and keep them out of sight," Dagger told Paige. "I'll park the cars out back, out of sight. Then I'll take a look-see around the place."

With the Colt Woodsman tucked in his waistband, Dagger prowled the grounds. The huge home would be perfect for a day or two. It would take those in the Company sympathetic to Pig that long to wade through the corporate tapes and discover the home really belonged to the Burrells. Dagger had no doubt that they would be discovered.

He thought as he walked, attempting to compartmentalize the issues. Why the massive cover-up? he pondered. It all has to be leading to something very large — but what?

Dagger dismissed the notion it was something

that *he* knew; he had been too far from clandestine operations too long to be a real threat in that area. True, he did know some things that would be damaging—but they couldn't be proved.

Was the attack on Kit staged? If so, for whose benefit? Was it done to pull them all together so Pig's people could wipe them out en masse?

He thought that might be it. But he felt there was much more involved.

But what the hell was it?

As he walked the grounds, his eyes flicking over the manicured lawn, taking in every possible hiding place, Dagger concluded he was still far from the truth. And that irritated him.

He walked back to the garage and took an Ingram from the trunk of the rental car, carrying it inside. Paige and Kit met him in the kitchen.

"No milk or eggs, Dagger," Paige informed him.

For a moment, he was sourly amused. He hid that amusement. He thought of the times he had gone days, even weeks, living off the land in the bush, eating snake and monkey and wild onions and wilder potatoes, wiping scum off the water in order to get a drink.

And these people were worried about a fucking omelet.

Dagger's tone was dry enough to build the perfect martini. "We'll just have to make do during this period of extreme personal deprivation." He sat down at the kitchen table and began loading the Ingram's clips.

"The Secret Service carries those, don't they?" Ralph asked, his eyes on the lethal little spitter.

"Either that or the .45-caliber version," Dagger replied. He did not look up from his work. He carefully inspected each cartridge before inserting it into the clip. He looked for flaws that might cause the brass to jam up.

"Mr. Dagger?" Jimmy said.

"Drop the mister. Just Dagger."

"All right . . . Dagger. Why are those men trying to prevent us from seeing this through?"

"Because they don't want to go to prison, I should imagine. I've been in the bucket a few times. It isn't very nice." Damned if he was going to volunteer anything more, not until or unless he got all this worked out in his mind. Of course, he hid his smile, all that was subject to change at any moment.

"But they've been following us for days," Kit said. "They could have done . . . whatever it is they were—are—going to do many times. Why this waiting game?"

Dagger shook his head. "I don't know. But I do know—or sense might be a better word—there is a hell of a lot more to this operation than meets the eyes."

"Such as?" Mike asked. He lit his pipe and tilted the kitchen chair back on its rear legs.

Dagger surmised the man had seen one too many western movies. He resisted an impulse to hook a foot around one leg of Mike's chair and jerk.

"I was hoping one of you might tell me that," Dagger said, laying the Ingram aside.

Paige held a package of frozen bacon in her hands. She paused on her way to the microwave. "One of us?"

"Yes." Dagger glanced at her. "Think about it — all of you. The dossier your PI compiled has something to do with it, yes, but that report, by itself, is almost worthless in a court of law. Yes, the PI was killed, but I don't believe he was burned because of that dossier alone. I believe he might have stumbled on something else, or Pig's boys thought he had. That's why they burned him."

"Sure, he did," Mike said carelessly. "We all know that."

Dagger shifted his gaze. "What do you mean?"

"He was coming to see us when he was killed. That afternoon."

"I didn't know that," Paige said.

"I told Kit." Mike looked at the woman.

"I, uh, got kind of stoned that evening," Kit admitted. "I forgot."

"Wonderful," Dagger said. He resisted another impulse, this time to raise his right hand and cleave the table.

Mike looked at his brother. "I didn't tell you?"

"No, Mike," Jimmy said. "You didn't."

"Well," Mike said with a shrug. "No big deal.

Anyway, you saw him the night before — we all did, I think. I got a little drunk at the club."

"Why don't you tell us now?" Dagger prompted. "Tell all of us what you considered to be so unimportant."

Mike flared, slamming his chair on the floor. "I don't think I like your attitude, mister!"

"I don't care what you like or dislike," Dagger said. "What in the hell do you think this is: some sort of kid's game?"

"Hell, what difference does it make now?" Mike went on the defensive. "Rossieau's dead, isn't he? We're safe, aren't we? Those military intelligence types said we'd be all right if we just kept out of sight with you for a few days."

Dagger's laugh was almost cruel. "You poor, dumb shit. I guess if anyone with a dime-store badge to back them up told you that pigs could fly, you'd believe them. Citizen, let me give it to you the way it is: Pig Lester upped the ante on my head, just because I agreed to help you people. I have twenty-five thousand bucks on me. Twenty-five big ones to the man or woman who kills me. Now that kind of makes me uncomfortable, and your so-what-the-hell attitude give me a good case of the red ass. Now what did your PI tell you?"

Mike looked to his friends for support. He received none. He was met with stony gazes and ill-concealed anger. Only Kit kept her eyes downcast. Mike said, "I guess I screwed up, gang—I'm sorry." He looked at Dagger. "Rossieau said he had just talked with a friend—buddy was the word he used—in Miami. This guy is some kind of—wait a minute . . . no—used to be some kind of Cuban Freedom Fighter. Something like that. Was a mercenary, too, Rossieau said. And he was in the army here in the States. Intelligence, I think. Some letters."

"Letters?" Dagger asked.

"Yeah. SSA. Something like that."

"ASA?"

"Yeah! That's it. Rossieau was real excited about it. But he said he was afraid he was gonna get zapped. He meant killed, didn't he?"

"Yes. Go on."

"That's about it, I guess. Rossieau said his buddies in this Cuban thing in Miami—those nuts, always wanting to invade the motherland, who the hell believes anything they have to say?—told him they had intercepted some kind of government communique or something." Mike laughed. "Aw, come on, people!" His confidence was restored. "This is fairy-tale stuff. Mumbo jumbo."

"What did they intercept?" Dagger asked. "And how did they intercept it?" He knew the Cuban resistance forces in South Florida had one of the best electronic sweepers this side of the CIA.

"How, I don't know," Mike said. "But—" he chuckled—"this is cute: Eagle-Fall." He slapped his leg and laughed long and hard.

Kit looked up, a startled look on her face. Paige wore a strange expression, head cocked to one side. Ralph and Jimmy looked confused.

Dagger stared hard at Mike for a long moment. Then he rose from the table, Ingram in hand, and walked out the kitchen door. He stood in the back yard.

Dagger was shaken. "Jesus!" he muttered. Not after all these years. It couldn't be.

But he was afraid in his guts it was true. It was beginning to add up. The columns began to look a little neater.

But why now? Why with this man? It made no sense.

Eagle-Fall.

The back door swung open, footsteps behind him on the stone walkway. Paige stood beside him.

"What is it, Dagger?"

"Trouble. Big trouble."

"What does Eagle-Fall mean, Dagger?"

He looked at her, thinking how beautiful she was, and how much he would like to make love to her.

Dagger expelled breath, sighed. "I'll tell you, Paige. But not the others. Not for a while. Paige . . . ninety-nine percent of the men and women who work for the Agency are good people: highly trained, very patriotic people. And they do good, very essential work for this nation.

Many of them risk their lives for this country, working as Black Agents, deep moles, in jobs you or any other civilian could not possibly comprehend. But sometimes mavericks get past the tests; sometimes good people crack under the pressure. Brilliant people, but just a bit overloaded in the love-of-country department.

"If Robert Kennedy had been elected president back in sixty-eight — and he probably would have been — there are some people who felt, *feel,* that would have been a disaster for the nation. I don't know. I am not a political person. I grew very sick of the whole political scene years ago. Quit keeping up with it when I saw the nation moving more and more toward socialism.

"But . . . a few people within the Agency came up with Operation Eagle-Fall. Just in case Robert Kennedy was elected. Now, understand this, Paige: The president didn't know of this; the DCI of the Agency didn't know of it; the Joint Chiefs, the FBI — none of them had any idea of this plan. This was strictly the brain child of three men. But Pig Lester, who has been a gun for the Company for years, was to kill Robert Kennedy. If elected to the presidency. Eagle-Fall. The top eagle falls. Simple.

"Well, Sirhan beat Pig to it. Another black mark in American history. I thought that was the end of it. Obviously, I was wrong. And don't ask me how I know all this. I won't tell you."

"Was Sirhan paid to kill Kennedy?"

"Not that I know of, Paige."

"The Agency didn't do it?"

"No. That I can tell you for a fact: No. If it had been an Agency touch, the code name would have been retired. They'd have never used the same code designation twice. Not one that heavy."

"All right, Dagger," Paige said, disgust in her voice. "You've taught me a bit of American history. Not that I couldn't have lived quite well without it. But I'm confused and frightened. What does Eagle-Fall mean now?"

His eyes were bleak as they touched hers. "It means, Paige, the President Menen is going to be assassinated. Probably within the next twelve to fourteen days."

8

Dagger slept for a few hours, then went through his exercise ritual—something he had missed the past few days—while the others slept on. The house was quiet. After luxuriating under the shower for fifteen minutes, then drying off with a huge, obviously expensive towel, he went back to bed and slept for another two hours.

When he awakened, he felt that old, familiar warrior's feeling wash over him. And S.B. Dagger knew he was back in the business to stay.

All right, he thought, lying in the huge bed, under freshly laundered and clean-smelling sheets, where do I start?

He began counting up—or down—his options. And they were few. What agency of the government could he trust fully? He couldn't think of any. He felt the heads of agencies could be trusted, and felt sure all would be appalled to learn of Eagle-Fall; but Dagger also was very aware of the fact his call would never get through to them. Calls would be monitored, traced and blocked.

With something this big, the Secret Service would surely be compromised—it would have to be to insure the plan working—so the phone, again, would be out of the question. Any meeting with the Secret Service would—at least until he could work something else out—have to be eyeball to eyeball. And that would mean chancing a run into New Orleans and leaving Paige and her friends alone. And unsupervised. Dagger didn't like that idea at all.

And he didn't know if he could trust any of the five civilians. Paranoia is something a person learns to live with in any type of clandestine occupation.

Paige entered his mind. Dagger looked down at his sheet-covered lower body. He was amused to see he was partially aroused.

The bedroom door opened. Dagger's hand closed around the Colt Woodsman on the bed beside him.

"Be a shame to let all that go to waste," a woman's voice touched him in the semidarkness of the room.

Kit.

She closed the door and moved silently across the carpet. She was clad only in a shorty nightgown. She wore nothing under the wisp of fabric.

She sat on the edge of the bed and put a soft,

warm hand on Dagger's chest, feeling the strong, slow thump of his heart.

She moved her hand slowly down his naked chest, her fingers playing in the mat of chest hair. She found the hem of the sheet and flipped it. He was naked.

"You got a thing for Paige?" she asked.

"No," Dagger said. "At least I don't believe I have a 'thing.'"

She grasped his growing hardness, feeling the muscle slowly come to life under her touch. "Nice," she said, her voice husky. "Thick. Real thick. Be fun gettin' all that in."

Dagger let her talk. He really didn't want this woman — sexually — but damned if he could figure out a way to put her off without Kit setting up a squall, waking up everyone in the house.

She stroked him, her small hand working up and down. The muscle grew under her touching and urging. Beads of sweat formed on Kit's face.

"Jesus!" she finally said. "You ever think of goin' into the movies? Who was your father, anyway, Trigger?"

Dagger thought that amusing, but he kept his face as impassive as possible, considering the situation. Kit moved once and the nightie was gone, in a flimsy heap on the carpet. She had a good body, trim and firm. She slid on the bed beside him, pressing her hot nakedness against him. Again her hand sought him, manually loving the stiff manhood. She shifted and straddled him, guiding him, moaning, biting at her lower lip as the bulk of him filled her.

She cried out several times as she pushed downward, taking him, forcing him into the wet, tight warmth. Dagger watched her face: It was twisted into a mask of pleasure/pain.

He let his eyes drift to her breasts: The nipples were full and aroused. He brought his hands from her undulating hips to cup her breasts, feeling the nipples hard against his palms.

She climaxed seconds after he entered her, and Dagger lost count after the third shuddering summit. There was nothing fancy about her love-making—nothing kinky; she just settled down into a steady rhythm, up and down. Old fashioned slap and tickle.

It seemed to Dagger Kit rode him for an hour, but he suspected it was more like fifteen or twenty minutes. When he exploded inside her, she sighed and then slumped forward, breasts pushing against his chest. She rested for a few moments—she'd done all the work—until her breath slowed and evened. She stirred and kissed him on the lips and slipped from him. She stood by the side of the bed and shrugged into her gown. The odor of sex lingered faintly in the room.

"You don't have a whole hell of a lot to say," she said with a smile. "But I never had anything that hurt me and felt so good at the same time. Bye now."

She was gone, bouncing across the room and out into the hall. The door closed silently.

In the adjoining room, Paige pressed her face into the softness of pillow and hated them both. Bitch! she silently railed at Kit. I hope you get pregnant.

But I could have walked through that door the same as Kit, she reminded herself. She listened to the sounds of Dagger's shower running. She was filled with many emotions. Two of which she recognized, grimly, as love and hate.

Paige's initial greeting that afternoon was definitely not the warmest Dagger had ever experienced. They met in the garden behind the plantation home.

"Excuse me," Dagger said, smiling. He knew what the matter was. "Please allow me to step back just a bit. I'm susceptible to frostbite."

"Don't consider yourself a VIP," Paige snapped at him, her eyes flashing fire — among other things. "Kit would screw a dog, and probably has."

Dagger barked at her.

Paige was dressed in fashion jeans that outlined everything she wanted noticed — which was plenty. Her shirt was unbuttoned just enough to tantalize. Which it did. She flushed at his barking.

"Yes," she said, the color deepening on her face

and neck. "You would definitely be of that species. Cur, no doubt."

"Ease off, Paige. I didn't go to her; she came to me."

"Do you always stick it in anything that comes along, wagging its tail?"

"Why are you so angry about it?"

Her flush grew darker still. She opened her mouth, then shook her head, electing to remain silent.

"Sorry I fell from grace, Paige. But I'm human, not a god. I learned a long time ago to eat when I can, sleep when I can, and make out when I can. Notice I did not say: make love."

"Well . . ." Her anger abated slightly, then slipped from her as the humor of the situation touched them both. A small smile shaped her lips. "At least you two could have been a little more discreet."

"Don't think I didn't want to knock on your door." Dagger was honest with her. "Don't think for a moment I haven't wanted you. You'd be wrong. But you made it clear from the outset you call the shots as to when and where. Or didn't you mean that?"

She refused to look at him, refused to reply. She was uncertain of her emotions. Did not know whether to yield or retreat.

"Kit is easy come, easy go," Dagger said. "Sex means nothing to her. Just a few moments of pleasure without the pure feelings that should accompany the act. I've met her type of woman all over the world. But you, you're different."

She half turned, to face him. The scent of early flowers drifted around them, the renewal of the cycle of nature and earth's odors created a surreal type of mood between the two players on life's ever-changing stage. Live oaks draped mysteriously with dark Spanish moss loomed over the man and woman. The Mississippi River surged and rolled and slowly wound its way south just a few miles from the stately old mansion.

"Why am I so different, Dagger?" she whispered the words, her intimate tone only making the mood more heady. "I listened to you and Kit . . . making it today and wanted to be in her place. So why am I so different?"

"That confuses me, Paige. Why with me? Two completely different people, nothing in common. Two different worlds, You're a wealthy, educated person. I'm a beat-up ex-soldier. Why?"

She laughed softly and moved closer to him. Her breath was warm on his face. "I've had my fill of pretty boys, Dagger. And if you make something crude out of that, I'll sock you, I swear I will."

He chuckled, rich laughter in the late afternoon. "Why, Miss Paige, honey," he mimicked rich Southern. "I do believe you would."

"Bet on it."

"One thing for sure," Dagger said, "I am no

pretty boy."

He put a hand on her shoulder and felt her body heat through the light shirt, warm on his palm. She moved closer, her breasts just touching his chest. Suddenly, she felt herself picked up bodily and tossed to one side, behind a waist-high running hedge, Dagger on the ground with her, one hard hand covering her mouth. The breath was knocked from her impacting with the earth.

"Don't move," he whispered. "Be silent."

He removed his hand.

She put her lips on his and whispered, "What is it?"

"We've been made," he said, returning the murmuring kiss, responding to her lips.

He felt her lips move in a smile. *"You've* been made, Dagger. *I* haven't — not yet."

Here, Dagger thought, is one hell of a woman. "Two men, with pistols, over by that line of bougainvillea, and you're thinking about sex."

He heard her soft chuckle and slipped from her, rising to his knees. The late afternoon sun cast long shadows over the huge estate, and Dagger made use of the sun-rimmed dusk to hide his moves as he stalked the men. He kept his back to the sun and stayed low, by the running hedge. He just could not believe Pig's men had found them so quickly.

But they had.

And that could only mean one thing: As Dagger had suspected, the operation was big, real big.

Dagger shifted the M-10 from left hand to right as he looked through the hedge. He recognized one of the men: J.B. Mohney. J.B. was a thoroughly despicable type who, Dagger recalled, liked his girls young—very young. And J.B. usually confused pain with passion, cries of agony for whimpers of pleasure.

The thought of his own sister came to Dagger, sending dark waves of fury over him.

He shook them away and sent his sister back to her grave. There was no time for that. Not now.

Dagger did not recognize the second man. He knelt by the hedge and listened to them talk.

"I tell you they're here!" J.B. said. "I just got a gut hunch. We gotta get to a phone and call in."

"Gut hunches," the other man said, disgust in his voice. "You pull Pig up here on a goose hunt, and he'll be more pissed off than he already is. And he's jumpin' up and down now."

"We'll check it out," J.B. said. "Just remember: We have to take them alive. Keep the Bear in mind."

The what? Dagger thought. The Bear. What the hell is he talking about?

Dagger looked down at the M-10 and pivoted the fire selector 180 degrees to full auto. That almost-mandatory visual check was the only thing Dagger disliked about the little spitter.

J.B.'s partner turned just as Dagger stood up

from his squat. He pointed his pistol at Dagger and opened his mouth to say something. His words were jammed in his throat as the Ingram stuttered like a muffled duck with a speech impediment. The man bent forward, then pitched on his face as he was slammed in the belly with half a dozen 9mm slugs.

"Stand easy, J.B.!" Dagger called. "or I'll cut your legs off at the knees and let you bleed to death." Without taking his eyes from J.B., he said, "Pick up my brass, Paige."

"Your what?"

"The casings. The shiny, copper-looking things on the ground."

"Oh."

J.B.'s hands were frozen in the air.

"Put your hands behind your head, J.B. Lace your fingers. You know the routine. Now, walk over here to me."

J.B. was no fool. He knew Dagger and knew his reputation. He knew Dagger would not hesitate to kill him. But he had to run at least one bluff.

"Pig's on the way, Dagger. Give it up — you don't have a prayer."

"You're a liar, J.B. I heard you and your buddy talking." The agent on the ground kicked his legs and drummed his feet as death took him. "Get your butt over here, J.B."

J.B. looked at the dead man and felt sick to his stomach. As he walked the short distance, his mind was racing, reaching for survival. For years, ever since joining the Company, J.B.'s only drawback as a field agent had been his low tolerance for pain. That and the fact he was a coward. He had always dreaded the thought of being taken alive and tortured. And death pills were not standard issue for stateside agents. But he would rather face what Dagger had to give than return to Pig and his insane rages of fury at an agent's failure.

"I'll deal, Dagger," J.B. said quietly. "I'll let you know that flat out."

"Depends on what you got I might want," Dagger said, holding the Ingram like a pistol. "But, J.B., you'd better tell me the truth first time I ask for it, or I'll make living awfully unpleasant for you."

J.B. picked up on the real menace in Dagger's voice. He began to sweat. He had heard what Dagger did to the men who molested his sister. Made him nauseous for a week. "I swear to God, Dagger, I'll tell you everything I know."

"You better swear to someone who knows you, J.B. Walk in front of me, to the house."

Full dark, and the night creatures hummed and flapped their wings and crawled and called in the gloom around the old home. Dagger had left J.B. trussed up and alive in the basement, secured with wide adhesive tape wrapped around his ankles, his wrists and his forearms, behind his back. The strongest man in the world would have trouble getting out of that.

Dagger wondered about the basement, since he didn't think plantation homes ever had basements. He'd never heard of one that had a basement. He decided this cramped little room must have been added later.

"Hell, what difference does it make?" he muttered.

There had been no need for physical persuasion with J.B., something Dagger had known from the outset. All he had to do was show J.B. a pocket knife, blade open, and the man began babbling like a person strapped to a medieval rack.

The problem was, J.B. didn't know that much. But Dagger wanted to keep him alive for insurance, once, or if, he got to the Secret Service and they believed his story. Far-fetched as Dagger was sure it would seem to them.

Dagger found the agent's car, parked in the woods behind the estate, drove it to the house and hid it in the garage, the dead man in the trunk. Dagger knew the guy would start to get putrid in thirty-six to forty-eight hours.

Coming to the plantation house, J.B. had said was a hunch on his part. Nothing more. He had seen the home and asked in town who lived there. Was told nobody. But he had driven around the back and seen the cars parked in the garage—figured them to be ones he was looking for.

Dagger thought about that, finally accepting it. The garage doors had been open. So OK.

One thing J.B. did tell him was his belief that the Secret Service had been penetrated years before. For sure, the White House police had been compromised.

"Who are they?" Dagger asked.

"Don't know."

"How many?" Dagger had pressed.

Didn't know that either.

"Who or what is the Bear?"

"It's a person."

"Who?"

"Don't know, Dagger—I swear it."

Dagger cursed as he walked into the sitting room of the home and confronted the quintet.

"So what's going on?" Mike asked. "Jesus Christ, Dagger, you just *killed* a man!"

"Yes," Ralph said. "My God, the police will be here and we'll all go to—"

"Shut up," Dagger told them. "The police won't be here, and nobody gives a shit about the dead agent. We're being hunted," he told them bluntly. "It's down to life and death from now on."

One of these people had to be the Bear—but was J.B. lying? Was the Bear not a person but a code name, some Agency designation, or was it the key to unlock this mystery box?

He didn't know.

And he couldn't tell them anything until he found more pieces of the puzzle and fitted them together.

If he could.

And he'd damn well better be quick about it.

Dagger said, "One of you—at least one of you—saw something years back. Or one of you or all of you knows something. Someone among you holds the key to this puzzle. So backtrack and try to come up with it."

"You know what Eagle-Fall means, don't you?" Ralph asked.

"Yes," Dagger said, "I do."

"Would you care to enlighten us?" Kit asked. If she felt anything after their brief encounter earlier that day, neither her face nor tone of voice indicated it.

Dagger wondered if her screwing him had been done so someone in the house could slip out and get to a phone to call in to Pig? Or had she done it after their liaison? Or had anybody?

Damn!

Dagger looked at Paige and saw her dislike of Kit evident on her face. Jealousy, he wondered? What a strange and different group of people.

Briefly, he told them of Eagle-Fall. Not of its original meaning, only what it meant at this time.

"Well, the answer is quite simple," Mike said, his arrogance returning in a rush. If it ever left him. "We'll just call the Secret Service. Let them handle it. Then we can all go home." He smiled at his burst of genius.

Dagger wondered how many games the man had played without a helmet. "Sure, Mike," he said. "Sometimes the best plan is the least complex. However . . . may I punch a few holes in your strategy? Thank you.

"One: How would you suggest we get to the Secret Service? They've been penetrated.

"Two: What solid proof do we have that anything is about to happen to the president?

"Three: As big as this thing is — and it's getting bigger — you want to be the one to meet with the Secret Service?

"Four: We've got a minimum of fifteen, a maximum of forty agents chasing us with orders to — "

Mike held up his hand. "OK, Dagger — all right! I get the message. So what do we do?"

"Form our own little think tank for a few hours. One of you might remember something. Let's get to it."

But by eleven o'clock, they were no closer to solving the riddle than when they started. All they had accomplished was to become quarrelsome and irritable with each other, and the think tank had degenerated into petty bickering, finger-pointing, and some catty backbiting. From both genders.

Dagger took it as long as he could. "Knock it off," he finally told them. "Friends are becoming enemies. I'll take the first watch, Jimmy — then

I'll wake you."

The younger Shaffler nodded his head.

Ingram in hand, Dagger stepped out onto the darkened upper gallery to begin his lonely vigil.

In a motel room in Baton Rouge, Pig Lester glared at the gathering of agents. "All right," he said savagely. "We got to assume J.B. and Smithy bought it. They were supposed to report in at 1800 hours." He glanced at his Rolex. "They're too far past due. They were assigned to sweep northwest of here—the New Roads area. Get some sleep. We'll converge on that area in the morning."

Dave Church dialed the DCI's private residence in Fairfax, Virginia. "I'm in New Orleans, sir, and something is definitely in the wind, and it stinks. Sir? Are you sure your home phone is secure?"

"As certain as I can be," Harrison replied tersely. "I've got to trust the agent who electronically swept it last week."

"Who was it?"

"Jennings."

Church breathed easier. "He's solid, sir."

"All right. Give me what you have, Dave."

"Record and scramble, sir."

Harrison punched the trigger of the phone/

corder on the night stand. The incoming and out-going conversation would be unintelligible to anyone monitoring. The phone was rigged to automatically record unless he cut off the machine.

"Done," Harrison said.

"We have a gathering of mavericks here, sir. I have personally identified twenty-two ex-agents or still-active agents, with one or another intelligence group. I have reason to believe more are on the way. Whatever it is, sir, it's very big."

"Dave, can I trust Fritzler?"

"No, sir," Church replied quickly. "Don't let him in on anything."

"Dave, if I can't trust my assistant DCI, who can I trust?"

Church gave him a list of men and women. "Trust those people, sir—for the time being. There will be a lot more, but give me time to work it out. Those I just named are solid. Now then, our man in Atlanta reports that the word first went out on Dagger to kill him. Then the word came down to keep him alive. He also reports that Dagger bought a trunk full of weapons and ammo and other gear from the gunrunner, Dog. Dagger was traveling in the company of a woman. The Dalon County, Missouri sheriff's office—who are very tight-lipped concerning Dagger, old family in that part of the hills—just ran a make on a Ms. Paige Burrell, who'd been asking directions to Dagger's house. Seems she hopscotched over a large part of the nation getting to Dagger." He related to Harrison as much of the devious route of Paige as he had been able to uncover in his short investigation.

"What about this Burrell woman?"

"Clean. Big money. Old money. Rich."

"She certainly traveled a strange route getting to Dagger," Harrison mused. "Now, how does she tie in with all this?"

"I don't know, sir," Church said with a sigh. "But Ms. Burrell and four of her friends have disappeared. And so has Dagger. And there is this: A Ms. Kit Volker—one of those who disappeared with the Burrell woman—was attacked a few nights ago, in her apartment. An apparent kidnapping attempt. Two men, at least. She set up a howl and they had to abort it. Unless it was planned that way."

"Dave—this is getting confusing. Where in the hell is all this leading?"

Again, that sigh. "I don't know, sir. Mr. Harrison . . . I keep getting, well, some rumors from the underground."

"What underground?"

"We have plants in Miami, sir, among the Cubans. It's nothing firm, sir, but a . . . an old code name keeps cropping up."

"What code name and what does it mean?"

"I'd . . . really rather not say on any kind of phone line, sir."

"I see. No! I don't see. Dave, I'm getting some foul breezes from all this. It may be my imagination—I hope so. Nevertheless, I want to meet with you at twelve. Can you get a flight out within the hour?"

"Yes, sir."

"I wish to use an Agency plane."

"Don't do it, sir. Haywood, one of those I mentioned, is a pilot—has a private plane. Get him to fly you to Atlanta. I'll meet you at the airport. If I may make another suggestion, sir?"

"Certainly, Dave. As you well know, I am relatively new to the spook business."

"Leave a note for Fritzler that you've gone to some sort of meeting: the Colorado Coon Hunters convention or something."

"I'll try to come up with something a bit better than that, Dave," Harrison said dryly. "All right, I'll see you at dawn."

"Yes, sir. Oh, Mr. Harrison?"

"Yes, Dave?"

"Come armed." He hung up.

Harrison looked at the buzzing receiver in his hand. Come armed! The DCI grimaced. He hadn't fired a handgun in years. He sat on the edge of the bed and removed the cassette tape from the phone/corder, replacing it with a fresh one.

His wife stirred beside him, opening her eyes, looking at him in the dim light of the small bed lamp.

"What is it, Sherman?"

He rose, looking for his robe. "I'll be gone for

a day, Mary. Maybe a night, as well."

"And you can't tell me where." Not a question.

"Correct, honey. Sorry."

"Grown men playing cops and robbers," she said disgustedly. She turned her face to the pillow. "I wish to God we had stayed in Denver."

So do I, Sherman Harrison thought, padding to the bathroom for a shower.

He wondered where Mary had put his pistol. He hoped she hadn't hidden it again. He'd feel like a fool getting off the airplane carrying a double-barreled bird gun.

Dagger sat on the upper gallery of the pillared home and gazed out at a row of dwarf pines, arranged in a pattern of descending size. Beyond them and around them, jasmine, honeysuckle, iris, camellia, and huge, old, live oaks dotted the grounds of the huge estate.

Dagger cradled the Ingram in his big hands as his eyes swept the darkness of his perimeter. In a few hours, noon at the latest, Pig would have people swarming all over this area. Dagger would have to pull his crew out and run.

But where?

He immediately rejected the idea of any city. Dagger did not like cities, and he knew the conclusion of this chase would, in all probability, be a fire-fight. He did not want any innocents killed or hurt. With all his years of combat, Dagger had seen too many innocents killed, caught up in the real tragedy of war. The very young, the very old.

Much like those preyed upon by the slime who slither in the streets of America, with a gun or knife or club or ice pick, brutalizing and robbing and killing and terrorizing.

He pushed that thought from his mind, and, as all combat vets must, pushed the horror of warfare away as well.

Then, as his head cleared, Dagger's mind began tying up some loose ends that had been flapping about: Paige and her friends were all within two years of each other in age; all had attended LSU during the turbulent years that marked the winding down of the Vietnam war. And Paige had told him that all of them had attended lectures given by Karl Crowe.

All right. Was Crowe the key to unlock this puzzle, or was he just another door in the maze of puzzles and dead ends?

Dagger rose, pacing the upper gallery, his eyes on the dark grounds, his mind busy attempting to further unravel fact from fiction. No point in awakening anyone at this hour with questions; he would talk to them later. Maybe then he would get some answers.

And stop it from turning bloody.

Jimmy relieved him at three o'clock. Dagger gave him Kates's .38.

Jimmy woke him a few hours later with the news that his brother, Mike, was gone.

EAGLE-FALL + 12

Agency Station 12—Atlanta. Dawn.

"Certain members of air force intelligence are acting hinky," Parker, the Atlanta-based Company man said. "At least that's the feeling I got out at Robins AFB. And army and navy are all uptight about something."

"Conclusion?" Harrison asked.

Church had met his boss at the airport, then traveled to an interstate rest area just outside Atlanta, on I-20. Haywood drove. There they met with Parker and one of his associates, Hartsel, who was stationed in Savannah.

Parker said, "I go along with Church: Something big is in the wind."

"But what?" the DCI pressed.

"Eagle-Fall," Church said softly.

Haywood's head jerked up, his face paled. A senior agent, he was in his twenty-fifth year with the Company. "You've got to be kidding!"

"I spoke with Hank McNeal just hours ago, in

Miami," Church said. "One of their electronics people picked it up from a very innocuous radio dispatch. He thought it so innocuous he became suspicious, found the code within. You know how those guys love to tinker with our codes? Well, they broke this one."

Harrison wore a very annoyed look on his face. "Who is McNeal? What guys? What codes? And what in the hell is an Eagle-Fall?"

Hartsel said, "McNeal worked for us years back — still does contract work from time to time. He was one of our people who went in the Bay of Pigs in sixty-one. His father was American, mother Cuban. His father was tortured to death on the Isle of Pines by Castro's goons."

Then he told Harrison about Eagle-Fall.

The DCI sat with his mouth open, face pale. He opened and closed his mouth three times before managing to get a word past his lips. "Jumping Jesus Christ!" he almost shouted. "Do you mean to tell me the *Agency* planned to *kill* Robert Kennedy?"

"No, sir," Church calmed the man. "Not the Agency — just a few people within the Agency. But no one will ever be able to prove that."

"Who, specifically, within the Agency?"

"It was Fritzler's idea, I believe, at first. But he found support from others. Lester's bunch — Section Five — was to burn Kennedy."

"I can't believe this!" Harrison said, heat in his tone. "This is . . . why, it's monstrous!"

"Oh, you can believe it, sir," Church replied in his usual quiet manner. "We've had some — have some — real bananas in our ranks. Most of them are gone, now, but a few still remain."

"But what has Eagle-Fall got to do with now?" the DCI asked. It was really very pleasant in the rest area, but Harrison wiped his suddenly sweaty face with a handkerchief.

"That," Church responded, "is what I would like to know, sir."

Harrison was silent for a few seconds as the awful thought came to him. He lifted his eyes, his gaze touching each man around the table. "Do you, any of you, believe the president to be in danger?"

There was an uncomfortable silence for a few pulsebeats. Hartsel stirred, then said, "I don't know, sir. Intuition tells me yes. But common sense asks: Why should *this* president be in danger? This man has the support of both houses, the majority of the people, and even the goddamn press seems to like him. We've got a man in the White House who not only believes in a strong military and intelligence system, but who is also responsive to the needs of the minorities, the elderly, the ERA-types . . . hell, this man is really a people's choice. What would be the point in touching a man like that?"

"I will never grow accustomed to the quaint euphemisms you people use when 'kill' is what you mean," Harrison said. He shook his head.

Sighed. Looked around the table.

Harrison continued. "Parker said he felt certain members of air force intelligence were behaving strangely. How about the other branches of intelligence?"

"O'Brian of army got zapped," Hartsel said. "After speaking with Dagger."

"Kaplan of navy just got transferred to Scotland," Parker said. "TDY'd in one hell of a hurry. And he was a friend of O'Brian."

Haywood said, "Same with Harland in ASA. He was TDY'd from Washington to Greenland, for God's sake. Real quick move. Like ten minutes notice. Jesus," he said, disgust falling from his mouth. "I spent a month in Greenland one day."

"Odd," Harrison agreed. "Too many quick moves to be mere coincidence. All right—what about VP Doyle?"

"Hell," Church said. "He was checked nine ways to sundown. Air corps during World War II, decorated fighter pilot. Recalled during Korea, won more medals as a jet jockey. Very rich man, old money. Owns farmland and factories in Iowa and Illinois. First-class all-American boy type. Straight as an arrow."

"Yes, I agree," Harrison said. "I like him. Very trustworthy type. Good man. Loyal. Smokes a nice brand of pipe tobacco, too. All right, gentlemen, let's sum it all up and see what we have concrete."

9

"I don't know where he could be, Dagger," Jimmy said. "He sure as hell didn't drive out of here. I would have heard him leave."

"Shit!" Dagger spat the vulgarity. His face tightened as he picked up a lone figure puffing up the drive. "Here comes the jock now." He glanced at the others. "Get packed. We're pulling out of here in a few minutes."

Dagger faced Mike in the foyer of the mansion. "Where in the hell have you been?"

"I jog several miles every morning," Mike puffed, grinning arrogantly at Dagger. "And if you don't like it, you can go to hell."

Dagger almost hit him. There was no doubt in his mind that he could open Mike up like a can of beans and pull his guts out. Mike was in good physical shape; but Dagger knew he had never had the good-guy ideas trained out of him, still believed in that myth called a fair fight, had never killed with his hands, had never faced death and beaten it.

The words inscribed on that C-ration box by an unknown Marine at Khe Sahn in 1968 came to Dagger: For those who fight for it, life has a special flavor the protected never know.

Dagger smiled at Mike. Something in the smile forced Mike back a step. His eyes grew wary. Coins jingled in one pocket of his jumpsuit (Rompers for grown men, Dagger always called them); Dagger thought that odd.

Why would a man carry change with him when he was jogging?

Maybe to make a phone call.

"You dumb shit," Dagger said softly. "I've got a dead man stuffed in the trunk of a car out back; we've got twenty-five, thirty agents—maybe more—chasing us, looking to kill us all. Now I don't give a damn for your life, pretty-boy, but there are other lives involved. So from this moment on, if you want to go somewhere, you ask me first. You understand all that?"

Mike's opinion of Dagger was even lower than Dagger suspected, but there is an aura of mystery surrounding men who volunteer for the military's special units, and of those who have served with what many experts call the toughest fighting men in the world—the French foreign legion— and those men who have fought as mercenaries. Some of those men cannot punch their way out of a wet paper bag, and will be the first to admit it—to close friends. But there are others still who exude danger simply by walking into a room, by the look in their eyes, by the way they carry themselves or smile.

Dagger was one of the latter.

Mike's returning smile was somewhat forced. "And if I don't?"

Dagger's gaze never wavered.

"Someday," Mike said, "when this is over, you and me, buddy, we'll see who is the better man."

"Your option," Dagger replied, "but I already know."

He walked away, leaving Mike standing in the foyer, feeling a bit foolish.

Dagger told the group to clean up their living quarters and kitchen. "Leave everything as we found it. Don't leave hair in the sinks, wet towels around, dirty dishes, and so forth. Pig and his bunch will be sure to search the place, but they'll be in a hurry. We might just pull this off and have a place to return to. Let's move it."

They pulled out an hour later. Kit rode with Mike and Jimmy. Paige and Ralph together. Dagger drove the agent's car, the dead man stiffening in the trunk, J.B. tied up in the back seat, a blanket covering him.

Before they pulled out, Paige had asked, "What are you going to do with the dead man?"

"We'll head west," Dagger told her. "As much as we can that is. I want to pick up 105 at Krotz Springs, south. I'll dump the dead meat somewhere between there and I-10."

She put dark eyes on his face, searching eyes. "And then?"

"I've got to keep you people alive — out of the hands of Pig and his bunch. And I've got to get to the Secret Service. And I've got to pump you all for information you think you don't know."

"I don't understand."

"You know something, Paige. One of you — all of you. Something that will tie this jumbled package up neatly. It'll fall into place, you'll see. Right now, we've got to get to Baton Rouge and you all have to get some cash. Cash some checks at small branch banks, where you're known. We're going to be running for ten days — maybe longer — and that gets expensive. I've already told the others to do the same."

"Isn't that risky?"

"Yes. But it has to be done. Stay with the caravan. When I stop to dump the meat, drive on past, I'll catch up with you. If we become separated, we'll link up at the truck stop. Remember it? Good. Take off."

She turned, then kissed him, pressing against him. "Don't forget, Dagger," she whispered against his mouth. "We have a date."

He gently pushed her away. "Don't be a fool, Paige. Get on out of here. Find yourself a nice lawyer or accountant or computer programmer. Even a pretty-boy." He smiled. "We're worlds apart."

She smiled, kissed him again, then walked toward the car. She called over her shoulder, "Sometimes worlds collide, Dagger. Ours have. I'll see you in Baton Rouge."

Dagger watched her leave, his eyes taking in all that woman walking from him. He touched his finger tips to his lips, her kiss still warm on his mouth.

Damn fool, he thought. Both of us.

Dagger prowled the medicine cabinets of the mansion; he could not find what he sought. He had asked Paige if she had any barbiturates. She gave him a bottle of Valium. He told J.B., "You either take these willingly or I'll jam them down your throat."

"No need to get hostile. I'll do as I'm told. Dagger? This tape is really hurting me. My hands and feet are numb."

"You're breaking my heart, J.B. I'll loosen the tape when you're all beddy-bye. Now open your mouth."

In half an hour J.B. was yawning hugely. In forty-five minutes he was out cold.

Between Krotz Springs and I-10, Dagger pulled off the road and waited until the highway was clear. He jerked open the trunk, manhandled the stiffening body of the dead agent, and dumped him into a brackish bayou. Dagger was back in the car and rolling within ninety seconds. J.B. snored peacefully on the back seat.

* * *

"Gentlemen, I don't feel we should tell the president of our . . . suspicions. Not yet. We all feel the Secret Service has been compromised. So," Harrison said, "let's count it up and down and add it up. Let's start with the bottom line: Who do we trust?"

The men compiled a list of forty men and women whom they felt they could trust to bring into the operation. They violated Company policy and coded the operation The Jasmine Affair.

The DCI looked at the list ruefully. "What a sorry business," he spoke grimly. "Forty people out of a list of thousands."

"Sir?" Hartsel said. "Most of the men and women in the Company don't know, and won't know, anything about what we're doing. Begging your pardon, sir, but you're relatively new to this game. We—" he indicated the others—"have spent out entire lives in a shadow world. Sometimes the left hand doesn't know what the right hand is doing. And in many cases, sir, it's better that way. Hell, it *has* to be that way."

Harrison nodded his agreement if not his understanding. He remembered his wife's comment of the previous night. At this moment, he wished to God he was back in Colorado. Lovely this time of year.

"We can put Fritzler on the top of the list," Harrison said. "My assistant DCI. The son of a bitch!" he cursed, which was quite unlike him. He looked around him. "And General Mitchell, of course, is in this up to his three-star ass. But who is the third man?"

The agents all shrugged. No one knew. No one wished to venture a guess.

"High up?" Harrison tossed it out.

Nods of affirmation.

"Anybody care to guess in what department of government?"

"Pipe smoker," Church said. "And that is only hearsay. That's all I ever heard about him."

"That's all any of us know about him," Haywood said. "And that could well be a deliberate false feed."

Harrison sighed. His head was beginning to ache. He felt like he was in a box and the lid was being nailed shut. They couldn't take it to the Bureau; the Bureau—they all suspected—had been compromised along with the Secret Service.

"Anybody got an aspirin?" Harrison asked.

St. Francisville

"Pig!" Young radioed in. "You were right. Burrell's parents own property up here. They just bought a mansion outside St. Francisville. Corporate name. We're just a few miles away."

"We'll wait for you."

Five minutes later, Pig told them, "Young, take two men and go in the back. I'll take Bitsy and Lisa and go in the front. Move out. The rest of you people hang tight."

A fast search of the house revealed nothing. They concentrated on the grounds. None of them was worried about local interference: They all had IDs showing them as BATF agents.

"Blood on the ground over here, Pig," Lisa called. She pointed to a broken hedge. "Looks like someone fell heavily. I'll look for brass."

"Don't bother," Pig told her. "Dagger would have removed all that." He walked to the combat scene. Kneeling down, he inspected the area and then grunted. "One man. Dagger took out either J.B. or Smithy."

"I hope it's Smithy he took alive," Bitsy said.

"Yeah," Pig mused aloud. "J.B. gets diarrhea of the mouth at just the mention of pain. But J.B. doesn't know that much."

"He knows what went down in sixty-nine," Pig was reminded.

"Yeah, but he can't prove it." Pig looked at the two women and felt a stirring in his groin. Lisa and Bitsy were both attractive women. Getting a little long in the tooth, but that didn't matter to Pig. What mattered was, like Pig, they both enjoyed their sex rough and kinky. To say the trio were all slightly unbalanced would be putting it most subtly.

The women looked at each other, picking up on Pig's vibes. Sweat formed on Bitsy's upper lip as she thought of past moments with Pig. And Lisa.

"Where are Burrell's parents?" Pig asked. He

knew, but didn't want the others to know he did.

"Europe, for the summer."

"Why no guards at this fancy place?" Bitsy asked.

"They never use them," Pig told her. "Don't know why." Pig looked at his team. "Young, you and the others head on back. You know what cars they're driving, and they took J.B.'s car. Find them. Check the rental car agencies in Baton Rouge, New Orleans, Lafayette. The cars they're in are getting hot; they'll maybe have to change. They may be running out of cash, try to cash some checks. They don't know what a surprise they have waiting for them when they try it in a bank. It's just a matter of time. We'll find them." He shifted his piggy eyes to another agent. "I'll get in touch with Fritzler. He'll roll the computer tapes, find out where, or if, any of the others own property. They may try to hide out there. Cover all Secret Service offices and Bureau offices in this state. Also Jackson and Biloxi, Mississippi."

"We'll be spread pretty thin, Pig."

"So I'll tell Fritzler we need more people," Pig said. "Mitchell's got the manpower at his disposal."

"Pig?" Young asked. "What if Dagger gets to the Secret Service or the FBI—bypassing our people there?"

Pig's eyes were bright with anticipation. "Then we burn some government boys and girls. Eagle-

Fall goes down as planned. The clock is running. Nothing stops the clock. Nothing. You understand?"

"We got it, Pig."

"Then move it! Take Cooper with you. Me and Lisa and Bitsy'll be along later. Meet you all in Baton Rouge. The rest of you guys fan out. You got your orders." He smiled. "Relax, gang. We got time, we got the power on our side. Dagger is just one man with a group of amateurs. And remember, pass the word, make it plain, you know they have to be taken alive."

"Right, Pig."

"Move it."

When the agents had gone, Lisa said, "You're lying to them, Pig. Are you trying to get rid of as many of them as possible before EF day?"

"You got it, honey."

"I like it." She grinned. "Loose lips sink ships, huh, Pig?"

They all laughed at the World War II slogan.

Pig hid his car in the garage and the trio walked into the mansion.

"This is dangerous, Pig," Bitsy reminded him.

Pig laughed as they entered a grandly furnished drawing room. "I never fucked in a place this fancy." He looked at the expensive imported rugs. He pulled both women to him, fondling breasts and crotch. "Let's get cum on the carpet, babies."

"I think we're ahead of them," Dagger told Paige. "But not by much. We'll get some cash and then take off. And we've got to get rid of these cars."

"I want that dossier in my safe-deposit box," she said.

"It won't be there, Paige. I'm thinking it was never there. If it wasn't taken outright, then your box has been sealed by some government agency—probably the IRS. Bet on it."

"I'm going to call the bank."

"Your option."

She returned from the phone, her shoulders slumped in defeat. She got in the car and stared at Dagger. Her eyes seemed dull. "Go ahead, Dagger, get it over with. Say I told you so."

"What's wrong?"

"I'm under heavy audit. I can't open my safe-deposit box. It's been sealed. The IRS has frozen all my assets."

J.B. slept peacefully in the back seat, covered with a blanket.

Dagger nodded his head, his expression containing an element of worry. "Bigger and bigger," he said. "So they've got people within the IRS. It doesn't surprise me."

"The government *can't do* this!" Paige protested, getting angry, losing her defeatist mood. "This is supposed to be *America*."

"The IRS can do damn near anything they

want to do, Paige. Even legitimately, they've got far too much power and control over the citizens. Well . . . so much for cashing checks at banks. The word will have spread among the banks. We'll cash a number of small checks where you shop for groceries, booze, clothes, gas, so forth. Then we'll drop your rental car off and call the people to come get it."

She touched his arm. "Dagger—I've a friend who is in the Caribbean for three weeks. She left me the keys to her car. We could use that. And I know Jimmy has a friend in Port Allen who works offshore on a rig; he is an engineer. They use each other's cars now and then."

"Good thinking. Let's do it. I sure would like to know if Pig has the Federal Building staked out. But finding out would be too risky, take too long. I'll just have to assume he does and try somewhere else later on."

"You don't sound very optimistic, Dagger."

"I'm not. Paige, what Crowson and Knight— whatever their real names are—said the other night might very well be true: I could be hot with the Feds. They might agree to a meet and set me up. I might get maverick agents and they'd come in shooting. Damn!" He hit the steering wheel with the heel of his hand. "I'm in a box. OK, we've got to switch J.B. from car to car. Follow me out of town."

The three-car caravan headed northwest out of Baton Rouge, on a state road. At Zachary, they turned east on another state road and, when the highway was clear, Dagger made the switch, leaving the agent's car in the drive of a falling-down, old farm house.

Behind the wheel of Paige's friend's car, a Buick, she asked, "Where are we going, Dagger?"

He grinned. "To New Orleans. To spend the night."

"I'm running out of personnel," Fritzler told Pig. "And Mitchell has committed all the men he is going to let you have. I'm sending all I have left to you. You find Dagger and those people and sit on them for a time."

"Maybe that isn't the best way, sir," Pig said, smiling as he said it. He was naked and so were the women. He had called Fritzler, collect, from the Burrell mansion. Lisa and Bitsy were on the carpet, loving each other, and Pig felt an erection build as he watched the women. "I got an idea, sir, but it might take a day or two to work it out."

"All right," Fritzler said. "Let's have your grand scheme."

"John," President Menen said to his chief-of-staff, "you look worried. What's wrong?"

John Cruse, a tall, erect-in-carriage man, with the same eyes and complexion of the president, smiled and lit his pipe. "No, William, nothing is the matter, not really. It's just been a long day, that's all. That, plus the fact that I'm worried about you. You haven't been yourself lately."

President Menen looked at his longtime friend, friends since college. Cruse had worked tirelessly to get William Menen elected, first to Congress, then into the White House. Years of struggle for both men.

Should I tell him? Menen pondered. No, he decided. Why complicate his life with more problems than he's already forced to carry around. God, the man practically runs the White House.

Menen smiled, the gesture transforming his face into that of a person much younger, erasing the lines placed there by holding onto the reins of probably the toughest job in the world.

"No need to worry about me, John. Everything is normal: The Russians are accusing us of espionage. We're denying it. We're accusing them of violating human rights; they're denying it. The Middle East has exploded again. Central America has guerrillas running around, blowing up this and that, all for the sake of liberty, of course. Labor is accusing me of being anti-union; the teachers are saying it's not their fault we have functional illiterates graduating from high school. Our courtrooms have become revolving doors for punks and hoodlums. The ACLU just said—so I'm told—that I have the mentality of the hanging judge, Parker, of Fort Smith fame.

That nut in Iran is flapping his big mouth again, spouting his usual line of bullshit. You want me to continue, John?"

Both men laughed, and the laughter felt good to both of them.

"No, William," John said, shaking his head. "But it is good to know everything is normal."

"John," Menen said, glancing at his appointments calendar, "I don't have anything pressing this afternoon. How about eighteen holes?"

John's face broke into a broad smile. "You got a date, William."

The president laughed. "Just don't beat me too badly, John."

Ralph Volker burst into Dagger's room through an adjoining door, and came very close to getting shot for his impulsiveness. He paled as Dagger slowly lowered the Colt Woodsman.

"Don't ever do that again," Dagger warned him. "Not ever again."

"Yes, sir." Ralph wiped suddenly sweaty palms on his trousers. He felt his heart slow its frantic beating.

"What's the problem?" Dagger asked. "The IRS seal your bank account, too?"

"Worse than that, Dagger," Mike said, walking into the room. "We just spoke with our attorney in Baton Rouge. We've all got heavy-type warrants out for us." He was shaking from anger.

"We've been set up! They got warrants out on us for dope-pushing—I mean the heavy stuff. They claim we're into all sorts of crap. Kiddy-porn to prostitution, the federal people went into our homes—so they claim—and found all sorts of pictures, dope, funny money, ties with organzied crime, double bookkeeping in our businesses. Goddamn you, Dagger, do you realize that in less than twenty-four hours we've all become *wanted fugitives?*"

"Welcome to the real world, Tiger," Dagger said with a smile. "You still want to go to the police?"

Dagger's relaxed pose on the bed and casual tone of voice irritated Mike. "I don't like you worth a damn, Dagger. You know that?"

"I'll probably cry myself to sleep, sonny."

Mike flushed with anger and spun around, stalking from the room.

Ralph sat down in a chair. "Mr. Dagger, I have a confession to make."

"I'm not a priest, Ralph."

"I'm not Catholic. Dagger, I'm scared."

"Join the club. So am I."

Ralph shook his head. "No . . . I'm sorry, but I don't believe you are. You may be somewhat apprehensive, but you're not scared. I think you're probably looking forward to a showdown. You're a gunfighter.

"Dagger, my attorney says the case against us is overwhelmingly strong. That we could all go to prison. I have never kept double books in my life and will not deal with any person who has. I run an honest business. No Mafia ties. This is a setup, Dagger."

"I'm sure it is, Ralph."

"Why did they do it, Dagger?"

"To force your hand. If you were to cooperate with them—so they would like you to believe—all charges would be dropped with an apology."

"But you don't believe that?"

"No. Maybe at first they would have. Now it's gotten out of hand. These warrants were probably set in motion several days ago; they couldn't stop the process."

The young man sighed. "We talked it over, Dagger. All of us. Even if we could, we won't be coerced into giving up this . . . quest for justice."

Dagger sat up on the edge of the bed. His smile contained that knowing element. That: I've been where you're about to go, boy. "Bet only on yourself, Ralph. Not on anyone else. We have two weak links in this six-link chain of ours, and they could go either way."

"Mike and Kit."

"You got it."

"So what are we going to do?"

"You people are going to stay put. I'm going to make a phone call."

Dagger walked down the street to a honky-tonk, got a fistful of change, and slid into a phone booth, closing out most of the sounds of a whiny, too-loud country band. He dialed a number in Miami.

"No names and I'll keep this short," Dagger said. "Kind of like a short sword. You know who this is?"

"Si," Hank McNeal said. "I do now."

"We both know the Company — among others — has your phone wired. You remembered that place where we met the last time I shipped out to the Dark Continent?"

A short pause. *"Si."*

"I'll call you there in half an hour. You'll be tailed by people who might like to silence you permanently, so you'd better call some of your buddies to take care of that little problem."

"De acuerdo." Hank hung up.

Dagger took a taxi to another part of the city, another honky-tonk, another phone booth. He had the operator assist him in locating the number of the Spanish cafe in Miami. Hank came on the line.

"De donde buendo, compadre?"

"Alone, mostly," Dagger replied. "I prefer it that way, if you'll recall. How hot am I, Hank?"

Hank laughed from across the Gulf. "As hot as a virgin nun with a fistful of stiff cock."

Dagger returned the laughter. "My friend, you'll do time in purgatory for that crack."

"Compadre, I'll never get *out* of purgatory."

"Hank, what am I up against with this one?"

"Ah, old friend, I wish I knew the whole story.

But it is betrayal. Far worse than that awfulness we experienced at the Bay of Pigs. It goes very high, I am thinking. Although I can prove nothing, I think it goes all the way up."

"The White House?"

"I think so."

"Eagle-Fall?"

"Most definitely."

"Jesus Christ, Hank—why that? Why now, with this president?"

"That I do not know. But it is something about which I have given much thought. I can come up with no answers that satisfy."

"Has the Bureau been compromised?"

"To some small extent, *si*."

"The Secret Service?"

"To a lesser extent."

"How do you people do it, Hank?"

Hank laughed. "We talk much but say little. And we listen all the time."

"I need the name of a man I can trust in the Secret Service."

"Ed Williams of Atlanta would be one. Bill Gormly of D.C. would be another. I believe you can trust most of the Secret Service. But if you're thinking of talking to one of them, try Williams or Gormly." He flipped through a notepad and gave Dagger the numbers.

"Can you help me on your end?"

"Si!"

"You get in touch with Williams. Tell him I'll be

in contact with him. Tell him what we discussed and that he can trust me. OK?"

"That's a big ten-four."

Dagger chuckled. "Progress is really corrupting you Cubans, Hank."

"I heard that. Dagger? Be careful, *mercenario*."

"Careful is my middle name, Hank."

"You can go to hell for telling lies, pal."

"I'll meet you there."

"That's a big ten-four."

10

The tension in the motel rooms was evident when Dagger returned. Paige sat stiffly in a chair, anger in the set of her chin. She looked straight ahead, eyes smoldering with banked heat. Jimmy and Ralph looked equally upset. Kit and Mike sat together, backs against a wall.

"What's up?" Dagger asked. He glanced at J.B. The man was wide awake, the gag over his mouth. His eyes were frightened.

"You got no reputation to protect, Dagger," Mike said. "I do—we all do. OK, so we lost people years ago. We're not going to bring them back no matter what we do now. I say we take this deal the powers-that-be offered us, and forget all about this hopeless vendetta we started. I just got off the phone with my lawyer."

Anger flared hot in Dagger. He felt tension grow in him. "How long did you talk, you dumb bastard?"

Mike held up a hand. "Relax, Dagger. I'm not

totally stupid, as you must believe. I talked for one minute, no more. Not enough for a trace."

Dagger relaxed. "Did your attorney try to keep you talking?"

Mike looked confused for a moment. "Yeah . . . come to think of it, he did. But he's a talker."

"Uh-huh. Go on."

"OK," Mike said, "so we all know what they're doing is illegal. The federal people, I mean. But what choice do we have? Come on, tell me: What choice?"

"Like I told Ralph. It's a setup."

"But our attorney knows of the problem," Kit said. "What harm could come to any of us when he knows about it?"

"Maybe nothing," Dagger replied. His eyes touched each person in the room. "And maybe your attorney—and I gather from your conversation you have the same one—has been bought. You said he tried to keep you talking. Maybe the Company is holding something over his head? Think about it, and while you're thinking about that, give this thought: The doctor who 'just happened' to be on the scene when your PI had his mysterious heart attack, anybody know if he and your mutual attorney are friends? How about it?"

"Doctor Rossetti," Kit said. "Yeah. That's interesting, Dagger. None of us ever put that together."

Jimmy had a very distressed look on his face. Only Dagger seemed to notice it.

Kit said, "Yeah. He and Charles Cleveland—our

attorney—are friends. I know they play golf together every week, weather permitting."

"Things beginning to fall in place now, Dagger?" Paige asked.

"Little by little." He looked at J.B. and reached for a knife in his pocket.

A dark stain appeared on the front of J.B.'s trousers as Dagger opened the knife, running his thumb lightly over the edge of the blade. J.B.'s eyes bulged and he struggled against his bonds.

Brainwashing from misguided parents, out-of-touch college professors, and goody-two-shoes foam from the mouths of liberals that all people are good shocked the men and women in the room into silence. Paige put her hand on Dagger's arm.

"What are you going to do?"

Dagger turned to J.B. He smiled like a wolf baring its teeth.

J.B. fainted.

"Clean my fingernails," Dagger said. "What else?" He chuckled. "Just wanted to see if J.B. knew more than he told me. He does. I'll get it out of him. But you people can relax—torture is not my forte. Get some sleep. We'll be pulling out just after midnight."

Mike looked up. His face was a mask of defeat. "Where are we going?"

Dagger grinned. "Why, back to the mansion at St. Francisville, of course."

EAGLE-FALL + 11

"Fritzler," Harrison said, "there is something that needs to be done, and I believe you are the man for the job."

Fritzler narrowed his eyes behind his lightly tinted eyeglasses. "Yes, sir?"

"Tomorrow morning, you're heading west."

"I am?" Fritzler blurted the words. He caught himself. "I mean, yes, sir, of course. But why am I heading west?"

"I want you to personally evaluate—in writing—our operations in Hawaii. And when that is done, you will wait there for further orders. I'll probably be sending you on to Japan."

Fritzler's mouth dropped open. He stared at the DCI.

"Did you hear me, Roy?"

"Oh! Oh, yes, sir. Certainly, sir." Goddamn him! Fritzler silently raged, the space between his ears a boiling cauldron of hate. What a time for me to go station-hopping.

Harrison smiled reassuringly at his assistant. "You're the only man I could trust to do this, Roy. You'll see what I mean when you get out there. The station is not operating efficiently enough to suit me. You'll see. You're the one who can straighten it out." And I hope you fall out of the plane, you traitorous bastard.

"Do I take anyone with me, sir?"

"No. And you'll fly military. I don't want any attention drawn to you."

Buying a little time. Separating the top men in this . . . despicable act of treason.

Harrison desperately wanted to go to his long-time friend, President Menen, and tell him of this; Church and the others wanted him to do that. But Harrison wanted to hold off until more proof was found. No need to create panic now; no need to put more pressure on the person in the most pressure-packed job in the world.

Besides, Harrison reminded himself, they needed more proof — something solid. They had no proof that anything was about to go down. Nothing but rumors and strange occurrences.

But he knew something was happening. Felt it in his guts.

But what?

He would have to wait. He was no trained field agent; his was a political job. And, Harrison silently concluded, it should not be.

11

Exhausted after their hurried trip back to St. Francisville and the Burrell mansion, Dagger let his charges sleep on. He untied J.B. and shoved him in a shower stall, tossing a bar of soap in after him.

"Wash your butt, J.B. You're beginning to smell like a goat in rut."

"But I still got my clothes on!" J.B. howled, dancing under the spray of hot water, the fat on the man jiggling in time with his double chins.

"Toss them out to me," Dagger told him.

He was not terribly worried about J.B. attempting any escape or doing anything drastic. J.B. had been, for all practical purposes, out of the field for ten years, and he had been a lousy agent all during his active tenure with the Company. He had spent most of his time on campuses recruiting. That and trying to get the panties off the youngest girls he could find. His one exception had been his stateside work with Section

Five. And that didn't require much sense, only savagery and perversion.

Dagger had never known and often wondered during his short time with Section Five why that section had ever been allowed to form in the U.S.A.

Now he thought he knew.

It was a cover for Eagle-Fall. A long-term, very clandestine operation that might take ten or twenty years before the trap was sprung.

But he still didn't know why it had to be with President Menen.

With J.B. showered and shaved, Dagger handed the man a sheet. "Wrap up, J.B. Just like a mummy. Then we're going to the basement. One way in, one way out."

A glint of hope sprang into J.B.'s eyes. "You're not going to tie me up?"

"Nope. But the first time you try to escape, I'm going to break all the fingers on your right hand."

J.B. paled.

"Slowly. One at a time."

J.B. began to sweat. "Dagger. I'll cooperate with you. You name it, I'll do it. I give you my word: no trouble out of me. I'm tired of running and hiding from my past."

Dagger's reply was a grunt. He knew J.B. was not only a coward, but a liar and a cheat as well.

With J.B. safely stashed in the basement, the heavy, oak door bolted from the outside, Dagger slipped from the house and drove to a pay phone about a mile from the mansion. He phoned Atlanta Secret Service, asking for Ed Williams. Ed was on the horn in ten seconds.

"You spoke with a friend of ours in Miami?" Dagger asked.

"Yes."

"Your phone secure?"

"I . . . don't know. But I want to hear this."

"I got J.B. Mohney. He doesn't know much, but he says he'll tell all."

Silence.

"What's the matter? Goddamn you, Williams! Don't try putting a trace on this call."

Silence.

"Answer me, you prick. You got ten seconds."

"Settle down, pal. I had a visitor, that's all. A secretary. Now you listen to me: Something big and ugly is in the wind."

"You're telling me? I'm standing out in the breeze."

"Be quiet and listen, Dagger. For a change. This thing is so big I'm running blind and scared—I told Hank that and I'm telling you that. I don't know who to trust. The Service has been compromised. And I'm not trying to trace your call. I've known and trusted Hank for years. If he says you're five by five, that's it."

"I'm open to suggestions, Ed."

"Aren't we all? Look, due to some unforeseen miracle in President Menen's schedule, I have the next two days off." The Secret Service often works days and weeks without a break. "I'll talk to a couple guys I know I can trust. Then I want to meet with you and J.B. But where?"

This time it was Dagger who was silent, suspecting a setup.

"Dagger? I'm not trying to set you up. How do I convince you of that?"

"Well, I sure as hell won't tell *you* where *I* am."

"I don't blame you. You're hot, man — real hot. Just keep your cool."

"OK. How much did Hank tell you?"

"All he knew."

"I figure we have ten or eleven days before Eagle-Fall," Dagger dropped it on him.

"Jesus Christ!"

Dagger tried to pick up on any act in the Secret Service man's tone. He could detect none. Dagger had no choice. He had to trust someone. "I'll meet you in Meridian, Mississippi, Ed. You name the spot."

Williams gave him a phone number to call that evening. Dagger suspected it was a pay phone and as it turned out, he was right. Williams was taking no chances on his office phone being tapped. "We'll settle on a motel then. I'll talk with some people I can trust in the meantime."

"OK. But I'll be with a crowd. I can't leave them alone. They're all amateurs."

I think, he amended that.

"I'll want to talk with them as well. I'll be

alone, Dagger."

"We'll see you then."

Dagger let his people sleep on. He checked on J.B. The Valiums had dropped him into a deep sleep. He looked like a fat King Tut.

Dagger took the watch for a couple of hours. He knew he had taken a chance leaving the mansion unguarded, but it was a chance he had to take. He did not believe Pig would send people back to the mansion, since backtracking was not something Pig liked to do.

Dagger was tired. Going full-tilt for many hours had taken its toll. He finally woke Ralph up and then took a shower, hitting the sheets. He was asleep in two minutes.

"You're in charge, Pig," Fritzler spoke from Washington. "The DCI is sending me out to Hawaii for a week—maybe longer. I don't like it, but there is damn little I can do about it without raising suspicions."

"I don't like it either," Pig replied. "You might be gone on EF day."

"Can't be helped. Mitchell will take over my job upon my departure—as far as this operation goes. But down there, Pig, you're running the show."

"I don't like that bastard, Fritzler. I don't trust him."

In Washington, Fritzler smiled. And he doesn't

like or trust you, either, Pig, Fritzler thought. But on EF day, if all goes according to plan, you and your people will all be dead. "He's a good man, Pig. Just remember this: Our orders come from the top. We all take orders."

In Louisiana, Pig's smile was grimly satisfying. He thought: And maybe you won't return from the land of hula girls and palm trees, you prissy prick. "Yes, sir, Mr. Fritzler. I will sure remember that."

"I'm counting on you to wrap up our little problem down there, Pig. Take care of it."

"Personally, sir."

Fritzler broke the connection. "Ugly savage," he said.

Pig looked at the buzzing receiver. "Son of a bitch."

Something warm and soft and satin smooth slipped into bed to snuggle up to Dagger. That something was naked, too.

None of us may come out of this alive, Dagger thought. So why not take as much pleasure as possible when it's offered?

He turned, gathering the woman into his arms. Her breasts pushed against his bare chest. With his right hand, Dagger caressed her belly, then moved downward to the dark triangle between her legs. His fingers found the moisture of her, parted her, and entered.

She sighed against his mouth at this welcome intrusion.

"And all this time," Dagger whispered, "I thought you were a lady."

Paige said, "There are no ladies when the lights go out, Dagger."

Her fingers sought and found the lengthening, thickening mass of him and stroked the hot muscle. She gasped her pleasure at the bulk.

The two of them spoke only the silent words of building desire as they touched, fondled, caressed, stroked and positioned themselves — one ready to give, the other ready to receive.

He brought her to readiness; she stroked him to fullness.

Then, in a bedroom of the 150-year-old mansion that already held more secrets within its curving stairways and antique furnishings than are contained in any whodunit, the old home shared still another secret as man parted the legs of woman and slid into the wet, not, giving constriction.

"Make it last and last, Dagger," she whispered. "We have all the time in the world."

And in the building mist of passion, Dagger could not help but think: Keep on believing that, honey. I've already killed two men in this operation, and you people can't get it through your thick skulls that you could all get your tickets punched at any time.

What in the hell is the matter with civilians,

anyway?

Dagger concentrated on pleasuring the woman, driving into her, taking her with one long thrust. She almost screamed as more maleness than she had ever experienced filled and stretched her.

She gripped his thick arms and hard shoulders and kissed his mouth, the fire in both of them reaching inferno heat. She murmured in lover's language as a climax shook her, another building just seconds behind the first.

Then the act grew gentler for a time, slower paced, each pushing, pulling, rubbing friction between the lovers bringing sighs of pleasure from both of them.

They shifted on the bed, Paige assuming dominance, straddling him, working up and down, while her long hair flew about her face. He cupped her breasts, then slid one hand downward, to gently caress her clit.

They tore the sheets and tossed pillows to the carpet in their frenzied lovemaking, not caring if anyone overheard them.

They experimented with positions, for a sweaty hour rewriting the Kama Sutra. The grandfather clock in the hall ticked, time moving silently and steadily past them. Neither cared.

His stroking was measured now, each long plunge giving her every centimeter of his being, from tip to belly.

"Now!" she cried. "Now, Dagger."

He exploded within her as she experienced the most shattering and numbing climax of her life.

When her head cleared, she was startled to find herself bent over the end of the bed. She had never before liked that position, thought it degrading. She changed her mind on this day.

He picked her up in his arms without effort and she was amazed at the power of the man. She did not know of another man who could manhandle her as if she were a child.

And she did not know if she really liked that power within the man. Not that much. It made her feel . . . well, helpless.

They lay on the bed, wrapped in each other, the sweat drying, the passion cooling, their hearts slowing, their sex returning to normal.

"Are you sorry that our worlds have collided, Dagger?" she asked, running her hand over his hard right arm, feeling the muscles ripple under her touch.

"No. Not if you're happy with it."

She smiled. "I think we're going to make it, Dagger. I really do."

Dagger said nothing.

Thousands of miles away, in Europe, another hunt had begun.

EAGLE-FALL + 10

Dagger had made the call to Williams; the time and meeting place had been set. He gathered his little band of reluctant troops and headed out. Dagger drove the lead car, with Paige beside him. Mike was in the back seat with J.B. Jimmy, Kit and Ralph followed several car lengths behind.

"You got your act all rehearsed, J.B.?" Dagger asked.

There was no bluster left in J.B. And no hope. The hours of confinement had worn him down. His face was haggard-looking and he was shaky. "No act, Dagger. I'm done with that. I'll cooperate. I don't know much, but I'll tell the Secret Service what I do know and take my chances."

There was a note of sincerity in J.B.'s voice that Dagger had not detected prior to this. J.B. was ready to spill his guts. For the first time, Dagger felt that maybe — just maybe — they might all come out of this in one piece.

They checked into the motel in Meridian and

Dagger asked for William's room number. He tapped softly on the door. The door swung open, carefully, and Dagger looked into a man's face.

"Name?"

"Williams." He held out his ID with picture.

Dagger gave the man his international driver's license. "Do we talk here or in my room?"

"Your room. Let's do it."

It was easy for Dagger to see the man was under a tremendous amount of strain.

Welcome to the club, Dagger thought.

Dagger kept the introductions brief. Williams sat down in a chair and glared at J.B. His contempt for the man was obvious. "All right, Mohney. Tell your story."

When he finished, Dagger gave him two Valiums, tied his hands and sat him in a corner.

Williams then questioned each of Dagger's party, tape-recording, as he had done with J.B., each word. The five could tell him nothing they had not already told Dagger. Williams dismissed them and waited until they had filed from the room before turning to Dagger.

"It's hard for me to believe the Secret Service has been penetrated. Almost beyond belief."

"Everybody has their price, Ed. I don't have to tell you that. Besides, we don't know how many years this was in the making. You know about Section Five?"

"Unfortunately."

"I think that was the beginning. Just be careful

who you trust, that's all."

Williams's eyes were tormented. "That's the problem, Dagger. Damn it, who do I trust? Where do I go with this?"

"How about those guys you told me about?"

"One is on vacation and the other is on overseas assignment. I *know* my boss isn't in on this. I'd stake my life on that."

"That's exactly what you're doing," Dagger reminded him.

"Yeah," Williams said, "how right you are. And the president's life. And my sworn duty is to protect his life at all costs. I'm going to talk with Gormly first — take Mohney to him. Where can I get in touch with you?"

"We're going to be moving and shifting locations often. Give me your home phone number. I'll get in touch with you."

"Don't you trust me, Dagger?"

Dagger sighed, looked at his big hands. "Yeah — I want to. Yeah, I do."

"The Company's been penetrated; the Bureau's been penetrated; the Service has been compromised. Eagle-Fall. But damn it, Dagger, I don't understand why anyone would want to burn *this* president."

"I told you about the word Bear, didn't I?"

That stopped Williams cold. "You think the Reds?"

"I don't know. Maybe. Probably. That's your job. Look, can you do anything about those warrants and subpoenas on Paige and her friends?"

Williams shook his head. "I doubt it. I wouldn't know where to start without blowing what cover I have. You think the IRS has been compromised?"

"Don't you?"

Williams sighed, stood up, stretched. "Yeah," he said shortly. "I do. Well, you know where to reach me. I'll wait till dark, then slip Mohney out of here. Take him to Atlanta. We'll see where it goes from there."

Dagger nodded and the two men shook hands.

"Sure you won't change your mind and tag along with me on this?" Williams asked.

Dagger's smile was tight. "Pig would just love to catch us all in a big box."

"Yeah," the Secret Service man agreed. "You're right. Stay loose, Dagger. If anything happens to me, get in touch with Gormly in D.C." He gave Dagger Gormly's home phone number.

Dagger backtracked to Jackson, then headed northwest to Arkansas. He felt he could not risk going back to St. Francisville. He had checked his maps and decided they would head to the resort areas of Arkansas and rent a couple of cabins, maybe on the White or Buffalo River. Pose as fishermen (he looked at Paige — fisherpersons?) on vacation and just let Williams and his bunch handle the problem from here on in.

Dagger and his charges would just drop out of sight and lie low.

Sighing wistfully, Dagger thought: would that it were. He knew for almost a certainty that would never be the case. *He* was now numbered among the hunted. But why? Was it something he knew, some *one* he knew?

Was it because of his knowledge of Eagle-Fall? Or something else?

He had to put it all together.

Maybe in the peace and quiet of the Arkansas timber, by the waters of a river, he would have time to think.

Maybe. If someone didn't shoot him first.

"Mr. President," the chief-of-staff placed the revised schedule on Menen's desk in the Oval Office. "We have had a change in plans, sir."

Menen looked up from his work. "Oh? And why is that, John?"

"A week from this coming Monday you will have to leave Camp David a few hours earlier. I have taken the liberty of cancelling those few appointments. You and Mrs. Menen will not return here, to the White House. Instead you'll go by helicopter to Andrews AFB where you'll board Air Force One to Los Angeles. I just got this change a few moments ago."

"Why not return here first?"

"Time, sir." John tapped the revised schedule

on Menen's desk. "That, ah, unpublicized meeting you agreed to attend?"

Menen nodded. "With that wavering western governor. Yes. I just wish to hell he'd go on and join the Democratic Party and get off the dime."

"He wants the meeting time changed for some reason or another. He wasn't specific, just insistent."

"Sit down, John." The president waved the man to a chair. "Damn it, I thought that meeting was set for Tuesday?"

"It was." A flash of irritation touched the man's features. He sighed. "I tried to talk him out of it."

"Damn! That Tuesday meeting was his idea in the first place."

"I know, William." He could but shrug the unreliabilities of traveling politics.

"Oh . . . crap!" President Menen said. "This means I've got to work all Sunday afternoon when I had hoped to do it on Monday. There goes our golf game, John."

"I'd just beat you again," John said with a smile.

Menen laughed. "Yes, there is that to consider. All right, John. I shall so inform Mrs. Menen."

In Los Angeles, two men stood on a bluff overlooking the highway President Menen's motorcade would travel. One man looked nervous, occasionally wiping sweat from his face with a large handkerchief. The other man watched the nervousness with an amused expression on his tanned face.

"You're sure this is going to work?"

"For the fiftieth time, Mr. Warwick: Yes, I am sure it will work."

"You're not going to do any further dry runs?" the Company man asked.

"No. No point in that. It would only increase the risk of detection. Besides, I know the exact speed the president's limo will be traveling. I've computed distance and speed. I know exactly when to detonate."

"You're certain the . . . charges will explode?"

The mercenary known worldwide as The Gunner smiled. "For two million dollars, Mr. Warwick — yes, I'm certain. You didn't bring me all the way from England because I'm an amateur."

"Yes," Warwick said quietly. "Your reputation did precede you, Mr. Manchester. Very well. One more time. On the morning of Eagle-Fall, a man will come to your hotel room."

"My man," The Gunner corrected.

"Yes. Certainly. Your man. The banker. He will verify that two million dollars have been placed in your account in Bern. You will then do your job."

"If the job fails, or if I have to abort because of any error on my part, the monies will automatically be switched to another account—then returned to you through a Belgian bank."

"Yes. Now let's go over it one last time," Warwick pressed the mercenary.

The Gunner laughed, exposing square, strong teeth. Very white teeth. "No sweat, Warwick. Everything is done with electronics. When the timer—which will be attached to the president's limo by your man with the Secret Service here in L.A.—passes under the eye, which is installed and in place down there—" he pointed—"the explosives will detonate."

"And you're certain they will ignite?"

"Ignite is not precisely correct, Warwick, but we'll let it suffice. Yes, I'm certain. I've blown up railroads, bridges, dams, buildings, planes, cars, tanks, trucks, factories—and individuals. Now there is a real challenge. One person. Oh, and don't forget that kike cafe in Paris last year. Yes, the charge is dry and will remain so—not that wet or dry makes a damn bit of difference—and will explode when the eye tells it to. That entire section of construction work will come down on the president's limo. About fifteen tons of it. At the same instant, the charge under the highway, in the tunnel, will blow upward. The limo will be caught between the simultaneous explosions. Menen doesn't have a prayer. The president, the driver and the limo will be squashed flat as a manhole cover. Since the plans call for this entire interchange to be rebuilt, look at it as saving the

American taxpayers money." The Gunner laughed.

Warwick shuddered. His mouth was dry at just the thought of it all. Like stepping on a roach. He wished he would be here to see it. All that blood and stuff. He was not aware of his slight erection and his hard breathing.

But The Gunner was and it amused him. He silently wagered that Warwick liked little girls and little boys to get his perverted kicks.

He was right.

"Route change?" Warwick asked, bringing himself back from his clouded perversions of the mind.

"Not likely. Construction has begun on the highway opposite this site. Can't get through — overpass will be closed. Down there — " he pointed — "on the two-lane on this side of the presidential route, a small accident will occur just seconds before the motorcade passes. A produce truck will be driven by what appears to be a non-English-speaking Hispanic. Total confusion. No, the plan is ninety-nine percent assured. This is the only way the president can go."

Warwick grunted. "My superiors do not plan on failure, Mr. Manchester. But what if this plan of yours does not succeed — because of some unforeseen reason?"

"If I feel I can still pull it off, I will. But your cost will double. How many times do we go over this?"

"I don't like your doubling the cost. I told you that."

"Can't be helped. If I have to use that rented room and rocket to kill him, my risk factor will be astronomically high — against me."

"I see."

The Gunner laughed. "I doubt it, Warwick. You've spent your entire tenure with the Company in administration."

Warwick ignored that. "This will be our only meeting. Good luck." He turned and walked away.

The Gunner looked at his retreating back. "Bloody queer fool!" he said.

Paige tossed the Arkansas paper in Dagger's lap. "Page four," she said. "Bottom left corner."

Dagger read the article with a feeling of despair — a sinking, almost bottomless emotion of hopelessness. "Jesus," he said.

The short article from the AP was about an auto accident in Alabama. A Secret Service agent, Edward Williams, and a passenger — not yet identified — in the car were dead.

He reread the article, then balled up the paper and hurled it into a corner of the room. "That was no accident," he said. He rose to his feet and began pacing the floor of the cabin. Ed was right: Someone in the Atlanta office is working for the other side and had had him tailed. Probably his office and home phones were bugged. He grimaced. "Just like Gormly's will be."

"Maybe they followed us here?" Mike said, looking around furtively.

"But we checked all our cars for devices," Jimmy replied. "And we certainly took a devious enough route getting here. None of us picked up on anyone following us." He looked at Dagger. "Did you?"

Dagger shook his head curtly. "No. We were not followed."

He looked around the room at the people. But? He let that thought drift back into the dark regions of his mind.

The cabins they'd rented were isolated. The nearest town was miles away. No neighbors within shooting distance.

Kit began weeping, the strain finally getting to her: the knowledge that her life could be taken any moment finally coming home to the woman. Her brother patted her shoulder for a few seconds, comforting her.

"I feel like we're all in a great big box!" she sobbed. "And the sides are closing in. I want this to be over with. I want it to stop."

Ralph glanced at Dagger, motioning him to step outside. Dagger followed him out to the porch. "We've got to do something, Dagger. And we've got to do it quickly, before we all come unglued."

"I'm open to suggestions."

"That's the problem. I don't have any. I was hoping you might."

Dagger waited silently, sensing the conversation was not yet over.

"I'm not a flag-waver, Dagger. And the military turns me off—cold. I'm glad my number wasn't called in the draft. Does that make you angry?"

"I believe in compulsory military service," Dagger informed him.

"I don't."

"Your option."

"Well, no matter. Dagger, our president is going to be assassinated—or an attempt is to be made on his life. Maybe now I can prove myself in your eyes."

"There is nothing to prove, Ralph."

"Don't interrupt!" Ralph said sharply.

Dagger smiled. He rather liked this young man.

"I mean it, Dagger. I think we all have to put personal safety behind us and do our best to warn President Menen. I say we get on the phone and we start calling FBI offices—all of us. We make so many damn phone calls to so many offices, somebody will have to do something. And we call the press. Tell them. Let them smear it all over the front page and the radio and the TV."

"And then what happens?" Dagger asked. "This: The people behind all this mess will just slip back into their holes—and they've been buried deep, Ralph, for years—and wait for another time and place. Oh, some small potatoes might be picked up but even that is doubtful. You people have no proof, Ralph. Nothing of substance. Nothing. The press isn't going to risk libel suits on your word alone. Think about it: You people are wanted fugitives. Some government agency has proof that you people—all of you—are dopers, have ties with organized crime, are into kiddy porn—the whole slimy bag. And that proof, rigged as it surely is, is strong enough to stand up in court. There are a lot of people in this world who will do anything for money, and that includes lying—very convincingly."

For a moment, Ralph looked defeated. Then his features hardened. "All right, Dagger—so what do we do? Are we to just sit back and watch our president assassinated?"

"No," Dagger said, "but it won't do any good to run out and start blabbing about it, either. I'd like to get President Menen's schedule. Whatever is going down is going down in about ten days. Maybe we can figure out when it's happening if we know where he's going."

"Well, we're not that far from Little Rock. They'll have all the major dailies. One of us could go in tomorrow and pick up a dozen or so. Maybe one of them will carry the schedule."

"Yeah. Maybe. But there is only one problem after we do figure out where the man is going to be."

Ralph looked at him. "What's that?"

"Figuring out a way to get to the killer before the killer gets to the president."

12

The voice was harsh and demanding. Perhaps the only person in the world Pig had any respect for. Respect mingled with fear.

"Pull out all the stops, Pig. Find them. You-know-who has to be taken alive."

"Goddamnit," Pig swore. "I think it's time for us to put priorities in line. We've got to burn all of them."

"No," the man said. Pig could hear him sucking on that damned pipe over the phone. "The Bear and the kid are too important to us. No more questions about it."

"I got a plan."

"I know. Fritzler told me. It's a good one. It will go into your record. Our superiors are pleased with you. The plan has been implemented."

"Thanks a bunch."

"Get them, Pig. Time is running out."

The connection was broken.

"Bastard!" Pig slammed the phone into the cradle. "I'll kill you when this is over."

Sherman Harrison had made up his mind: He was going to tell the president and let the devil take the hindpart. He looked at the newspaper clipping, crumpled now, where he had balled it in anger and frustration. The clipping contained the story of Ed Williams, Secret Service agent, dead in an auto accident in Alabama.

"Like hell it was an accident," Harrison muttered.

And the man with Ed. Somebody was sitting on his identity. The Service had released that the passenger was a hitchhiker.

"I don't believe that either," Harrison said aloud.

And neither did any of his newly acquired confidants. None of them bought any of the story. Haywood and Church said Williams was a fine man, one who simply could not be bought off — a man devoted to his job and his country.

Sherman Harrison and President William Menen — Willie, to his very close friends — went back a long way. Years. All the way to the freshman days of college. Sherman and Willie and John and Lewis Doyle. Same fraternity. All buddies of the closest kind, and Harrison trusted them all. But on this matter, Lewis and John would have to be excluded. Sherman didn't like that, but this was just too damn big for a lot of people to be privy to it. Too awesome in scope. And just too dangerous.

Power play! The phrase jumped into Sherman's brain. No, he rejected it. That would be impossible in a country this size . . . unless the military were in on it.

Maybe they were, that thought entered his brain.

God! He hoped not.

But no, he rejected that outright. Something of that magnitude would have been picked up by some intelligence-gathering operation somewhere in the world.

No . . . this was a bit more insidious. Something played very close to the vest. Maybe for years.

But who would stand to gain the most?

And he didn't like the thought that jumped into his head: his old friend, VP Lewis Doyle.

Sherman could not accept that. Not at all.

Pipe smoker, Church and Haywood had said. That much they knew about him. Lewis smoked a pipe. But so did John Cruse and Doug Farmer.

Hell, he knew two dozen men and one woman in high government office who puffed on a pipe.

Sherman punched a button on his desk and within seconds Haywood walked in.

"Yes, sir?"

"Let's do it," Sherman said.

With Haywood at his side (Church was still

down south, chasing leads), the men drove to the White House. Haywood and Harrison both carried brief cases. Haywood's brief case contained a compact PSE machine—a psychological stress evaluator—and a de-bugger. In Harrison's brief case, he carried his old .38-caliber Chief's Special (he found it only after waking up his wife the night of Church's call; she told him she had stuck it down one of his waders).

Harrison knew Willie would not welcome this intrusion; he liked to spend Saturdays alone with his wife. But that couldn't be helped.

The men breezed past the guards in the rear, the Secret Service men in the White House, and went straight up to the president's living quarters. Menen looked up, his slight frown vanishing quickly when he saw who his visitors were.

"Sherman," Menen said. "It's always good to see you. Who is your friend?"

Haywood was introduced. Menen shook his hand, then turned to Harrison. "You look very serious, Sherman. What's on your mind?"

"I want you to call in your head of Secret Service, Mr. President. Lorne Holt. Just him. I would also like it if you would ask no questions at this time. Just bear in mind this is something of the gravest national concern."

The president looked at his longtime friend for a moment. He's put it together, Menen thought. Finally, Menen nodded his head. "All right, Sherman. The intrigue is fascinating. I can assume the interruption in my family's planned activities for the afternoon is worth it?"

"It is, Mr. President," the DCI informed his boss.

The men sat and stared at one another in silence for several minutes until Lorne Holt strolled in. Holt, a tall, well-built man in his early fifties, stood calmly in front of Menen's desk in the Oval Office.

Harrison wondered what in the hell the head of Secret Service was doing at the White House on a Saturday afternoon.

"Sir?" Holt asked Menen.

"It's not my show, Lorne," Menen said. "It's his." He shifted his eyes to Harrison.

Holt faced the DCI. "Sir?"

"Would you please lock the door, Lorne?" Harrison asked.

Harrison expected a buildup of tension at that order. Instead he was surprised to see smiles flit across the faces of both Menen and Holt. Harrison wondered about that, but said nothing.

The doors to the Oval Office locked, Harrison nodded to Haywood and the Company man opened his attache case, removing the compact de-bugger: a small, highly sophisticated, computerized piece of equipment that would tell the operator if any listening device, unauthorized by the president, existed within the room.

He fanned the room, after signaling the men to remain quiet about what he was doing.

The president's phone was tapped.

Menen's face tightened in rage. Holt balled his fists. Harrison waved the men into another room and motioned for Haywood to fan the area.

The room was clean.

Haywood, at Harrison's nod, removed the PSE machine from his brief case.

"That's a lie-detector machine," Menen said.

"Yes, sir," Harrison said. "Mr. Holt, if you will please sit down, I'm going to tell you and the president a story. A story both of you will find very difficult to believe. I did, at first, but I am now convinced beyond any doubt of its validity. After I conclude, Mr. Holt, I am going to ask you to take a PSE test."

"We know some of the story already, Mr. Harrison," Lorne said. "But I'll answer any question you care to ask — truthfully," he added.

Harrison nodded his head. "I suspected as much when I saw both of you smile. All right, gentlemen, here it is."

Harrison began his story, starting with the woman in the Agency's computer section and then going to the gathering of the agents in New Orleans. He left nothing out. He told them of the Agency's Section Five teams. About Dagger and Hank McNeal and Paige Burrell and her friends. The murder of O'Brian of army intelligence. The transferring of Kaplan and Harland. And finally of General Mitchell and Fritzler and the mystery man. Then he told them of Eagle-Fall.

Holt sat shaking his head, cursing under his breath. Menen blinked a couple of times, then said, "This Eagle-Fall must be my planned assassination. That the way you see it, Lorne?"

"Yes, sir. So all our information was wrong. It wasn't the Reds; it was our people all the time."

Menen was thoughtful for a moment. "Or so it appears on the surface, Lorne."

"Yes," Holt agreed. He looked at Harrison. "We knew — suspected — the Service had been compromised. As well as the Bureau and the Company and some of the military's intelligence-gathering units. How much time do you think we have, sir?"

"Ten days, according to my people's estimation."

"To Eagle-Fall," Holt said.

"Yes." Harrison told Haywood to put away his PSE equipment. "Mr. Holt is not part of any plot to kill the president."

Holt said, "Seems to me that Dagger and these other people are being tossed to the wolves, so to speak."

"By us," Menen added.

"I think that is the way it must remain," Harrison said. "At least for the time being."

Dagger called the cafeteria in the Treasury Building at noon, EST, and had Gormly paged. On this run, luck was with Dagger.

"This is Dagger," he said. He heard Gormly suck in his breath. "If you think Williams and Mohney bought it by accident, then you believe in Santa Claus."

"I don't know what to believe. You might be who you say you are, and then again, you could well be someone else."

"I'm Dagger. Williams's phone was bugged. That's how they got him and J.B. I would imagine your phones are tapped as well — both office and home. Think about it."

"That's . . . interesting."

"You know what's going down?"

"I may have spoken with Ed."

"You know Hank McNeal?"

"I may have heard the name."

"I'll have Hank call you. Give me a verification word."

"Bizarre."

"I'll get back to you in half an hour. You want me to call you same place?"

"No. That might create suspicion." Gormly gave him the number of a pay phone in Georgetown. "I've used that number from time to time. It's secure. If it's busy, keep trying."

Dagger hung up, then called Miami. They agreed on a safe phone, and within minutes Hank was back on the line. Dagger brought him up to date, gave him Gormly's check word, and the two men chatted for a moment.

"The freeze is on, Dagger," Hank said. "Nobody saying anything on the air."

"You've heard nothing?"

"Not a belch. Everyone is staying quiet down here, and for a Latin community, man, that's weird!"

"When this is over, we'll have to get together for a drink, Hank."

"Several of them, *mercenario,* with a couple of Spanish fireballs, of which I am at least familiar with one or two."

"Not to mention your wife," Dagger needled him.

"Leave my wife out of this," Hank laughed.

"See you, Hank."

"Luck to you, Dagger. I'll call Gormly."

Dagger waited for a few minutes, then called the number in Georgetown. Busy. He waited, then tried again. Gormly picked up.

"What's going on up there?" Dagger asked.

"Very quiet hysteria," Gormly replied. "Among very senior agents of several government agencies."

"How many of your people can you trust?"

"All of my team," the Secret Service man replied tersely. "I couldn't tell you first time you called, but I made damn sure of my people about two hours ago, after Lorne Holt strapped me to a PSE machine and put it to me. I had one man in my section whose story didn't wash. He was suddenly taken with a severe case of appendicitis."

"Did he live through the operation?" Dagger asked.

"We're not barbarians, Dagger! He's only under heavy sedation, that's all."

"Get rid of him, Gormly. Pump him and then shut his mouth."

"Goddamn you, Dagger! I don't take orders from you." A few seconds of silence followed, punctuated only by line noises. A heavy sigh from Gormly's end of the connection. "Your suggestion was taken under consideration for a time. It was finally rejected. Only time will tell if we made the right move. What can you give me in the way of constructive information?"

"Don't trust any of Menen's aides. Don't trust any of the Bureau that haven't been checked out. Don't trust the VP. You know the rest."

"Thank you so very much," Gormly said dryly. "You are a veritable well of information. By the way, Dagger, an old buddy of yours is missing from his home base in England. For several weeks, as close as we can figure it. Maybe longer. Probably longer. What can you tell us about Guthrie Manchester?"

"The Gunner? He's no buddy of mine."

"You were mercs together in Africa."

"I once found a Gaboon viper in my blankets, Gormly. That didn't make me and the snake bosom buddies. The Gunner is a cold-blooded killer for hire. He's killed children, old women, priests, rabbis—you name it, he's burned it. And he is very expensive. Works out of a pub he bought in England. I vaguely remember someone telling me he'd retired about the same time I did."

"Yes. Something brought him out of retirement."

"The challenge of killing a president would do that."

Gormly made an ugly noise. "I really wish you hadn't said that, Dagger."

"Gunner is an egomaniac. I didn't believe he would stay in retirement when I heard it. I don't believe he ever retired. I heard he's been killing Jews in France."

"The Libyan Connection?"

"Possible."

"You keep such nice company, Dagger."

"Screw you, Gormly."

"You're not my type. I don't like hairy women. Are you familiar with Gunner's M.O.?"

"Yeah. He likes to blow things up. Big bang type. Gormly, before I waste ten dollars on newspapers, what's the president's schedule for the next ten days?"

"Why?" Instant suspicion in the agent's voice.

"Because I'd like to figure out where the assassination attempt will be made."

"You leave that to us. The way I get it, you people are having trouble staying alive."

"You people need all the help you can get, pal. Listen: One of the people with me, maybe more, knows something about this affair. I don't mean to imply they are directly involved, but Pig and his bunch have — I think — been doing their best to take some of them alive. Now you chew on that for a time." Dagger would say no more about it.

"I don't know, Dagger."

"I'll be in touch." Dagger hung up in disgust. But he could understand the agent's reluctance.

"All right," Pig told his bunch. "We know they met with Williams in Meridian. We don't have to worry about J.B.'s mouth any longer. He and Williams have been iced.

"A gas jockey says a party that fit Dagger's people filled up just outside Meridian and headed toward Jackson on I-20. The Shafflers own property up in north Louisiana. Our people say they didn't go there. They've played out their hand in Cajun country; they won't go back there. We've got them on the run." He looked around him, meeting each pair of eyes. "But where?"

"Where did the second report originate?" Bitsy asked.

"Pine Bluff."

"Maybe he's heading for Little Rock to hole up?" an agent suggested.

Pig shook his head. "No. Dagger don't like cities. He likes plenty of room to move. He's got this thing about killing innocents. I got a hunch he thinks this is going to turn into a firefight and he's looking for room to maneuver. I think he's heading for hillbilly country. Maybe near a river. A fishing camp, maybe. It'll be isolated."

"How come you know so much about Dagger,

Pig?"

"Because I hate the bastard!" Pig spoke through gritted teeth. "And I want to see him dead."

"Lot of country up there to check out, Pig," Art Tappen reminded the man. "And we're running out of time."

"We got time. You people hit the ground running on this. Fan out and check every real estate office in this area." He thumped a map. "Dagger is there—bet on it."

"President Menen will spend the weekend at Camp David," Jimmy said, after his brother showed him an article in a paper. "He'll be going on to Los Angeles on Monday."

"That's Eagle-Fall day," Dagger said. "Ten days from now. And don't think the Secret Service hasn't figured it out—they have." A flash of memory surged through Dagger's mind: the picture of Gunner Manchester with a LAW in his hand during a fight on the Mozambique border, years back. But the range of that weapon was limited: two hundred meters and the rocket became erratic. Six hundred and fifty feet. That would have to be The Gunner's last resort, and his price would double if he was forced to go that route.

The route!

There it was. The route. The Gunner would probably use explosives along the route. Somewhere along the route the presidential motorcade traveled that day.

But where?

He would have to get to Gormly with that . . . that what? Fact? No—just a hunch. As for the LAW, yes, Gunner would use that anti-tank weapon if forced into it. But the big bang would be his choice—his style.

Dagger was curious though as to why kill President Menen? And why now? That nagged at his mind, darting and nipping at him. There was just no reason. Double-cross down the line? Triple-cross? Power play? Or was the president's assassination a ploy? Something to cover up something much larger? Jesus God! what could be larger than killing a U.S. president?

And maybe somebody—like the Reds—was holding something over a person's head?

But whose head? And was that the way to go?

Dagger picked up an old magazine left behind by a previous occupant and looked at the color photo on the cover. A full head shot of a man.

Dagger paused for a moment, studying the picture. He lifted his eyes, quickly taking in each person in the large room of the riverfront cabin. He returned his gaze to the picture, then again lifted his eyes to study the men and women in the room.

He tossed the magazine aside and rose to his feet. "I have to make another call. You people stay close and armed. Pig has memorized my dossier; he will have figured out the general area I'd take you people. So stay loose."

"What!" Gormly almost screamed the word. "That is impossible, Dagger."

"You check this out—quietly—and you'll find I'm right. That hit on Burrell, Shaffler and Volker back in the sixties was no accident. Bet on it. Pig is playing both ends against the middle on this one. Has been for years. Waiting for the right moment, a moment he knew was coming because he knew that sooner or later Eagle-Fall was going down. I know the bastard. And Fritzler is not the top man. Bet on that, too."

"There has to be more," Gormly said.

"Yes. And it's got more twists than a snake. But it all comes down to this: Someone—for whatever reason—is going to kill President Menen. Or try."

"You keep reminding me. Jesus," he moaned. "And I don't know who to trust. God!"

"I don't think He can help us on this one, Gormly. This is up to just us mortals."

13

Dagger almost walked into the middle of a hot argument. The quarreling voices stopped him on the porch of the cabin. He sat down in a chair and listened.

"Sissy boy," Mike's voice reached him. "I don't much care what you like or dislike. I don't take orders from you."

"Dagger said to stay close to the house," Ralph said, more than a touch of anger in his voice.

Dagger had been observing Ralph, taking in the flat-footed way he walked, the lean but rawhide toughness of the young man. He felt Mike was in a lot deeper water than he realized.

"Screw Dagger — and screw you, too."

Dagger smiled.

"Don't use that language in front of the ladies," Ralph warned him.

Mike laughed. An obscene bark. "You really don't believe your darlin' sister is the picture of virginity, do you, sissy boy? Hell, she banged

226

half the jocks at LSU and sucked off the other half. She's swallowed enough cum to flood this valley."

Dagger listened to the sound of a wooden chair being pushed back.

Ralph got to his feet. "Would you care to step outside with me, you wooden-headed semi-cretin?"

Mike laughed at him. "Sissy boy, tangling with me, you're about to play in the big leagues."

"Is that right?" Ralph retorted. "Well, I don't know what you'd know about that, Mike, since that's something you weren't good enough to do, right?"

Mike flushed. "I think I'll just tear your goddamn head off for that crack, sissy boy."

"Then shall we adjourn outside?" Ralph suggested. "I see no point in smashing up the cabin."

Dagger let them go, hearing the back door of the cabin open and close. Might be an interesting fight, he thought. It will at least relieve the tension, take their minds off the chase. He rose from the chair and walked around the corner of the cabin, leaning against a tree. Paige came to his side.

"They're going to fight," she said, real concern in her voice, mingled with, Dagger thought, just a bit of excitement.

"Yeah, I know. I heard them bitching at each other from the porch."

"Aren't you going to stop them?"

"Nope."

"Ralph is going to get seriously hurt and humiliated." She said it with all the somberness of a gypsy fortune teller. "Mike is bigger and stronger."

"But not necessarily tougher," Dagger told her. "Sometimes the bigger and stronger men find that weight and strength used against them. I have seen close-combat instructors prove that time and time again. Quite painfully, I might add."

Dagger smiled faintly at Mike's antics: The man was doing deep knee bends, jumping up and down, flexing his muscles, shadowboxing and making snorting noises through his nose. He reminded Dagger of an ape at a zoo in front of an audience.

Ralph was standing quietly, hands at his sides, watching the show. "You ought to go on the road with that show, Mike," he said.

"You won't be saying that in a minute," Mike told him.

Dagger again smiled.

"What do you find so amusing?" Paige asked. "You smile at the strangest things."

"I've seen it all before, Paige. A hundred times in a dozen countries. It's nothing new." He looked at Ralph. "Hit him, kid," he whispered. "Now—hit him!"

"But Mike's not looking!" Paige protested, disgust in her voice. "That wouldn't be fair. He isn't ready or set or whatever you call it."

"That's one of the tricks to winning a fight, Paige. There is no such thing as a fair fight — not outside the ring and its rules. You have a winner and a loser and that is all."

Paige glanced at him, her eyes flat, showing no emotion. "What a horrible outlook on life you have."

Dagger grinned at her. "It's called being a realist, Paige."

Mike had ceased his leaping about and looked at Kit. He grinned nastily at her. "To the victor go the spoils, baby — even if they are a little bit used."

Kit spat at him.

Mike laughed and turned, off balance, to say something to Ralph. He didn't make it. In the crude vernacular of barroom brawls, Ralph knocked the shit out of him. He did not hit him with a fist, but with his foot — a high, graceful ballet kick to the side of Mike's head. The kick dropped the bigger man to the ground.

"Finish it now, Ralph," Dagger whispered, more to himself than to Ralph. "Kick him in the mouth or the nuts — but finish it." But he knew Ralph could not, would not, do that.

Paige looked at him, contempt in her eyes. "That's dirty fighting, Dagger."

"Sure it is. What do you think a brawl is, a Sunday school picnic?"

She looked away.

Ralph let Mike crawl to his knees, then to his feet. Blood dripped from a small cut on the side of Mike's head.

"You son of a bitch!" Mike cussed him, balling his big hands. He swung at the smaller man, Ralph easily ducking the wildly thrown punch.

Ralph put a hard karate chop to Mike's left kidney, bringing a grunt of pain from the man. He doubled his right fist and brought it down hard in the center of Mike's back, directly above the spinal cord. Mike dropped to his knees.

"Give him a knee or a boot in the face," Dagger muttered, almost under his breath. "Smash him, hurt him, bloody him."

Paige folded her arms under her breasts and glared at Dagger.

"Don't let him get to his feet, boy," Dagger muttered.

Jimmy and Kit stood quietly, side by side, Kit biting her lower lip, watching their brothers brawl.

Mike lunged at Ralph, knee tackling the smaller man, bringing him down, smashing at Ralph with heavy fists, drawing blood from Ralph's nose, snapping the man's head back.

Mike was roaring with anger, sensing victory as he pounded his opponent.

Ralph rolled away from the punishing fists, sprang to his feet, and lashed out with a foot, catching Mike in the face, bloodying his mouth and nose. The blood spurted from Mike's face.

"Now you're cookin', kid," Dagger said with a grin.

"You're disgusting," Paige told him, not taking her eyes from the two men locked in combat.

"I repeat, Tootsie: just a realist in a world full of dreamers."

"Tootsie!" Paige muttered.

This time it was Ralph who took the offensive. With blood on his face, the smaller man assumed the classic karate stance and went to work with short, brutal, hurting slashes and blows, working his hand and fist like machine-driven pistons, punishing and bruising Mike's arms and shoulders and face.

Mike spun away and tried to grab the smaller man in a bear hug to wrestle him to the ground— maybe fall on him. But Ralph would have none of it. Slipping away, he slammed the knife edge of his hand onto Mike's thick neck, then brought his left fist into Mike's stomach, just above the belt buckle.

Hurt, Mike shuffled backward, no spring left in his legs. He backed off, still in the boxer's stance. He had a confused look on his face. This was not working out the way he'd planned. Little non-jocks don't do this to big jocks.

Mike had read too many of his press clippings. And believed them.

Ralph did not let up. Lashing out, he kicked Mike on the kneecap, bringing a howl of pain. Mike bent down, grabbing at his injured knee, and Ralph put a foot in the man's face, smashing the mouth. Mike fell back on one side and Ralph kicked him just above the groin.

Mike screamed as the breath left him in a rush. He gagged and gasped on the ground.

The fight was over.

Mike puked up his lunch. He held up one hand and wiped his mouth with the back of his other hand. "All right," he panted. "OK. Jesus. That's it. You fight like a madman, Ralph."

"I was mad," Ralph panted. He stood over Mike. He suddenly grinned and held out his hand. "Come on," he said. "Let's get cleaned up."

Mike looked up at him, shook his head in disbelief, then returned the grin. "Give me a few more seconds to grow up a little more, Ralph." He laughed, blood from his mouth and nose spraying the ground. "I needed what you just gave me, Ralph. But I sure wish there could have been an easier method of learning." He took Ralph's hand and got to his feet.

Mike swayed for a moment, then said, "You'll do, Ralph. You're OK. I sure don't want any more of you."

They walked off toward the pump at the rear of the cabin. They had their arms around each other's shoulders and were laughing.

"Ain't that sweet?" Dagger muttered. "All lovey-dovey. If they try to kiss each other," he said, knowing it would bring a hot retort from Paige, "let me know. We'll room them together."

Paige put hands on hips and glared at him. "Dagger, you are perfectly *awful!*"

"I only have a few seconds," the voice spoke. "Then I'll be missed. The people in Europe have been located. What do you want done with them?"

"We discussed this," General Mitchell said. "Why go over it again?"

"Because I want them taken now."

"No. Keep them under constant surveillance. We don't touch them until the Bear gives the word. Everything now hinges on Pig."

"Anything from Fritzler?"

"No. And that has me worried. I'm wondering if Harrison smelled something and looked toward Fritzler as the source. It could be that was the reason for sending him to Hawaii."

"It really doesn't make any difference," the voice replied. "Everything is go. Eagle-Fall's on Monday, the twenty-fifth."

The general's reply was low-pitched. "I don't know."

"What do you mean?"

"It's going sour. I can feel it, sense it. There has been unusual activity among intelligence groups the past twenty-four hours. I smell a rat. And what about our man in the Service who was hospitalized?"

"I thought about that. So far as I can gather,

his attack of appendicitis was legitimate. It was ruptured. He isn't in good shape. But go on, get it out of your craw. I know there is more on your mind."

"I smell a double-cross."

"No. Who could it be?"

General Mitchell was silent for a few ticks of the clock. "I hope it's not you," he finally said.

He hung up the phone.

The pipe smoker stood listening to the buzzing of the receiver. Double-cross, he thought. Yes, that thought had entered his mind—more than once. And the more he thought of it, the more real the possibility was that more than a double-cross was taking place.

He dialed a number through the mobile operator.

In a moment, Pig's voice came on the line. "Pig here."

"Kill them all except the kid."

"What!"

"You heard me, Pig."

"No way. Do you know what you're saying? The Bear is a deep, deep plant. I've got to have word from a higher authority than you to do that."

Pig's reluctance only deepened the man's suspicions. "There is no other way, Pig. We're down to only a few days and counting. We don't have any choice in the matter."

Pig slapped a hand to his forehead. "Jesus!"

The pipe smoker laughed. "Now, now — you know we don't subscribe to that mumbo jumbo."

Pig thought he saw a way out: a way to make himself shine in the eyes of his superiors and get rid of Mitchell and the pipe smoker. "All right," he said. "But I want it in writing — in your handwriting. Get it to me. Send it Air Express to Little Rock. I don't move unless I have it. But you'd better notify our European contact to firm it up over there."

"As you wish, Pig. But are you forgetting who is in charge?"

"You just do it, partner."

"You've got to change your plans, Mr. President," Harrison said, urging the man, his friend.

"You believe my office staff, up to the highest, has been compromised, Sherman? Is in on this . . . madness?"

"Yes, sir. I do. I can't prove it, but it has to be."

"Insane," the president muttered. "The nation has gone insane."

The president looked at Lorne Holt and nodded minutely.

Holt lowered his eyelids in understanding.

"No!" Menen said. "No. I will not bow to this madness. Let's play it all the way through. I want to see this to the end."

Harrison and Haywood rose in protest. Lorne Holt sat calmly, quietly, saying nothing. He waited for the hubbub to die down.

Only he and the president of the United States knew how the final outcome would be handled. Others would be brought in at the last moment — the very last moment.

President Menen said, "To think that Doyle or Cruse is part of this, or behind it is . . ." He shook his head. He looked as though he had aged five years in as many minutes. "Sherman, we've both known them for years. All the way back to college. They called us the Four Horsemen when we played football. We . . ." But the president knew his sour words were hollow and bitter on his tongue. It had to be one of them. "No," he spoke, his voice filled with regret, "I'm wrong and you're right. But if it is one of them — or both of them, as the case may well be — let's give him enough rope to hang himself. Both John and Lewis are out of the White House at this moment, but I have appointments with the both of them later on. I don't want you people here. That might create suspicion." He looked at Holt. "What about this Gormly?"

"He's solid. And he has been in touch with Dagger."

"All right. Pull Gormly in on this and tell him to cooperate with Dagger."

"Sir!" Harrison protested. "The man is a damned mercenary."

"He is also a solid, red, white and blue American, Sherman. I know a little something about him. No—don't ask me how I know. Or why. You both had best go now. I'll see you gentlemen in the morning."

Harrison and company filed out.

Menen looked at Holt. "It's time, Lorne."

"Are you sure, sir? I mean, are you absolutely certain of this? Once this is set in motion, it will be extremely difficult to stop."

"I'm certain, Lorne. I really wasn't until a few moments ago. This nation must survive. And if that can only be accomplished by a group of men and women acting outside the written law—then so be it. I believe we have included enough safeguards. Set it up and put the operation on hold. We'll—*I'll* decide later if and when they will ever be used. I only hope this Dagger lives through the assassination attempt. You know I will, Lorne."

"Yes, sir. If all goes as planned. You want me to call the money man overseas?"

"Yes." The reply was softly given. Menen sighed heavily. "God. That's what I'm playing, Lorne: God. And I'll pay for it. But if this republic stands, it will be worth the punishment." He looked into the eyes of Lorne Holt. "You're sure, Lorne, about Monday?"

"Yes, sir."

"Very well. It's a brave thing you're doing." He drummed finger tips on the desk. "I knew in my heart it had to be John when he came to me with that foolish story about the meeting date being changed. But I kept hoping against hope I was wrong. But he's not alone, Lorne. Lewis is up to his neck in this, too. But, damn it, Lorne — why? What in God's name do they hope to gain? And when and where did they begin to go sour? Why did they turn against this nation — and me? Unanswered questions. And how many more people in government and industry are involved? It's . . . staggering in scope, Lorne. And that is yet another reason why I want our plan to proceed. Tell me, what have your people found?"

"Very little, sir. They are buried deep. But I sure liked that information Dagger fed Gormly."

"You think it's true?"

"I'd bet on it, sir."

Both men smiled.

Menen said, "So it has to go back many years, right, Lorne?"

"Yes, sir. At least to the point where you entered politics."

"I'll miss you, Lorne. You're not only a good man, but you've been a friend."

"Thank you, sir. I'd rather go out this way than lie in a hospital bed, dying by inches, seeing the pity in the eyes of my family. This way at least will be quick — and very abrupt."

EAGLE-FALL + 9

They had established a rhythm that was mutually satisfying, and a position. They maintained that as both felt the juices of passion build from deep within, slowly simmering toward that sudden final boiling-over.

They reached the last climax together, and she shivered as he slowly eased from her; she sighed as he slipped his softening length from her and she closed her eyes to fall asleep in the satisfaction of sexual exhaustion.

Dagger slept for a few hours, his eyes popping open just after four in the morning, a gut feeling of alarm welling up strong within him. He eased from her warmth and quickly dressed, picking up and checking his weapons.

We've been made! he thought. But goddamn, how could it have happened so quickly? Unless . . .

He knew Pig's boys and girls were outside, waiting and watching.

He padded silently across the room and stared out into the darkness. He could see nothing moving. But his warrior's senses, honed fine, told him unfriendlies were out there. Time had run out: Alpha was about to meet omega. But Dagger didn't know what symbol he represented.

He was about to find out.

How many? was the question Dagger asked. And he wondered if they had taken out the guard. Four-thirty by his watch. That would be Mike on guard. He hoped the man had not maintained his watch off the porch of the cabin.

There! Movement caught his peripheral vision. Dagger clicked the Ingram off safety. He hoped whatever it was out there was not some drunk tourist, for if it was, this was going to be his last vacation on this earth.

Dagger squatted by the open window and waited, watching, his breathing quiet. Another shape took human form out of the gloom. This one had a gun in his hand. No tourist. Dagger lifted the SMG and squeezed the trigger, the powerful, little Ingram stuttering and bucking in his hands. The form was flung to the ground, legs jerking as hot pain tore his stomach and chest. The man flopped and screamed, then fell silent. Paige ran from the bedroom, her nakedness white in the darkness.

"Get down!" Dagger yelled at her. "Hit the floor."

Paige squatted down and slipped back into the

bedroom, grabbing jeans and shirt just as footsteps thudded in the early-morning darkness. Dagger swung the M-10 at the sound of someone leaping onto the porch. The shape was unfamiliar. Dagger pulled the trigger, the 9mm slugs knocking the man backward, off the porch. The man's head slammed against the stone walkway, producing an ugly, smushing noise.

"Fire at anything that moves out there!" Dagger yelled, just as the night abruptly changed into sparking gun muzzles and the whine of slugs as they ricocheted off the stone of the cabins.

He tossed Paige a pistol. "Shoot at anything that comes through that door without first identifying themselves."

"Where are you going?" she asked, her face pale and her voice shaky.

"Out there," Dagger replied and charged through the cabin, out the back door.

Dagger almost ran into a man as he leaped from the porch, hitting the ground in a combat crouch. So sudden was his exit that the man was startled, hesitating for just a second in bringing up and leveling his pistol. That was all the time Dagger needed. He squeezed the trigger of the M-10, putting a short burst into the man's chest. The slugs, at almost point-blank range, lifted the man off his feet and dumped him in a dying heap in the pre-dawn Arkansas gloom.

Dagger crouched behind the dubious protection of a small tree. He changed clips, shoving the almost-empty clip behind his belt. He waited. Thought he heard a woman's muffled scream. Listened intently. It was not repeated. Far down the road, a car engine roared into life, the tires slinging dirt and gravel as the driver fishtailed away from the death house by the river. The early-morning darkness grew silent with the post-combat hush only combat vets know so well.

"Dagger?" a voice called. Ralph.

Dagger shifted positions, darting to the slim offering of a stunted pine. No one fired at him. He ran, zigzagging to a cabin.

"Stay inside," Dagger told the man.

"Don't worry," Ralph replied. "I have absolutely no intention of sticking any part of me outside."

Dagger smiled at the man's open honesty. "Start packing up. We're pulling out. One got away—at least one. There will be more coming for us."

"Dagger?" Mike called from the third cabin.

"Yeah?"

"Kit is gone."

14

They were packed up and moving just after dawn, heading for Missouri. Dagger had inspected Kit's room, found the screen cut out, a vial of sodium pentothal and a bent syringe on the floor by her bed. They had gotten enough of the drug into Kit to addle her, but not enough to keep her unconscious. Hers was the scream Dagger had heard. Dagger's awakening had put a kink in their plans, delaying them long enough for Kit to come out of the drug and scream as someone was putting her in a car.

"But why take Kit?" Mike had asked. There was real concern in his voice, and Dagger suspected Mike's feelings for the woman ran even deeper than Mike knew. "It doesn't make any sense to grab her."

Dagger did not tell them of his suspicions. "Let's roll it," he said. "It's fish or cut bait time for us."

He put the bodies of the dead S-5 agents in one

of the cabins. He knew them all. Carl Wortham, Mel Keith, Art Tappen.

Dagger did not believe any of them would be missed.

"Well, now." Pig smiled. He cupped a soft breast and squeezed. "Look what we got here."

Kit hissed her fear and revulsion and jerked away from him.

Pig laughed at her.

He had taken the news of the loss of his three agents without any sign of emotion other than a wave of dismissal with one hamlike hand.

"Strip her down, boys," he said, loosening his belt. "And bend her over that table there. I get first pop at her, then you boys can flip a coin. My, isn't she a pretty, little thing? I bet she's got quite a bush on her."

Kit screamed and fought the hands that shredded the clothing from her, the hands that roamed her body, squeezing and fondling and entering her.

Hard hands, demanding and hurting fingers, both male and female, stroked and fondled and entered the woman. The hands forced her face down over a table. Hands parted her legs and held her firm.

Kit began screaming louder as Pig positioned himself behind her and shoved.

It would be a long day and night for Kit, and she had no idea why it was happening to her.

In Los Angeles, Gunner Manchester sat beside the pool of his hotel and enjoyed the view afforded him of scantily clad young ladies as they scampered and jiggled and bounced about — all of them knowing they were being observed during their human semblance of the peacock strut. They amused The Gunner. Women, he felt, were the same worldwide: They wanted to peel down to the barest slips of clothing and prance around in front of men; but just reach out and fondle one and see how fast one ends up in the pokey.

Gunner felt women were good for only one thing. If they didn't have a pussy someone would surely declare a hunting season on them. Just like deer.

Gunner's opinion of women was just slightly less than his opinion of the world's political leaders.

Gunner leaned back in his poolside lounger. He was not concerned about being recognized. He had shaved his moustache, had a nice tan and had dyed his hair.

He could be recognized only by someone who knew him well. And those men and women were not likely candidates for this plush hotel.

Everything was ready. Now all Gunner had to combat was time.

Lorne Holt tried, for the fifteenth time, to write a letter to his wife and two kids — both of them in college — attempting to explain why he was choosing this way out.

President Menen sat in the Oval Office and stared out the window. His thoughts were not of his planned assassination attempt, but of the group he alone had the power to put into operation: Zulu Nine. Nine men and women whose only function in life would be to kill criminals. The money was there, millions of dollars. It would take a team of auditors, working around the clock, twenty years to untangle the web of complicated legal turns and twists as to the how and why and where of the monies.

Odd, though, he thought, Dagger getting involved in this difficulty just at the time the man was being considered for a part in Zulu Nine. But he's a good man, tough and resourceful — he'll come through.

He punched a button on his desk.

"Yes, sir."

"Is Mr. Cruse in his office?"

"Yes, sir."

"Ask him to come in here, please."

John Cruse walked in, smiling, his pipe in his hand. "Mr. President."

"I've been thinking, John — about next Monday. Monday week, that is. I think I'd like to have you ride with me in the limo."

Cruse paled a bit under his tan. Menen thought he saw the man's hands tremble just a bit. Menen secretly, inwardly, smiled, enjoying putting the screws to the traitor. Even if for just a short time.

"Oh, I don't know, sir."

"Come now, John. I insist."

"Well—" John's mind was working rapidly—"I just . . . don't think I could, sir. You see, I'm needed ahead, as usual."

"Ah, yes, John. I keep forgetting how indispensable you are to me." Son of a bitch. "We've been friends for a long time, right, John?" Lying bastard.

"More than twenty-five years, William," Cruse said, relaxing and smiling. "All the way back to those ivy-covered halls."

"And the girls," Menen nudged him on.

"Ah, yes, William. Can't ever forget those lovely ladies."

"Yes, that's right. Can't forget the ladies. Long time ago, John." It will work, Menen thought. We are the same height, not five pounds difference in weight, and wear the same size suit. His hair is just a bit darker than mine, but at a distance, it will pass. "Oh, John, before I forget, since people do confuse us at times, what are you wearing Monday afternoon?"

"Why . . . I haven't thought about it, William. But now that you mention it, I certainly wouldn't want us to be confused Monday. Or any other time for that matter," he was quick to add.

I just bet you don't, Menen thought. Especially on Monday, the twenty-fifth.

"I think I shall wear the gray pin stripe, William. Yes, that's what I'll wear."

"Good. Then I'll wear the brown herringbone so we won't be confused." But I'll be carrying a gray pin stripe, you turncoat.

John stuffed and lit his pipe. He smiled at the president.

"How's your love life, John?"

"So-so." Cruse was now completely relaxed. "Since Mary died I've just been playing the field, so to speak."

"Ever think about remarrying, John?"

"No. No time for that, William. I'm married to my job."

Married to the Party, you mean. "Yes . . . and I do appreciate your . . . loyalty, John."

"Thank you, sir."

When Cruse left the Oval Office, he was smiling.

But not so hugely as President William Menen.

"I wonder what Kit is doing at this moment?" Paige asked.

"Getting screwed every way possible," Dagger said bluntly.

They were a few miles south of the Missouri line. Dagger and Paige in the lead vehicle.

"Then she must be enjoying herself immensely," Paige said, verbal claws extended.

"Not the way Pig and his people go at it, Paige.

I once heard of that bunch forcing a girl—an anti-war protester—to take on five guys at one whack."

She looked at him. Thought about that for a moment. "That is impossible, Dagger."

"No, it isn't." He told her, in considerable detail, just how it was possible.

She was silent for a mile. "That would not only be very painful, Dagger, but that is positively the most disgusting thing I have ever heard of."

His smile was anything but pleasant. "I should imagine so. Pig and his bunch are nuts, Paige. Twisted. They enjoy torture. Like to hear the victim scream and beg."

"And to think they were, or are, employed by this country."

"Russia has people just as bad, Paige. And worse."

"Yes, I'm sure they do. It doesn't make it right for us to use the same tactics. Were you needling me about Karl Crowe?"

"No. I wasn't even thinking about him. But people in this country have lost perspective as to what kind of government and ideology we're fighting with Russia and the Communist Bloc nations. Same as many people have lost perspective in dealing with criminals and other assorted street slime in this nation. Sometimes one has to fight fire with fire."

"I suppose so," she said quietly. The tone of her voice told Dagger she did not agree with him.

It came as no surprise, civilians being what they are.

They rode in silence for a few miles. "Where are you taking us, Dagger?"

"To a county just north and west of Springfield. Not too populated. Cuts down on the odds of someone getting hurt accidentally." He did not tell her he had kinfolks who sat in the sheriff's chair and the chief deputy's chair, or that he owned the property where he was taking them.

"High-noon time, Dagger?"

"You got it. I know that country, Paige; they don't know it. I was born around there. I'll stash you people in a safe spot, don't worry."

"Something has changed in you, Dagger," she said, putting a warm hand on his thigh. "I don't know whether I like the change."

"Showdown time, Paige. I don't run anymore."

She looked at him. "There is only one of you, Dagger."

"That will be more than enough."

There was no cockiness in his tone. Just fact.

He stopped once, in Springfield, at an army/navy surplus store, and carried a huge box to the car, stashing it in the trunk. Paige did not ask him what was in the box. If he wanted her to know, she knew he would tell her. She'd learned that much about Dagger.

Kit lay in a ball of hurt and shame on the floor of the cabin. She thought it ironic they were back in the cabin where she'd been grabbed only hours before. She was bruised and bleeding from the anus. Pig glanced at one of his men.

"Cabin's paid up for a week, Jordan. So you get elected to stay behind and watch the broad. You let her get away and your ass is fried meat, you understand all that?"

The agent nodded.

"I don't understand what Dagger is doing," Rich said. "He's making no effort to hide his tracks. Cooper said he found a Missouri map on the floor of Dagger's cabin. Got a county circled in red. Reckon he's trying to trick us?"

Pig snorted in contempt. "No. He's tossin' down the glove, so to speak. He's telling us to come and get him. All right. If that's what he wants, then that's what he'll get." He glanced at his watch. "We'll pull out now and get the supplies we need. Then drive to Springfield and get a motel, get some rest. We'll reconnoiter the area the next two days, take Dagger on the nineteenth."

"That's cutting it fine, Pig."

Pig ignored that. He knew what he was doing. He and one other person. "Get on the horn. Pull every agent we got up to Missouri. Tell 'em to roll it."

EAGLE-FALL + 8

Dagger looked out the window at the light mist that clung to the rolling hills and wooded valleys of the Missouri of his youth. It appeared very peaceful. Just under eight thousand residents in the entire county. And this spot was perfect for ambush.

Dagger smiled.

Dagger had hunted squirrels and rabbits in this county as a youth, and not that much had changed. Only one road cut through this region: a county-maintained highway. The interstate lay to his east, a small river to the west. Sparsely populated region.

He had checked all his weapons very carefully, and all his ammo. He waited at his father's old getaway house, as his dad used to call it. Dagger still used it when he wanted to "get away."

It was a five-room, native-rock cabin, and Dagger knew it well. He had helped his father build it, back when Dagger was twelve and thirteen years old. Before his "trouble"—as his parents called it—in Springfield: the dead man in the gutter with a busted neck. Trouble. Yeah. Before Dagger learned that he was as natural at killing as most men are at breathing. Years before his little sister—she wasn't supposed to come along, his parents had always said with a smile—was molested and murdered. Before his parents died.

Before a lot of things.

When his parents were killed in that accident, Dagger had been in Rhodesia, working as a mercenary. He had not made it back for the funeral. He had done his grieving on the plane. Stateside, Dagger had learned his father had left him moderately fixed as far as money was concerned. He began giving serious thought to retiring from the field. He had returned to the cabin to find it in slight disrepair and vandalized. He ordered a team of carpenters to fix it, modernize it some. Put in a pump house. Best water in the world. Right out of a deep well. Septic tank laid down. Big, comfortable den with fireplace. Kitchen. Three bedrooms. Big bathroom.

Again Dagger allowed himself a smile. The area around the cabin was cleared for three acres. The cabin stood on fifty acres. Timber. No fences.

Dagger turned to his small group. "Let me show you all something."

He showed them and told them why it would be extremely difficult for anyone to burn them out: The cabin was practically burnproof. Walls of stone. Shingles fire-retardant. Small windows with aluminum frames. The cabin did not have electricity. Water was brought up by a portable generator, gas operated; the pump house, which also contained the generator, was attached to the cabin. The pump house was constructed of the same native stone.

"Two doors," he told them. "One front, one in back. Steel door frames, set in concrete. The doors are oak, three inches thick. Dead-bolt locks. Any assault on this house by Pig will have to be done quickly and gotten over with in a hurry. Any sustained fire fight would bring the law. No one will pay any attention to an occasional shot or two. Pig will know all that. So he might use gas. That is why I stopped in Springfield: to buy masks for you people. I'm going into a nearby town now to buy food for a week. You won't see much of me for the next several days. I'll be out there." He waved his hand to the hills and hollows. "I'll be setting up booby traps for our guests. So don't any of you venture outside of the clearing. I'd prefer it if you stayed in the cabin. I'll bring back a box of paperbacks and magazines for you. So get together, make out your grocery lists. I'll get the food."

He stepped outside and went to the storage shed by the side of the house, to the rear. He left a frightened and badly rattled group in the house.

"Well, let's get our list made," Paige said. "It

looks like we're going to be here for a few days."

Jimmy was whistling merrily.

Ralph looked at Jimmy, then at Paige. She seemed relaxed. "You look calm," he said to her.

"Outside," she said. "Inside I'm all quivering mush."

All of them looked at Jimmy. He was just too calm.

Paige walked into a bedroom and shut the door.

"She's changed during the past few days," Jimmy observed.

"She's in love," Mike said with a smile. "And she's scared to death of her emotions."

"Yes," Ralph said. "Kit picked up on that day before yesterday. She told me about it."

"I hope Kit's OK," Mike said. "I, uh, kind of miss her."

"Can I at least put my clothes on?" Kit asked Jordan.

"Yeah." The man looked at her through uninterested eyes. "I sure don't want any more of it."

Kit climbed painfully to her feet. She swayed slightly from her brutal assault. She stood for a moment, allowing her head to clear. "I need to clean up."

Jordan laughed at her. "Yeah," he agreed. "You sure don't look like a beauty queen." He pointed. "The crapper's in there. You know the way."

Kit showered, lingering long under the hot needle spray. She sat on the commode and finished her toilet. She dressed in jeans and a denim shirt. Drying her hair, she fixed it as best she could, and finally stepped out into the den.

Jordan looked up from his magazine. "You look a whole lot better, baby." He took handcuffs from his belt. "Come over here."

Kit obeyed without question. Pig had told her what he would do to her—personally—if she acted up. She believed him.

Jordan put one cuff around her slender wrist and clamped the other to the wooden support of a chair. "That ought to hold you," he said, smiling.

"I'm hungry," Kit said.

"I'll fix something in a couple of hours," Jordan told her. "You just sit over there and keep your mouth shut." He returned to his girlie magazine.

"Why are you doing this to me?" Kit questioned. "I think I have a right to know."

Jordan wore an amused look on his face. "You really don't know, do you, kid?"

Kit shook her head.

"Well, I'll tell you this much, honey: Pig wants you alive for insurance. And that's all I'm going to tell you. Now you either shut your mouth, or I'll stick something in it and let you suck on that. Which is it going to be?"

Kit shut her mouth.

Jordan laughed at her. "We'll play some games tonight, baby — you and me."

"I can hardly wait."

Jordan chuckled. "Yeah, you and me, baby, we got three, four days to play. And I like to make the gals holler."

Kit shuddered.

Dagger returned from town. They stored the milk on a shelf built into the well — it would stay cool, if not cold. The rest of the supplies were dry and canned.

Dagger gave each of them a weapon; most of them taken from Pig's men. He gave Mike the .460 magnum the Dog had put on him. Mike looked at Dagger, then at the weapon.

"You play for keeps, don't you Dagger?"

"I do try, Mike."

"Now what?" Mike asked.

"Now comes the hard part," Dagger told them all. The group looked at him. "The waiting."

"When . . . I mean, well," Paige asked, "when do you think they'll come after us?" She handed Dagger a cup of coffee.

Dagger sat down and sipped his coffee. Too hot. He put it aside to cool for a moment. "Pig has lots of flaws, people, but his main flaw is overconfidence without the ability to back it up. I believe Eagle-Fall goes down Monday the twenty-fifth. This is the seventeenth. I think Pig

will first call for supplies that will enable him—
he thinks—to mount a fast, all-out assault once
he finds us. That will take him a day. One to get
here. One day to find us. But I might be a day
off. Probably the eighteenth or nineteenth."

"And then?" Ralph asked.

Dagger shrugged. "I start killing."

"Sir?" Church had phoned Harrison at his
home. "The agents are pulling out. All of them."

"Any idea where?"

"Not yet. But our man I put tailing Pig's bunch
reported a fire fight at a resort cabin—or
cabins—in Arkansas. He laid back and didn't get
involved—my orders."

"Good man, Dave."

"I had a friendly soul at our home base run the
Dagger family name. Used to be D-A-G-G-A-R.
French."

"Thank you for the lesson in genealogy."

Dave ignored the dryness. "Thank you, sir.
The elder Dagger—now deceased, as is Dagger's
mother—owned property in Missouri. Our Dagger likes the hills and hollows, likes to fight in
wide-open spaces. Dislikes cities. I think he's
taken his bunch up there."

"Dalon County?"

"I don't think so, sir. That's where Dagger
lives. I don't think he'd want to screw up his
home base. I'm going to pull out and stay behind

Pig's boys. I've got three car switches arranged between here and Springfield. In the morning, sir, have someone find out if Dagger owns property way out in the boonies of some county. If so, that's where he is."

"I can get the ball rolling on that today," Harrison said. "Dave? We're spread pretty thin, but I can let you have a few men I know are trustworthy."

"No, sir," Church replied after a slight pause. "I got one running ahead of me; we're getting together in Springfield. I'm just going to let Dagger have his day with Pig."

"He's just one man, Dave. For God's sake, we're throwing him to the wolves in this matter. He's up against fifteen or twenty agents. He's just one man."

Dave Church chuckled. "I believe I told you what some people think the initials S.B. stand for, sir."

"Yes, Dave, you did. But Dagger is still only one man."

"He's Ninja, sir."

"That order died out centuries ago, Dave."

"If that is what you choose to believe, sir."

Harrison sighed. "Keep in touch, Dave."

"Yes, sir."

Dagger ringed the cabin, in the timbered area around the stone house, with booby traps. He carefully dug and camouflaged punji pits — the twenty-inch-deep pits filled with needle-sharp wooden stakes. If the fall itself didn't break a man's leg or ankle, the sharpened stakes would inflict a terrible gash to the foot or calf. Dagger wished he had time to get some animal shit to smear on the points of the stakes; that would cause severe infection and blood poisoning. But he had a lot to do and was working against the clock.

He built a dozen swing traps and carefully hid the lethal booby traps. Using fresh, limber branches from trees, the limbs about the size of his wrists, Dagger bent them back and stationed them, attaching a very thin, almost invisible wire ankle-high on a route he felt they would take. Sharpened stakes were attached to the bent-back limb, rigged to strike stomach-high should anyone trip the wire.

The Japanese had perfected this trap on the islands in the Pacific during World War II.

Ask any vet who fought there.

That "other stuff" the Dog had given Dagger back in Georgia included four Claymore mines. Dagger would place them later. He wasn't worried about interference from the law.

The sheriff was Dagger's first cousin on his father's side. The chief deputy was Dagger's uncle.

Dagger rose from his work and smiled, looking around him.

"Here, Pig, Pig," he called. "Here, Pig, Pig, Pig."

"You just sign these." The voice was soothing. "Right where I've shown you, and the pain will stop, I promise you.

The white-haired man looked at his hands. Bloody. He looked at the torn tips of his fingers where his fingernails used to be.

"I don't know what you hope to gain by any of this," the tortured man said, his voice pain-filled. "My daughter will never go along with anything this . . . this far-fetched."

That got him a hard, gloved fist in the mouth. Blood leaked from smashed lips.

Somewhere in the great old house in West Germany a woman screamed.

The man cringed. "Is that?"

"Your wife. Yes." The voice was cultured, containing a slight European accent. "She does not bear up well to pain. Would you like to see her?"

"Yes." The word was pushed out of a broken mouth. Past stubs of broken teeth. "This is free Germany," the man said, struggling to rise to his feet. "You people must be communists."

"We're on the border. Yes, you're right with your assumption."

The man spat in his torturer's face, spraying him with bloody spittle.

The older man was jerked to his feet and half carried, half dragged down the hall to a room. The door was opened. He began weeping at the sight of his wife of thirty-five years.

The woman was naked. Tied to a chair. Wires that would smash her with charges of electricity were attached to her breasts and to her inner thighs. Her legs were spread obscenely wide, lashed to the legs of the chair.

"Give the loving husband a vivid demonstration," the voice ordered a bald bear of a man.

A button was pushed. The woman lunged against her bonds. She screamed in pain. She bit her tongue and chewed her lips until the blood poured from her swollen mouth.

"Enough!" the man cried. "For the love of God — I'll sign. Stop hurting her."

The current was cut off. The woman slumped in the chair, only half conscious. She had soiled herself. The room stank.

The husband and wife were taken to a spotlessly clean room. Bright lights highlighted the medical facilities therein.

"See to their needs," a man in a white jacket was ordered.

Several hours later, the husband and wife were taken to a lushly furnished study. A small fire was burning in the fireplace, for the night was cool by the mountains. The man and woman looked haggard, but they had been bathed, their wounds dressed, and they were clad in clean but wrinkled pajamas.

"How is your hand?" the tortured man was asked.

"It hurts."

"Your fault, sir. Can you sign your name in a legible manner?"

"Yes."

"Very good, sir. Excellent, I should say." The man placed a pen on the table. "Now, then, Mr. Burrell, if you will sign right there on the line indicated."

EAGLE-FALL + 7

They waited.

The four of them waited and watched a man change in front of their eyes.

Dagger.

He had not spoken a word in hours. He had sat in a corner of the cabin, on the floor, and seemed to put himself into a trance. Not one muscle moved. Not even his eyelids. He seemed not to be breathing. But of course, they all knew that was impossible.

Wasn't it?

At four o'clock in the afternoon, Dagger abruptly rose from the floor and walked into a bedroom. When he emerged fifteen minutes later, he was dressed in camouflaged field clothes and had tied a camouflaged bandana around his forehead, covering his hair. Another camouflaged bandana covered the lower part of his face. Only his eyes were visible.

They were utterly void of expression.

He wore light, camouflaged boots on his feet, his field pants bloused at the tops of the boots.

He did not make a sound when he moved.

Around his waist, attached to and hanging from a camouflaged web belt, Dagger carried a coiled length of piano wire, with wooden handles attached. In a pouch on his left side were several Shurikens of various sizes. The pointed throwing stars were lethal in the hands of an expert. And Dagger was that. He carried his .41 in a holster. Two speed-loaders. In a clip pouch, he carried five clips for the M-10. He carried his knives strapped to his lower legs.

"Ninja," Ralph said.

"Hai!" Dagger spoke for the first time in hours. He stepped to the doorway, walking out into the late afternoon's waning sunlight.

Dagger paused in the doorway, his eyes touching each person in the den. "Don't anyone leave this house for any reason. I will kill anyone that I find in the timber."

The door closed and he was gone.

"What is a Ninja?" Paige asked.

"A secret society of martial arts experts," Ralph replied. "It supposedly died out several centuries ago. But most people knowledgeable in martial arts history never believed that. The true masters just went underground with it. Ninja-trained people are the most dangerous people in the world. Very few non-orientals are masters of that forbidden art. I would imagine Dagger is the exception."

"He looks . . . competent," Mike said.

"At least that," Ralph said.

Dagger took one of the Claymores and an electronic timer and detonator and walked through the woods to the dirt road—the only road leading to the cabin—and placed the man-destroying Claymore facing east. He set the timer to blow the charge when he hit the switch, up to five hundred meters away. He rigged a half dozen tin cans filled with pebbles and swung them from east to west; another line of pebble-filled cans went north to south. He hung the cans on thin, black wire, at ankle height. The cans were concealed behind bushes and in thick foliage; the wire would be visible only if someone were looking specifically for it.

Dagger slipped back in the woods a few hundred meters and made his mean camp for the evening in a thicket of briars, crawling in under the needle points at full dark. He went to sleep after eating some cheese and bread, washing it down with sips of water from his canteen.

Dagger awakened every hour to listen for five minutes. He observed the calls of night birds, mentally absorbing them, and called to the birds. They answered his calls. Dagger would go back to sleep after listening to the returning calls of the birds. A man-made birdcall will echo—a bird's call does not.

He slept well, despite his hourly awakening and listening, and was refreshed when he awoke an hour before dawn. He did an hour of isometric exercises: pitting one muscle against another. Then he retreated into his mind for half an hour, clouding everything there except those facts necessary for survival.

Then he was ready.

He waited.

EAGLE-FALL + 6

"The White House is secure," Lorne Holt informed the president. "And so is our L.A. office — except for one man. You know who that is."

"Yes. Go on."

"I have taken the liberty of including Powell of FBI in with us. Needless to say, he was, at first, stunned, then furious. Working with Harrison at CIA, and our own trusted people here in D.C., Powell has ferreted out four maverick agents, but they don't know they've been made. We plan to keep it that way for as long as possible."

President Menen nodded his head. "Any word from Dave Church?"

"No, sir. Harrison thinks — with the information he gave Dave the other night — he's probably tucked away close to Dagger's father's old hideaway cabin, waiting for the action to start."

"One man against how many, Dave?"

"Probably fifteen."

"That doesn't seem possible."

"You don't know Dagger."

Dagger drew first blood just after eight o'clock in the morning. He took the point agent out with a star, driving a point into the man's brain from a distance of thirty feet.

The man died without making a sound.

Dagger did not know the man.

Dagger dragged the body into the woods, covering it with brush, and again assumed his vigil by the thick brush.

He knew that once the point man did not call in, Pig would realize his man had been burned and the other agents would be cautious.

It would do them no good.

Dagger waited motionless. Only his eyes moved. All senses working at full capacity.

Then he heard movement to his left. He remained still, seeing only what his peripheral vision would allow. Dagger saw the hands first. A woman. Then she came into full view. Bitsy. Dagger knew her slightly. He did not believe he had ever heard her last name. That was not uncommon among agents in the field. Not that it would have made any difference. He would still have to kill her.

He waited, watching, listening, alert for any trap. Bitsy was very good; she had been through some thorough training at the hands of experts. Probably at the farm up in Maryland. Dagger let his right hand slowly drift to a boot knife. He exploded from the thicket as Bitsy passed by. Dagger almost decapitated her with the razor-sharp knife. Her head flopped back and forth as he silently lowered her to the ground. The blood pumped from the gaping slice just under her chin.

Two down.

Dagger shifted positions a few meters and squatted down, reviewing in his mind the number of Pig's people he had taken out. Seven. No, six. J.B. had died with Williams. Well, that still came to seven. Pig would have to be getting short.

And some of Pig's people would bug out on their own. Probably already had. They would have no stomach for something like this. And to hell with Pig.

"Dagger?" the whisper came from his right.

Dagger remained still.

"Pig wants to talk, Dagger."

I just bet he does, Dagger thought. With lead.

"Dagger? There is no need for more of this. You just back off and go your way. Name your price."

I thought it was Name That Tune, Dagger thought, smiling behind his face scarf.

Close to the cabin, there was a breaking sound, followed by a thud, then a hoarse bellow of pain as someone stepped into a punji pit. A man began screaming almost hysterically.

Into a life some rain must fall, Dagger thought, in keeping with the game-show theme. He tried to remember who sang that. Gave it up.

"Oh, my God!" the agent who had been calling for Dagger said.

He had found the body of Bitsy.

"What is it, Young?" another voice was added.

"It's Bitsy," Young called. "Her throat's been cut. Jesus! Her head's almost separated from her body. There's blood all over the place."

"You find Jimmy's body?"

"No. I don't want to either."

Pig called: "Dagger, you goddamned son of a bitch. I'll kill you for this, Dagger."

Dagger remained still and silent.

"Dagger?" Pig called. "How old was your little sis when she got poked up the ass? Six? Seven? I bet that was some tight stuff, Dagger."

Dagger's eyes narrowed, but he refused to play Pig's baiting game.

"You ever think much about that, Dagger?" Pig's voice was taunting. "You ever think about how she must have hollered when those guys spread those little legs and shoved it to her?"

Dagger did not move. Only his thoughts, and they were dark and atavistic, springing from the mouths of torchlit caves while huge beasts prowled the darkness of the Stone Age.

Someday, Pig.

"He's not going to play your game, Pig," Lisa

said.

"All right, Young," Pig called. "This is no good. Back off—back off."

Young backed off. Straight into Dagger's knife. Young had only one second of heart-pounding fear as the hand of Dagger covered his mouth and jerked him to the ground. Young felt the cold steel of the knife at his throat. One second of intense pain. One second of feeling his own blood pour from him. And then blackness.

Dagger held his hand over Young's mouth until the man ceased his jerking.

"Young?" Pig called. "Answer me, Young."

Gas escaped Young's cooling body.

A horrible scream floated through the timber just a split second after a twanging sound. Someone had tripped one of the swing traps, the stakes driving with tremendous force into chest and belly. The screaming died away.

"I'm done, Pig!" a man called. "Fuck you and this mission."

Several pairs of feet began running through the woods, the brains of the feet ignoring Pig's screaming and violent cursing for them to halt, come back.

"Pig, help me," the man from the punji pit called weakly. "Pig! No, Pig—please."

The boom of a pistol.

The pleading stopped.

You're a real nice fellow, Pig.

Dagger waited.

In the distance he heard one car start up, roar away, tires digging in the dirt.

Then he heard the sounds of the pebble-filled cans rattle. He removed something the size of a cigarette-sized package from a pocket of his field jacket and flipped the toggle switch. The violent explosion was harsh in the beauty of the budding wildflowers and leafing trees. Gurgling shrieks of pain ripped the morning coolness. Two screams of pain. One faded away as death laid its heavy hand on the man. The other man was still alive. Sort of.

"Jesus, Pig!" His shout was pain-filled. "My leg! I ain't got no leg."

Dagger waited.

"I can't stop the blood, Pig. Help me, for God's sake, help me!"

Dagger waited, waited silently for fifteen minutes. He rose from his squat and carefully, cautiously, made his way to the road, stopping often to check the terrain. He encountered no one. All senses told him Pig had pulled what was left of his group out and away from the zone of combat. On his belly, working under vines and brush, Dagger looked at out at the scene of carnage by the dirt road.

A squirrel began its chattering somewhere behind Dagger. Another squirrel replied. A bird called. Then another. A robin landed in a bush just across the road and looked the situation over. The robin hopped to the ground and began looking for something to eat. Dagger stood up. The robin took to the air.

The men must have been standing directly in front of the anti-personnel mine when it blew. One man was torn to bloody rags of meat. The second man had bled to death, one leg missing. It lay, almost shredded of flesh, some feet from the body.

Dagger slipped back into the brush and squatted, looking at the death caused by his hand. It was something he made himself do. If one can kill, then one can look at it.

A bit of verse came to Dagger's well-read mind: "I only know that summer sang in me. A little while, that in me sings no more."

He struggled for a time to recall who wrote it. Millay.

Odd, he thought, I should think of that now.

He thought of life and death for a time, squatting there, amid the green and flowering colors of budding young summer.

He felt no remorse, and knew he should feel . . . something. But he didn't. He never had. Not when, during and after, he killed that man in Springfield. Never after he had mauled those few loudmouths in high school who were stupid enough to try him in a fight. Not after all the men he'd killed.

Nothing.

Dagger's I.Q. was high — not staggeringly so, but the genius level nonetheless. But he knew —

had known since childhood—he was missing some important (so he was told) emotions. Dagger could love, had loved. Not wisely, but well. He knew that emotion. He wished he had never experienced it. Dagger did not weep—over anything or anybody. He could, he just didn't.

And, contrary to some reports from various personality profiles made on Dagger during his years in the army, Dagger did feel pity. He felt pity and shame at his country when he thought of the helpless elderly and the young. And he had compassion for those people. And for those that life had beaten down too many times: too many failures not of their doing; too many tries for the gold ring, only to find it made of tarnished brass. He had sympathized with those who could not for some mental flaw cope with life. Others. He felt compassion for them.

But he had nothing except contempt for those people who wantonly took from innocent others. Thieves and punks and street slime and thugs and muggers and rapists and others of that ilk could expect nothing from Dagger. Except a fist or a boot or a gun or a knife.

And Dagger despised organized crime. He thought that Godfather slop a sentimental pack of crap. If Dagger could have his way, he'd take anybody and everybody even remotely but knowingly connected with the Mafia or whatever those scummy bastards called themselves, and make the St. Valentine's Day Massacre of Capone's era look like a Sunday school outing.

Dagger had often wondered why someone in high power and wealth hadn't formed a group of men and women whose sole function in life would be to kill those turned loose because of "legal technicalities" by bleeding heart judges. Just plain criminals who prey on the innocent.

He would be the first to enlist.

He rose from his squat and left Edna St. Vincent Millay among the flowers of the forest while Dagger hauled off the bodies, stacking the pile of them like cordwood in the timber.

He stood looking for a time, looking at the grotesque pile, the faces twisted in that final second of death pain.

Then he wondered if he'd made his semi-annual payment to that mission that cared for little kids overseas.

He thought he had, but he'd best check his records when he got back to the house.

If he got back to the house.

Alive.

He walked away from the pile of bodies, his mind already canceling out the memory. He would dispose of them later. Or someone would.

"Mr. Harrison?" Dave Church spoke from his motel room in Springfield. "Dagger took seven of Pig's people out this morning."

"Seven of them! One man?"

"Yes, sir. Fifteen left the motel this morning. Five came back, packed their gear and took off. Then Pig and two others came in about fifteen minutes later. Those that cut out were a pretty shaken-up bunch. Pig is just mad."

"Using that both literally and as slang, Dave?"

Dave chuckled. "Yes, sir. I told you Dagger was one hell of a hoss."

"So you did, Dave—so you did. I feel better. I feel so much better I think I shall report this to the president. For some reason or other, he knows of this Dagger."

That's odd, Dave thought. Why would President Menen know of Dagger? They certainly don't run in the same social crowd. Well, he amended that, maybe not so odd. Dagger is a Medal of Honor winner.

He gave it no more thought. "I think the president would welcome some good news, sir."

"Yes. Oh, by the way, Dave."

"Yes, sir."

"All those so-called federal warrants that were out on Dagger's bunch? They've been dropped. All charges. Quite suddenly. The Justice Department has extended its apologies and all that. It has written to everyone it contacted and apologized profusely. Same with the IRS's freezing bank accounts and safe deposit boxes. I find that both interesting and amusing."

"Yes, sir. Amusing. Do I tell those at the cabin that?"

"How would you know of it, Dave? And what business is it of the CIA?"

"Good point, sir. You're learning."

"Dave . . . I don't know whether that is a compliment or not."

Dave was laughing at his boss as he hung up.

Kit woke up in the back seat of a moving car. The drug Jordan had injected into her had left her feeling lousy. And what Jordan had physically and personally introduced into her had left her feeling dirty and badly used. And sore. The man was a pervert.

"Where are we?" she asked. It came out: "Wurr ae e?"

"What the hell did you say?"

Kit cleared her throat and shifted her sore butt on the seat, attempting to ease the dull ache. It didn't help. "I said, Where are we?"

"New Mexico, baby. Heading west, toward the land of fruit and nuts."

"What?"

"California. Now shut your face and go back to sleep."

"I have to go to the bathroom."

Jordan sighed. "Baby, you pick the damnedest times to have to pee."

"Sorry to inconvenience you, master."

That got her a smack in the mouth, backhand from the front seat.

She cried for a few moments, sniffling into a

tissue. "I still have to go to the bathroom," she said.

Jordan pulled off the highway and got out, opening the back door. He motioned Kit out of the car. He removed her handcuffs.

She looked around her at the empty vastness of the desert. "But, I mean, what . . . where am I supposed to go to the bathroom?"

"Right out there, baby," Jordan said with a nasty smirk. He pointed. "Where I can watch."

Kit felt disgust wash over her—mingled with the revulsion and contempt for Jordan.

"All right," she said, turning slightly.

He laughed. He stopped laughing when she kicked him in the nuts.

Jordan howled and dropped to his knees, both hands holding and cupping his swelling testicles. Kit turned, stopped, walked back to Jordan and kicked him in the face, knocking him sprawling on the pavement.

She jumped in the car, dropped the gearshift into Drive, and roared off, leaving Jordan cussing and moaning and bleeding and vomiting in the middle of Interstate 40.

Kit kicked the speedometer needle up to seventy-five, then eased it back down to fifty-five. She did not want to risk getting stopped by a highway patrolman. She dropped her hand to the seat beside her and breathed a sigh of relief as her hand touched her purse. She felt giddy when she opened the purse and found everything intact:

driver's license, money, credit cards.

She saw a sign pointing to Santa Fe and whipped onto the exit. There were several things she knew she had to do: get rid of the car and rent another (her time spent with Dagger had made her wary); find a place to hide until she could work something out in her mind and/or get in touch with her brother or Paige. Or Dagger. She knew she could not risk a flight out. The airports at Baton Rouge and New Orleans, she thought, might still be watched by . . . those people.

She would get a few hours rest at . . . someplace. Rent a car in Santa Fe, maybe. Then run.

That was the best she could come up with at the moment.

She shifted on the seat. Somehow, kicking Jordan in his parts had made her sore butt feel better.

"Are . . . are you all right?" Paige asked Dagger.

"Yes. Fine." He removed his Ninja scarfs.

"We heard just the one large explosion."

He pulled his still-bloody knife from the boot scabbard and cleaned it. Paige paled, one hand going to her throat. Jimmy and Ralph stared. Mike swallowed hard.

"A snake makes little noise when it strikes," Dagger said.

"Old oriental proverb?" she asked.

"Probably. But it holds true in any nation."

"So now what do we do?"

"We wait, and give me time to think. I cut our odds by half."

"You killed a couple?" Mike asked.

"Seven," Dagger looked at him.

"Jesus!" Mike said.

"I don't think Pig will risk an all-out assault on the cabin or try another frontal from the woods. He knows I have the area booby-trapped. And he knows his people aren't as good as I am. I think what he'll do is sit it out and try to pick us off one at a time if we try to leave. I may be wrong. He may have lost so many people he might just pull out. I don't know."

"So we?" Jimmy asked.

"Wait it out," Dagger said.

15

Kit left Jordan's car in the airport parking lot and rented an Oldsmobile. She took Interstate 25 and headed for Denver. At Pueblo, she turned in the rental car and rented another from a different company. She stopped at a mall outside Denver and picked up a few articles of clothing and some makeup. She checked into a motel on the west side of Denver, under an assumed name, and after a long, hot soak in the tub, she tumbled into a deep sleep.

Dave Church hesitated again before reaching for the phone. He knew he was violating Company policy, but he felt Harrison was just too new to the game to really know what to do in times like these.

He made up his mind and had the operator get him a party in Hawaii—on the big island. When his party came on the line, Church waited for two heartbeats, giving the operator time to clear.

"Scramble this," he said.

A few seconds' pause. "Done."

"You are aware of what is going down?" Church asked. He knew his man did.

"The whispers are turning into shouts in some quarters, yes."

"Dagger is playing the game. You know that?"

"I heard. Dagger is a savage."

"He's a warrior."

"Your choice of words. But since we're playing semantics, what is the difference?"

Church ignored that. Professional killers sometimes had strange moral codes they operated by and under. "Can you reach Fritzler?"

"Certainly." The voice seemed offended that Church would have any doubt.

"Burn him. But it has to be an accident. We'll double your usual fee. But it *must* be an accident. We'll double your usual fee. No slip-ups."

"No pun intended?"

"That sounds good to me."

"Done."

Church sat back in his chair, a slight smile on his lips. One more problem taken care of.

EAGLE-FALL + 5

Morning dawned muggy on the nation's capital. In certain quarters, the old game of CYA was being played with more intensity than anyone could ever remember.

Cover your ass!

But for many, it was too late.

Carefully selected and tested agents of the CIA, FBI, Treasury and Secret Service moved quietly and quickly, placing many of the lesser men and women involved in Eagle-Fall under tight surveillance. They were very careful not to alarm anyone, including White House Chief-of-Staff John Cruse, VP Lewis Doyle or General Mitchell (ret.).

And business went on as usual.

"What do we do, Pig?" Lisa asked.

"I don't know, baby," he admitted. He held a crumpled piece of paper in his big hands. The directive from John Cruse to kill the Bear.

But there was no way Pig was going to do that. The Bear was his insurance policy, just as he was the Bear's stay-alive policy.

The phone rang in the adjoining room. After a moment, an agent stuck his head into Pig's room.

"The boss, Pig. All the warrants on Burrell, Volker and Shaffler have been dropped with profound apologies from the Justice Department and the IRS."

"Crap!" Pig spat the word. "What about Eagle-Fall?"

"Everything looks good there, Pig. It's still Go."

Pig rose from his chair. For a big man, he moved fluidly and with grace. "Get your gear together. It's all over here. No more for us to do except get our asses in a crack. Or—" and the words were bitter on his tongue—"get dead by Dagger."

"We now have reason to believe that one of the group Dagger is protecting is a Red agent," Harrison told Menen. "A deep, deep plant."

"I won't ask how you came to that conclusion," Menen said.

"Good," Harrison looked relieved. "Because I'm not certain I understand it myself."

Menen smiled his agreement. "It's a big job,

isn't it, Sherman?"

"Too big to be a political one, William. Far too big. That should be changed—but I know it won't be."

Menen said nothing.

Harrison brought him up to date, including what Dagger had done in Missouri.

The president smiled. He had been right in choosing Dagger. Quite a man. "Seven, Sherman?"

"Yes, sir."

Do I have the right to play God? the president once more questioned his mind. Do I have the right to unleash these men and women on society?

But I'm doing it *for* society's sake.

Still . . .

The phone buzzed. The president spoke for a few moments, the expression on his face a curious mixture of grimness and satisfaction. He hung up. Looked at Harrison.

"Did you order Fritzler killed, Sherman?"

"Good God, no!"

"Well, he's dead. He slipped in his hotel bathtub this morning. Broke his neck."

"It wasn't my agency's doing, William."

"Don't be too sure of that, Sherm. You've got Church running point on this thing, haven't you?"

"Yes, sir."

"He's burned more than his share of men—and

women — over the long years. Or ordered it done."

"I . . . don't think I like this job, Mr. President. I don't think I'm cut out for this. Intelligence-gathering is one thing. This other . . . " He shook his head.

"It's a lousy world, Sherm. And getting lousier by the day. But stay with it, old friend. I need you on my team."

"Yes, sir."

"At least one more traitorous bastard is out of the way," Menen said.

Sherman Harrison looked at him, a shocked expression on his face. "Willie, has the time spent in this office changed you that much?"

Menen shook his head. "I don't know. Maybe I always felt this way — latent, deep down. Just took this job to bring it to the surface."

The phone buzzed again. Dave Church calling for Harrison.

"I'm going to put you on speaker, Dave," Menen told him. "After you make your report to Harrison, I want you to answer each of my questions — truthfully."

"Yes, sir."

"Go."

"Pig and what is left of his bunch have pulled out. The Springfield police agreed to tap his phone and Pig ordered his other people — in Arkansas and down in Louisiana — to scatter and keep their heads down. I don't know where Pig went. I think it's time for me—or somebody—to break the news to Dagger's bunch about those warrants being withdrawn and all the rest of it. Dagger can take the strain; he's lived with it all his life. But I don't know how much more those civilian pilgrims can take."

"Hold off, Dave," Harrison said. "One of them may be a Red plant."

"A false flag! Goddamn," Dave cursed. "What else is going to crawl out from under this slimy rock?"

"I don't know. But right now our main purpose is to keep the president of the United States alive. Dave? Did you order the burn on Fritzler?" Harrison unknowingly slipped into the slang of the Agency.

Silence on the line.

"Answer the question, Dave," Menen told him.

"Yes, sir. I did."

Before Harrison could reprimand his agent, Menen put it all in a box and locked it up tight. "A job well done, Dave," he said. "I commend you."

Harrison could say no more about it. He sighed and said, "What about the Volker girl?"

"She got away from Jordan in the middle of New Mexico. Somehow. Kicked him in the balls and stole his car. We don't know where she is. But she's a gutsy lady. Hopefully, she's in hiding. Jordan is dead. One of the guns from the army's

Group Two Teams burned him in Albuquerque."

"Group Two Teams?" Harrison leaned forward. "Dave, what in the hell is a Group Two Team?"

"They're called Dog Teams, sir. I really don't think a telephone is the place to be discussing them."

"I'll tell you about them, Sherm," Menen said.

"*You* know about them, William?" Harrison blurted. He was suddenly sweaty.

"Yes." To Church: "Who popped Jordan?"

"Kovak's kid."

"He's working out well, then?"

"As good as his old man."

"What in the hell is going on around here?" Harrison jumped to his feet.

"Calm yourself, Sherm," the president said. "Dave? Did the elder Kovak ever soldier with Dagger?"

"Yes, sir. I think they were mercs together."

"Umm," Menen said. To Church: "Thank you, Dave. I want you to keep in daily contact."

"Yes, sir."

Menen hung up.

"William . . ."

Menen looked at the DCI. "You haven't heard a word about Dog Teams, Sherm. Believe me, it's for your own good and personal safety. If you insist, I'll tell you, but I would rather you didn't ask."

Harrison was quiet and very thoughtful for a

long moment. "I recall last year . . . no, almost two years ago, just after Wade had that heart attack and you asked me to step in as DCI. Yes—there was some kind of minor flap in our reading and analysis section about a book. A fiction book about Dog Teams."*

"It was fictionalized non-fiction, Sherman," the president said softly.

"The government of the United States has active, working Kill Teams, William?"

"You have them in your agency, Sherm."

Harrison's head jerked up.

"You just didn't have a need to know."

"I'd damn sure like to know more about them, William. Since I'm the goddamned DCI and liable to take the heat."

"If you decide to stay and if you really want to assume that pressure."

Harrison stared long and hard at his friend. "All right, William. We'll drop it. You won't change your mind about going to Los Angeles?"

"No. Don't worry, Sherm. Everything is set. Nothing is going to happen to me."

"Famous last words," Sherman muttered.

Menen laughed and rose from his chair. The meeting was over. He shook his friend's hand as they walked toward the door.

Before he opened the door, Sherman Harrison said, "Should you decide to run again, Mr. Presi-

*The Last of the Dog Team.

dent, I would appreciate it if you would not ask me to continue at this post."

Menen smiled. He had already decided that his old friend was just too moral a man for the job. Nice guys have their place in society, but not in high-level government jobs. One has to be part son of a bitch to hold those.

Sad, but the way of the world.

"If that is your decision, Sherm, I shall certainly respect your wishes, of course."

Sherman clasped his friend on the shoulder. "Thanks, Willie."

"They're gone," Dagger told the quartet. "Pulled out. Something big has gone down. I'll try to find out what. You people stay put. But stay alert."

Dagger had called his Uncle Walt at the sheriff's department, and Uncle Walt had called the Springfield Police Department.

Dagger drove into a small town and called Hank in Miami.

"What's the word, Hank?"

"You just have to be the luckiest man alive, Dagger," Hank's words sprang out of long distance. "We don't have to switch phones; all the bad guys have tucked their tails between their legs and cut out. Damn!" he said. "I would have bet the odds would get you on this one, old buddy."

"They still might, Hank. This isn't over by a long shot." He brought Hank up to date.

He could hear Hank sigh and then quietly curse over the miles. "Dagger, ol' buddy — you're home free. All charges have been dropped against your stalwart little group of justice-seeking civilians. With much government bowing and scraping and apologizing. Your group is free to return home and pick up their lives. Let them do it, Dagger, and you do the same. Don't push this, *mercenario*."

"There is only one problem, Hank."

"Oh?"

"One of the five is a Red plant."

EAGLE-FALL + 4

Dagger called Gormly and told him of his suspicions. Gormly told Dagger they had already figured that out but thanks anyway. Go home. Forget it.

"Just turn them loose?"

"Your part in this affair is concluded, Dagger. Just do what you're told and forget what you know — about everything."

"I think I'll see it through to its conclusion, Gormly."

"Get in the way, Dagger, and you might get stepped on like a bug."

Dagger laughed. "Speaking of bugs, Gormly, I left seven of them — squashed — stacked in the woods about a mile from my daddy's cabin. You know where it is. You better send someone to do something about them. Before they start to stink — and need explaining. You still think you can step on me like a bug, Gormly?"

Gormly made a choking sound. "Dagger, you

293

goddamn . . ."

Dagger hung up in his ear.

At the cabin, Dagger told them, "Go home. It's all over."

Mike looked at him. "Just like that? God! How anticlimactic can something be?"

But one of them was looking at him strangely, a slight smile on the lips.

The four of them packed, the tension in them slowly unwinding. Paige came to Dagger's side. Put a hand on his arm.

"Please let me stay with you, Dagger. I'd feel a lot better."

"I'd like that, Paige. But I've got some hard traveling to do. It's going to be dangerous. You need to get back and see about your business. I'll be in touch when this is all over."

"I . . . think I'm in love with you, Dagger."

"Don't, Paige. Don't do it. I told you before, we are of two different worlds. Go on back to yours and let me return to mine."

"Back to the wars, Dagger?"

"Something like that."

"Dagger . . ."

"It has to be, Paige. Listen to me. I'm a warrior. I can't even visualize me in your world, surrounded by your friends, living your life style. Think about it, Paige. Can you see me there?"

"Yes." Her reply was choked with emotion.

"Then you're letting your heart overrule your mind. Give it some time, Paige. Let both of us cool some. Then we'll talk."

Dagger could see the beginning of tears in her eyes. "All right. You promise?"

"I promise."

He spent an hour removing his booby traps. He did not want to zap some nature lover all enthralled watching an ivory-billed woodpecker or a yellow-bellied sapsucker screwing. Then he locked up his house and had Paige drive him into town, to the bus station.

"The bus station, Dagger?"

"It's just about a forty-minute ride to my house, Paige. I can use the time to unwind." He kissed her mouth. "I'll be in touch, Paige. Oh — don't depend too much on Jimmy. I mean it, Paige. I can't tell you more, but stay away from him."

"Jimmy!"

"Remember what I told you about obeying orders, ma'am?"

"Yes, Sergeant," she said, then kissed him with enough heat to sizzle.

He watched them go until the cars had faded from view.

"Dagger." The voice came from behind him.

He turned. Smiled. "Hello, Uncle Walt."

The men shook hands. "You been raisin' some hell back in the timber, boy?"

"I've been busy, yes, sir."

"Did you leave a mess in the woods?"

"Someone will be along to take care of it."

"All right. I'll check on it in a couple of days. You all through here?"

"I . . . don't know, Uncle Walt. Maybe."

" 'Bout time you thought of gettin' yourself a good woman, boy. Settlin' down. I reckon your dad would like that. Might help him rest some easier."

"Maybe. If you believe that."

"You don't, boy?"

"No, sir."

The older man shook his head. Sorrowfully. "I never could figure you out, boy. Never could get close to you. You keep all people at arm's length?"

Dagger smiled. "Only the men."

His uncle hitched up his gun belt. "I hope." He returned the smile. "See you 'round, son."

"Bye, Uncle Walt. Thanks."

"That's what kin is for."

Lorne Holt sat in his office, studying the route the presidential motorcade would take from the hotel to the meeting with the governor. No big, publicized affair. Very quiet meeting before the governors' conference began. Lorne knew The Gunner liked the big bang type of take-out. He thought he knew where the planned assassination attempt would take place. He circled the spot with a red marking pencil.

General Mitchell looked out the window of his

office. He knew nothing of Fritzler's death. Did not know about Jordan's death. Did not know about the quiet surveillance of many of his people. Did not know all his calls were being monitored and traced. Did not know many of the people calling him were being placed under quiet surveillance.

Did not know he had only four and a half days to live.

Kit stayed close to her motel. She had tried calling her brother and her friends. No answer. She didn't know what to do. She forced herself to remain calm.

John Cruse sat in his office and felt something stir in his guts. Some . . . *thing* was just not quite right. But he couldn't pin it down. Warwick had told him just that morning from L.A. that everything was fine—looked good from his end. No, he had not heard from Pig or the Bear. Did not know where they were. Didn't care, Warwick said. Just wanted this over with and phase two put in operation.

Cruse had told him to hang on and in. The clock was running and Eagle-Fall was counting down.

Vice President Lewis Doyle had worried himself into an ulcer. His stomach felt as though it had a fire in it.

God! he thought. How could I have been so stupid as to ever trust Pig?

What am I going to do?

President Menen sat in his office and drummed his finger tips on his desk. He was still uncertain about Zulu Nine. Knew that something like it was certainly needed, but did he have the right to unleash something of that magnitude?

What were the odds of it getting out of control? He didn't know.

Damn! He didn't know what to do.

But he knew one thing for certain: He didn't have much time to ponder the problem.

EAGLE-FALL + 3

Dagger sat in his den and looked out the window, looking at and seeing nothing.

His mind was carefully and methodically going over every aspect of the men and women he had just shepherded into and out of danger. The men and women he had killed for.

He counted it down:

Vice President Doyle was being blackmailed by someone, or some group, the knowledge of Kit Volker, his illegitimate child held over his head. And there was no doubt of that. Kit's father was VP Doyle.

But who or what was doing the blackmailing? And why? Dagger didn't know.

He was ninety percent sure Kit was not the Red agent.

Mike was just too stupid.

Paige had nothing to gain from it. She was a wealthy young woman with the whole world at her finger tips. There was nothing Dagger could come up with to tie her in with the Reds.

Ralph was a loyal American, even if he did have a difficult time putting that emotion into words.

Dagger remembered Mike's words at the Burrell mansion: "You saw him the night before, Jimmy. We all did, I think."

Mike had been speaking of Rossieau. And they had all told Dagger, in private, that Jimmy had been against hiring Dagger from the first.

It all pointed toward Jimmy.

Dagger stirred. For the tenth time that morning he vacillated between going and staying put. He wanted to be where the action was. Wanted to see this through.

He rose from his chair and went outside to work in his flower beds, carefully replanting some very delicate plants. His big hands were gentle with the plants, almost lovingly working the earth, patting it, his fingers touching the fragile stems.

He had not heard from Paige or any of the others. He wondered about Kit. Gormly had surprised him with a phone call, telling him about Kit and Jordan. And damn little else. The bodies were gone from the woods. Gormly sounded a bit repulsed at the way Dagger had left the bodies.

Dagger had told him he'd try to do better the next time. Be a little neater.

Gormly had hung up on him.

Dagger rose from his work. He looked toward the west. "Hell with this," he muttered.

He showered, packed a few things, locked up his house, and got in his Silverado pick-up and pulled out. He pointed the nose of the pick-up toward Los Angeles.

In Baton Rouge, Pig sat in the apartment of the Bear, waiting for the Bear to return from work. They had to get their heads together, had to salvage something out of this operation. The last time Pig had spoken to the Bear, from a pay phone in Arkansas, they had discussed the alternate. Bear had told him to put it in operation.

Pig shook his head. The Bear was even more cold-blooded than Pig.

Pig heard the key in the dead-bolt lock. The apartment door swung open.

" 'Bout goddamn time you got here. Where the hell have you been?"

"Doing some checking with our superiors. They want Eagle-Fall stopped."

Pig shook his head. "We can't. It's too far into Go."

"I thought as much. John Cruse is being set up, I think."

Pig was silent for a moment. He looked around the apartment. Didn't like it. Looked too faggy to suit him. "It figures," he said. "Mitchell?"

"No. I believe he is being set up as well."

"What!"

"Fritzler is dead. Someone broke his neck in Hawaii. Some of our people are under surveillance in Washington. Doyle is frightened out of his wits."

"Maybe," Pig said with a sigh and a smile, "all this is to our mutual advantage."

"Explain."

Pig waved the Bear to a chair and began talking.

16

As Dagger drove westward, his mind still mulled over the mystery—mystery at least to him. And he did not like the feeling of doom that had settled on him. Something was missing. It was as if, at least to Dagger, he was confronted with a puzzle made up entirely of square pieces. No way he would be wrong in placing them: It would be right to someone viewing it in abstract.

Dagger knew that nothing of this proportion ever ended with such a whimper.

He had missed something.

But what?

He wondered what was going through President Menen's mind.

"You've been very preoccupied of late, William," President Menen's wife remarked. "Even more so than usual. Want to talk about it?"

He looked at his wife of oh-so-many good years and smiled. She didn't know it, but she was about to come down with a bed-confining virus, compliments of the White House doctor. Menen hated to do it to her, but that was the only way he could keep her from accompanying him to L. A.

"Just have a lot on my mind, Doris," Menen said. "I'm sorry I've been distant. Did the doctor get in touch with you?"

"Yes. I saw him. Gave me a shot. Something about a virus going around. Said he hoped it wasn't too late."

"Good. We're scheduled to leave for Camp David in just a bit."

"We're packed."

She gazed at her husband. She knew something was wrong—something heavy weighing on him. But she also knew he would not tell her unless he felt it necessary. More than likely, he would not.

"William, did you read this article in the *Post?* It's awful." She held out the paper. "That poor old woman those young thugs attacked and tortured. My God! People aren't even safe in their own homes—especially the elderly. It's shameful. I wish there was something you could do about conditions."

President Menen nodded his head. "Yes, dear. I wish there was something I could do." There is. "But the liberals have me blocked on that. And the courts seem to enjoy spending billions of dollars of the taxpayers' money delaying any death sentence handed down."

He had almost reached the conclusion he did not have the right to play God. Could not in good conscience put Zulu Nine into force.

"Tortured her with cigarette lighters!" Doris was saying. "Then killed her by stabbing her with ice picks. Savages. And those damned free-legal people are saying the thugs should not be held responsible for their acts. Well, who in the name of God should be held responsible?"

William Menen tuned her out. He knew the story by heart: They were venting their rage at an uncaring society; they came from a broken home; they were black or brown or white or pink or polka dot. Or they had pimples.

No, he knew it wasn't all their fault. But a full eighty percent of it was. Maybe more than that. Why was this generation so different from his own? What made so many of this generation's young people so unfeeling and uncaring and savage?

Hell, he knew the answer to that, too. Liberalism, permissiveness, so-called progressive education, lack of discipline, lack of respect . . . Christ, the list was endless.

And the press. Oh, yes, let us not forget them.

Menen was sick of the entire scenario. Ninety-nine times out of a hundred what it boiled down to was the nation had packs of rabid dogs in human form roaming the streets, preying on the elderly and the sick and the helpless.

What America needed was a dog catcher.

EAGLE-FALL + 2

Kit was almost hysterical when her brother answered the phone in his apartment. Ralph had to explain to her several times that it was all over for them. He told her to stay where she was and he would come and get her. And Mike was coming with him. Mike had been awfully worried about Kit. Ralph told his sister he thought Mike just might be in love with her. Kit told Ralph she'd known that for years. She'd just been waiting for him to grow up.

"Well . . . hell!" Ralph said.

No, no one had seen Jimmy.

EAGLE-FALL + FIVE

HOURS

It had taken Dagger twenty-two hours to drive from Missouri to L.A. He had stopped only for gas. Just outside the city, he checked into a motel and slept soundly, a deep, almost hypnotic sleep. He moved very little in his sleep.

He spent the day driving the route he believed President Menen would take from his hotel to the meeting place. He backtracked three times, from the meeting place in San Fernando back to Beverly Hills. He picked out the three best places for The Gunner's explosive methods, then again backtracked, using a rental car so as not to draw attention to himself.

The governors were meeting in San Fernando.

And the thought came to him: Why? Why would the president stay in Beverly Hills when all the meetings were in San Fernando?

No. That was wrong. Why were the governors meeting in San Fernando? Why such a distance away from the president's hotel? Unless . . . one of the governors was in on it. Had to be.

Dagger again drove the highway, eliminating two of his ambush sites. He picked the one where the best vantage spot was, for he knew The Gunner would watch his work. But he would not be so close as to risk capture.

He turned in the rented car, picked up his Silverado from the parking area down the block and drove back to his motel. He was smiling as he lifted the receiver. Hell, he thought, if I'm going to do it, I may as well go first class.

He dialed the number of the president's hotel.

"President Menen, please," he said.

"That is impossible," a man's voice cut in almost immediately. "To whom am I speaking?"

"Dagger."

"I know the name. Why do you want to speak to the president?"

"I want to make a contribution to his political party."

"Don't be a smart-ass, Dagger."

"Put the president on the line."

A click as Dagger was put on Hold. Then another click. "Mr. Dagger. This is William Menen."

"An honor, sir." Then Dagger told him of his suspicions of one of the western governors.

Menen sucked in his breath. He said something to a party in the room. Dagger could not make out the words. To Dagger: "Very astute of you, Mr. Dagger. That is something that had not occurred to any of us."

"Who do you have set up to take your fall, sir?" Dagger asked.

Menen laughed. "Why would you think I'd do something like that?"

"Because I know you were a Marine Raider during World War II. You have a lot of close kills to your credit. You won the congressional for your expertise with a knife. And you're probably just as cold-blooded as any man I ever served with."

The president laughed. "Thank you, Dagger. Tell me, what are your immediate plans?"

"To kill Gunner Manchester."

"I wish you a lot of luck."

"Thank you, sir. The same to you."

Dagger hung up.

EAGLE-FALL

John Cruse stepped into the president's suite and was startled to see him in a gray pin-stripe suit. Just like the one he wore.

Cruse opened his mouth. "I . . ."

A gun was shoved into his back. "Keep your mouth shut, Cruse," Lorne Holt told him. "Or I'll blow your backbone clear out your stomach."

Cruse knew then he had been made, had played right into Menen's hands. A very slight smile touched his lips.

"How long have you known, William?"

"Long enough, John. Why, John? Why did you do it?"

"I worked a long time to help you get elected, Willie."

His use of the president's nickname got him a hard slap across the mouth. William Menen brought his hand back across his face in a vicious, backhand pop.

"Mr. President to you, Cruse," he was told.

"Yes, sir." Blood leaked from Cruse's mouth. "Mr. President. Why? For all its anti-capitalistic rhetoric, Mr. President, Russia is, for the most part, as capitalistic as America. At least as far as its leaders go. Power, Mr. President. And money, of course."

"Doyle's part in this?"

Cruse had no idea he was only minutes away from death. He felt Menen would use him for political purposes, flaunting him in Russia's face. He felt like talking. Why not? This was America—land of liberals. Ban the bomb. Take all handguns away from citizens and give them to criminals. Take a Punk to Lunch day. He'd be traded to Russia for some Russian Jew or other dissident. He felt sure of that.

"Kit Volker is Doyle's bastard child. To keep the mother quiet, and preserve his political career, Doyle had her killed—with our help. Through Pig and his S-5 group. After that, we had him in the bag. Unfortunately, this Karl Crowe thing came up shortly after Mrs. Volker was killed."

Cruse did not see the look that passed between Menen and a man sitting in a corner of the room.

The man rose and quietly exited out a side door.

Vice President Doyle had less than an hour to live.

"I don't suppose you'd care to tell me how many people are involved in this?" Menen asked.

Cruse smiled at him. "Not likely, Mr. President."

"We'll find them, John."

"Some of them, I'm sure. But we're buried deep, very deep. And that is all I have to say on the subject."

"It's time, sir," Holt said.

"Put him in the car."

John Cruse then realized what was going to happen. Why the president was wearing a gray pin-stripe. He opened his mouth to protest and felt the lash of the needle drive through the sleeve of his suit and into his arm. Within the space of four minutes, the powerful drug had addled him enough to make him thick tongued and easily handled. He was surrounded by agents and put in an elevator, hustled downstairs, avoiding the knot of reporters. He was placed in the back seat of the limo. Lorne Holt got behind the wheel. The small motorcade pulled slowly out of the parking area of the hotel.

Menen picked up the phone in his room and spoke to a man. "Have Kovak burn Warwick," he said.

He replaced the phone in its cradle and sat down at a table by a window. Lunch was brought in to him.

President William Menen could not recall ever so thoroughly enjoying a meal.

Lorne thought he knew where the big bang would take place. He was calm as he drove. He had taken a pain pill an hour before leaving the hotel and the drug had eased the gnawing in his guts. He had finished the letter to his wife and kids and given it to a friend to deliver when *it* was over. He had told her only that there might be trouble on this trip and he had volunteered for a dangerous assignment. But he knew she would read between the lines. She would understand. She wouldn't like it because he had not taken her into his confidence; but she would understand.

His insurance and his pension would more than take care of the kids' education and see that his wife would live comfortably.

He caught Cruse's eye in the rear-view. The man was groggy, spittle oozing from one corner of his mouth. "I wish I could kill you myself, you son of a bitch," Lorne told him.

Cruse mumbled something and slobbered on himself.

"Screw you," Lorne muttered. He reached for his mic, keyed it, and said, "Fifteen minutes, boys. Begin a gradual back-off."

"Luck to you, Lorne."

Lorne Holt hoped God would understand why he was choosing this way out.

"You'll never see it, Gunner," Dagger spoke to the back of the man.

The Gunner whirled, his hand moving toward a shoulder holster under his jacket. He froze when he saw the Colt Woodsman in Dagger's hand, the silencer screwed on.

The men stood on the crest of a hill more than a mile from the site of the planned explosion. Heavy binoculars hung from a strap around Gunner's neck.

"I had you in gun sights more than once back in Rhodesia," Gunner said. "I should have pulled the trigger."

"You mean Zimbabwe?" Dagger smiled.

Gunner spat on the ground.

"That's one thing we agree on," Dagger said.

"How'd you do it, Dagger?"

"I just looked for the best seat in the house."

"Put down that gun and I'll take you with my bare hands."

"That's a lie and you know it. I know you carry a hideout gun behind your belt buckle."

"Damn your memory!" The Gunner laughed, facing death as calmly as he had given it out. "We were made, weren't we?"

"That's right."

"President Menen isn't in the limo, is he?"

"Right again."

"Who is it?"

"Probably John Cruse."

"Yes. He was half the brains behind it all."

"The other half?"

"I know only the code name."

"The Bear?"

"That's it. I'd tell you if I knew. You know me that well, Dagger."

Dagger nodded his agreement. "General Mitchell?"

"Been on the Red payroll for years."

"Pig's a mole, isn't he?"

"For years. It's very deep, Dagger. And I've told you all I know."

Dagger believed him.

"It's a business, Dagger. That's all. That's something you could never understand. Just a business. Like a banker or a barrister or a shoe salesman. But you always had to have some cause to fight. That moral streak in you will get you killed someday."

Dagger smiled. "Or keep me alive."

Gunner shrugged his contempt for life in general.

"Any last messages, Gunner?"

"Yeah."

Dagger waited.

"Fuck you, Dagger!"

Dagger shot him twice. One slug entered his head at the tip of nose; the second slug took him directly between the eyes. The little, steel-jacketed slugs did not exit the head, just swelled it as they smashed brain and exploded fluid.

The Gunner fell forward on his face.

Five minutes later, one entire section of the interstate was blown to rubble and half of a massive overpass fell onto the presidential limousine, crushing and mangling beyond recognition the two men inside.

Dagger turned and walked away. He got in his pick-up and pointed the nose east, toward Missouri.

In Washington, Dave Church walked into General Mitchell's office and laid a .45-caliber semi-automatic pistol on the general's desk. Mitchell looked at the pistol, then at Church.

"Unless you want a very messy trial, General," Church told him.

One minute after Dave Church left the office, retired air force General Mitchell blew half his head all over one office wall.

Vice President Lewis Doyle was admitted to Walter Reed Hospital shortly after he heard the news of the attempted assassination of the president. A massive heart attack. He died moments after being admitted. Complications.

In Baton Rouge, Louisiana, Doctor Rossetti and a friend, attorney Charles Cleveland, were killed when the car in which they were riding collided with an eighteen-wheeler. The autopsy showed both men had large amounts of heroin in the bloodstream. It came as a shock to their friends to learn the men were drug users.

Never can tell about people.

In San Fernando, California, one of the governors at the conference drowned in the swimming pool. President Menen sent condolences to the widow.

Senator Larkin and Representatives Ballard and Cassard waited and wondered about their future. They were all caught in that unenviable position known as between a rock and a hard place. They could but wait. And hope. Since the three of them belonged to the Party, and the Party espoused no belief in God, prayer was out of the question.

But that all reverts to the old saying that there are no atheists in the foxholes.

The official statement released to the press was that President Menen had come down with some sort of virus and John Cruse was taking his place at the meeting with the governors in San Fernando.

Yes, it was a terrible tragedy.

No, we don't know who might have been behind the assassination attempt.

A madman, surely.

And in Baton Rouge, Jimmy Shaffler finally put in an appearance. Said he'd been out of town. Working.

17

"It was a timer attached to the rear bumper of the limo," Gormly said. "The agent who put it there has been taken into custody and placed in a mental institution in Virginia. His recovery is doubtful," he added dryly.

"Glad to see you boys are taking my advice," Dagger said. "Finally."

"I just flat don't like you, Dagger," the Secret Service agent said.

"One of life's little tragedies," Dagger said.

Gormly hung up.

Dagger dialed a number in Baton Rouge.

"Oh, Dagger!" Paige said. "I've missed you so much."

"And I've missed you, kid," Dagger said. "Has Jimmy returned?"

"Yes," she breathed, a note of intrigue in her voice. "He says he's been up in north Louisiana, seeing to his farm."

"You believe him?"

"No. I think you were right about him."

"Then I suppose I've got one more thing to do before I can wrap this up, right?"

"Dagger . . . do you have to kill him?"

"What would you have me do, Paige?"

"I've . . . I mean, he's been a friend for years. Can't you just . . . *talk* to him?"

"Maybe."

"Dagger? Can you come down this weekend? We've never been really alone. Let's spend some time at the mansion at St. Francisville. We can, well, play, if you know what I mean."

Visions of her nakedness pranced through Dagger's mind.

"I'd like that, Paige."

"I can hardly wait, Dagger."

"I'll see you tomorrow evening then."

"I'll be there, Dagger. Dagger? I love you. I know you have reservations, and you don't have to say you love me, but I know you do. You'll see. Hurry, darling, I'll be waiting for you."

She hung up.

"Yeah," Dagger said, slowly replacing the receiver in the cradle. "I know you will, Paige. You and Pig."

18

Dagger left his pick-up parked on a dirt road about a mile from the Burrell mansion. He walked slowly toward the mansion. It loomed up dark in his eyes. Swiftly and silently, he prowled the grounds, locating a man standing in the shadows of a huge, live oak. Once, he caught sight of a woman, but it wasn't Paige. Dagger figured it to be Lisa.

There was no moon, and a very light, almost invisible mist was falling, lightly sparkling the grounds.

Dagger could smell the jasmine.

The scent seemed out of place on this night of sudden death.

"I know you're out there, Dagger," the woman's voice came to him, the voice carrying through the gloom of night and mist and delicate scents. Trees loomed tall and stately on both sides of the estate road.

"Yeah, I'm here, Paige," Dagger said quietly.

He crouched some forty meters from her. Silver caught light and he could see she had a gun in her hand.

"Dagger, I didn't mean this kind of playing when I talked with you. Don't you want me, Dagger? Why don't you step out in the road where I can see you?"

"You must take me for a fool, Paige," Dagger said. He watched her eyes shift, locating him. The mist created pockets of shimmering light in her raven hair. He could not recall seeing her any more beautiful.

Or any deadlier.

The pistol in her hand, hanging by her side, did not move.

"Darling," Paige called, "don't be silly. Why are you doing this? Why did you slip up on the house instead of just driving up and coming on in?"

He laughed at her. "I have this thing about being shot, Paige."

"Darling, I believe you've taken leave of your senses! Why would I shoot you? Guns frighten me."

Dagger slipped further back into the hedge, thinking: Ol' Mr. Rattlesnake or Cottonmouth, don't be underfoot now.

"I hear you, darling," she called. "Slipping away. Why are you doing this? I love you."

You always hurt the one you love, Dagger thought. Safely hidden behind the bulk of an oak tree, Dagger said, "They got to you, didn't they, Paige."

"Whatever in the world do you mean, Dagger?"

"Cut the shit!" Dagger said harshly.

She tried another ploy. "They have my parents, Dagger—in Europe. They'll release them for you."

He laughed at her. "No way, honey. You see, I finally figured it out. You were the only one who could have set up Kit that night in Arkansas. You did it when I went into town to make a phone call."

"That's not true, Dagger."

"Yeah, it's true, Paige. That night, after we made love, we were talking? I asked you how you got your tennis shoes so muddy. You said you went for a walk. You sure did. Hiked right down the path to a phone."

Silence greeted him. Something moved to his right. Stopped.

"Took me a few days of thinking to recall what you'd told me. Has to be, Paige."

"No!" she screamed the word.

"Come on, Paige. You're lying and you're out of your league. You're playing with the grown-ups, now. You're in my ballpark. I've been doing this kind of work for years."

She shifted the pistol from her side, then lowered it. Dagger could see it was an automatic— .32 or maybe a .380. She did not hold it at all awkwardly.

"Paige, listen to me," Dagger called. "You know you people blew it. President Menen is alive. The Gunner is dead. Mitchell is dead, along with Warwick, Fritzler, Doyle, one governor, one doctor, one lawyer, and one White House chief-of-staff. You—"

"Shut up, Dagger!" Her voice was no longer loving. "You've been red-tabbed in our files for too long. When this came up, I was ordered to kill you. Hire you, then kill you. Then the orders came to keep you alive."

"So I could kill off as many Section Five personnel as possible."

"That's right, Dagger."

"Go on, honey."

"Honey! You bastard! When you told me back at your house you knew who killed Karl Crowe, I wanted to kill you right then."

"But Pig . . ."

"I didn't know Pig was the one who killed him. Now that I do, it no longer makes any difference." She laughed in the night.

"Crowe was working both sides of the street?"

"He had agreed to do that, yes. I seem to be one of those whose illusions have to be constantly shattered."

"Karl Crowe recruited you, years ago."

"Yes."

"Paige, for God's sake—why? You were born with that silver spoon in your mouth. Why throw all that away for a communist line of bullshit?"

"Because I was in love with Doctor Crowe. Knew it the moment I saw him. All the months we had together—they were wonderful. And even though he turned against his country, I'm still in love with him. His memory. The U.S. government blackmailed him into working as a false flag. I made up my mind I would make this government pay for his death."

"Must have been quite an affair, Paige. A fifty-five-year-old communist and an eighteen-year-old girl with stars in her eyes."

"He was gentle."

"And loving?"

"Yes."

"And kind?"

"Yes." She was crying real tears.

"And instead of just popping it to you right off the bat, he coaxed you along, recruited you, and then shoved the meat to you."

"You're a vile, filthy bastard, Dagger!"

He wanted to make her angry, and knew he had done it. She cursed him long and hard. As she swore revenge, Dagger slipped away, changing positions, edging closer, moving from tree to tree in the blackness. The weight of his .41 mag was comforting in his hand.

"Why don't you just call your buddies in the KGB and have them rescue your parents, Little Bear?"

She spun around, trying to locate him. "Goddamn you, Dagger—stand still."

"I guess I'll never understand all of it, Paige."

"Everything started crumbling around the edges. We didn't think our investigation would turn up anything," she said. "Rossieau was too smart for his own good."

"Jimmy?"

"He's nothing, has nothing to do with anything."

"Yeah, I know. I had some people check on his story. He's clean. You're quite the actress, aren't you, Paige? And as cold-blooded as a snake. Your parents are dead, aren't they?"

She said nothing.

"Transistors, computers, components. That's where dear old dead Dad's money is, right? Lots of overseas companies your father has stock in, or owns, through corporate fancy footwork. And who stands to inherit all his wealth? Dear, loving daughter, Paige."

"Keep digging your grave, Dagger. You're doing wonderfully."

Dagger was thoughtful for a quiet moment. "Paige? If ever a sorry bitch walked the face of the earth, it's you."

She laughed at him.

"How long have you known Pig?"

Again, that mocking laugh.

"You had your own brother killed."

"You're spinning this fairy tale. Keep spinning, Dagger."

Dagger was conscious of someone trying to slip up the side of the road, keeping in the deep shadows from the rows of live oaks. Dagger got a glimpse of a bald pate. Pig. The other man he'd spotted was still on the other side of the road. He wondered where Lisa was.

"Sad thing is, Paige," Dagger spoke softly, "all this is so unnecessary."

Dagger watched Pig slip to the shallow ditch, an M-10 in his hands. Silently, Dagger again shifted positions.

"What do you mean?" Paige called.

"Hell, honey. All Pig was doing was following orders. And knowing Pig, he probably taped a lot of them. Nobody can prove anything against any of you. He'd be a hero. Saving the country from a communist takeover, or some such crap. All he'd have to say is he put those legitimate intelligence agents on us to keep you and your friends safe — which is probably not far from the truth. He could have taken you people at any time. He didn't. And not one slug that night in Arkansas even came close to hitting anyone.

"And you, honey, you'd be just an innocent bystander, caught up in a web not of your making. Think about it: the bereaved daughter who lost her parents to the big, bad Reds." As he talked, Dagger used the sound of his voice to cover the cocking of his .41 mag. "The Volkers don't know about your Red connection, neither do the Shafflers. And I can be bought, honey. A lot of money and a couple of weeks of your good pussy and I just vanish, drop out of sight and stay deaf, dumb and blind."

Pig spoke for the first time. "Listen to him, Paige. I like what he's saying."

She snarled at him. "You're supposed to *kill* him, you fat bastard!"

"Shut up," he ordered her. "Killing him would just add more complications to an already screwed-up operation. He's smart, Paige. He figured out your brother's death and everything else, didn't he? Go on, Dagger."

"Somehow, Pig, the FBI, the Agency, all the other intelligence-gathering groups screwed-up on their quality control. They got compromised. But to date, you're clean — all of you. No one can prove a damn thing. All you have to say is you were working under Fritzler's orders, looking after the five civilians. Everyone else is dead. You can plead innocent, Pig, and I know how convincing you can be."

"And you'd keep your mouth shut?"

Dagger laughed. "You know it, Pig. For a hundred thousand and a couple weeks with Paige — I'm silent."

"Pig . . ." Paige said.

"Shut up!" he barked at her. "Think about it. We might kill Dagger tonight — we might not. So far he's been damned hard to burn. And killing him would just be something else we'd have to explain. This way, we could keep on working, our cover intact. And, like me, I figure Dagger has left a tape or two and some notes around to nail us."

"You got that right, Pig," Dagger lied.

"Paige?" Pig called.

"All right," she said quietly. Too quietly and too quickly to suit Dagger.

Dagger had all the agents spotted now. He had watched Lisa work her way noiselessly up to within twenty feet of him, across the road.

"When do I get the money?" Dagger asked.

"Tomorrow night," Pig said.

"All right," Dagger said, and stood up.

He shot Pig first, putting a round dead center in his chest. Pig's M-10 clattered and bucked in his hands as he went down, the rounds playing hell with the live oaks.

Dagger dropped to one knee and assumed a two-handed grip on the .41. He shot the unknown man in the face, the slug tearing off the man's jaw. Dagger charged Paige just as an M-16 cut the night. Out of the corner of his eye he watched Lisa fold up like a shattered doll.

He wondered where the M-16 came from.

Dagger hit Paige with a rolling block, knocking her feet out from under her just as she fired. The pistol went sailing from her hand. Dagger hit her twice, smashing her skull with the knife edge of his hand and using the fingers of his left hand, rupturing her larynx.

She jerked once and was still, blood leaking

from her mouth and ears and nose.

Dagger squatted on one knee as he watched half a dozen men leave the row of jasmine on the opposite side of the road, walking toward him.

He raised his .41. If he was going out, he planned to take a few with him.

EPILOGUE

"Easy, Dagger," a voice cautioned him. "We're on your side."

"Oh, yeah?"

"Yes. It will all be explained to you in a little while."

"What will?"

"Everything."

"I'm all aquiver with anticipation," Dagger said sarcastically.

Dagger stood by the row of jasmine and watched as a pick-up truck rolled down the road and the men dumped the four bodies in the back, covering them with tarps, tying them up like bundles of old rags, roping them together. The truck backed off, turned around and was gone into the misty night.

Dagger felt a fragrance assail his nostrils, something soft in his hand. He looked down. He had plucked a blossom from the vine and when Paige had been dumped into the truck, he had crushed the flower in his hand.

He let the crumpled blossom fall to earth.

"You ready to go to Baton Rouge?" a man asked Dagger.

"Why the hell do I want to go to Baton Rouge?"

"To board a plane."

"Why?"

"Because Air Force One is there. The president is on board. He wants to see you. We'll drive your truck to St. Louis. The president is scheduled to speak there tomorrow. You can pick up your truck then."

Dagger lifted his hand to his nose, inhaling the fragrance of jasmine.

"Were you in love with Ms. Burrell?" a man asked gently.

"I think I was moving in that direction," Dagger said honestly. He knelt down and rubbed his hand on the wet grass. He couldn't get that goddamn smell off his palm. He stood up. "Let's go see the man."

Dagger had met one president when the congressional was pinned on him back in sixty-seven. That president was a jerk.

This one impressed him.

They had been airborne for half an hour before Dagger was ushered into the cabin where the president was waiting.

"Sit down, Mr. Dagger," Menen said. "I have coffee and sandwiches. Help yourself."

Dagger did. He was hungry. But he still smelled of jasmine.

"The Constitution isn't working, Dagger," Menen said.

"Agreed, sir."

"We have rabble taking control of our streets. The courts are too lenient. What this nation is doing to its elderly makes me sick. The law-abiding citizen is getting the short end of justice."

"Agreed, sir." He didn't particularly care for mayonnaise on ham sandwiches but he didn't feel like he had the right to bitch about it.

"What do you think should be done to rectify the situation, Dagger?"

"Start killing criminals."

Menen smiled. "You mean a group of men and women acting as vigilantes? That could get out of hand."

"Yes, sir. It could. That's probably why no one has ever formed one."

"When you leave this plane in St. Louis, Dagger," Menen said, "you will — in all likelihood — never see me again."

"Yes, sir."

"Do you think it's time for such a group to be formed?"

Dagger leaned back in the comfortable seat and sipped his coffee. He said, "I don't know, sir. Something like that sounds good — I think about it from time to time — but it could get dangerous. Out of control."

"It's already set up and ready to go, Dagger. All I need is one more person."

"And I'm it."

"That is correct."

"It has to have a name."

"Zulu Nine."

"Nine people?"

"Yes. Men and women."

"Would we work together?"

"Not often. Sometimes."

"I like it."

"Yes." Menen smiled, leaning back in his seat. "I rather thought you would."

MORE THRILLING READING!